THE MAGICS OF REI-EEN BOOK 1

I0585345

THE HIDDEN PRINCESS

GEORGINA MAKALANI

ISBN: 978-0-6483372-6-3

For my grandmother,

Ray Smith

1

Lis closed her eyes and enjoyed the cool breeze blowing across her tanned skin. It pulled at her skirt, the fine material lifting up around her, and whipped through her long jet-black hair. The smell of sweet grass and blossom surrounded her, although the flowers had yet to bloom. She stepped through the field and felt the flowers open beneath her palms as she held her hands over them. She lifted her hands out wider, until her arms were level with her shoulders, then opened her eyes to watch the flush of colour wash across the field as every flower opened.

'I love how you do that,' Peng said, wrapping his arms around her waist from behind, his breath hot on her neck before he gently kissed it.

'Father doesn't love it as much as you do,' she said, her happiness dissipating somewhat. Her father allowed her to use her magic, to be who she was, but she was nervous doing so. There was always the underlying fear that they could be discovered at any moment, despite being so far from rest of the Empire here on their island home.

'You are safe with me,' Peng said as she turned in his arms and smiled into his dark eyes.

'I always feel safe with you,' she said, running her fingers through his hair. Unlike the other men of the Empire who wore their hair tied in smooth, neat buns on top of their heads, Peng let it fall free and long down his back. Lis pulled his face down to meet hers. 'If only we didn't have to wait for the summer festival to marry.'

'We don't have to wait to do everything,' he whispered in her ear. His breath tingled across her skin as he pulled her closer, holding her tight against his hard body.

'Someone is coming,' she said, reluctantly pulling away from him.

Peng looked around, then grinned as he looked back at Lis. 'We can wait,' he murmured.

'Someone is coming,' she said again, feeling an urgency and uncertainty she hadn't felt in some time. With little effort, she could sense the boat moving closer to their island. She lifted her skirt and moved as quickly as she could towards the house, eager to reach her father's side. It would have been easier to use her magic to create a path through the stalks, but she knew too well the dangers.

She was halfway to the house when the boat bumped against the side of the jetty. It was larger than their own family boat, but smaller than she would have imagined for the Empire—yet it carried the seal of Emperor Rei Shoashu on its sail. A small, stocky man disembarked, dressed in the golden colours of the advisors, and four soldiers joined him in heading towards the house. Lis slowed her steps as fear closed around her chest.

Why would these men come from the Palace Isle? What does the emperor want of Father now?

She waited for them to enter the house before she picked up her pace again. As she followed them into the house, a wave of uncertainty made her shiver. She moved slowly around the pond that filled the centre courtyard, and she heard them talking before she reached the main room. Lis knew she needed to stand beside her family, but she waited outside the door.

'General Long, you have done so much for the Empire of Rei-

Een. Emperor Rei Shoashu respects your wish for solitude and peace after your years of service. Unfortunately, we have grave news that will impact all the Empire.'

'Speak, man.' Her father's impatience was apparent, and Lis waited.

'We cannot continue until all your family is present. You have another daughter, do you not?'

Lis slid the door open just as her father nodded. The large room contained a long table, one wall open to the courtyard and pond beyond, with images of the Empire painted on various screens on the opposite wall. It was familiar, yet it all looked so different with these armoured men standing amidst it.

'Excuse me,' she said, bowing low to the short man, who wore the slanted hat of someone high in the emperor's advisors. Two guards stood unmoving at his back as she walked to stand beside her sister.

'We are all present,' her father continued. 'Tell us this news.'

'The crown prince, Rei Ta-Sho, is dead,' the little man said without any emotion at all.

Her mother's hand flew to her breast, and Lis took her sister's hand.

Her father waited.

'The crown prince was due to be wed this very summer, his bride trained and waiting,' the little man continued.

'This is very sad news indeed,' her father said. 'How did he die?'

The little man shook his head so slightly that Lis would not have noticed had she not been watching him closely.

Does he think we were involved in his death? she wondered.

'I thank you for coming so far with this sad news,' her father said, standing slowly from his chair. 'Please pass my condolences to the emperor and his family.'

'You may do that yourself,' the man said, bowing a little. 'For your daughter is of age.'

Lis looked at her sister and then her father. His features hadn't changed, and he stepped towards the little man.

'Explain yourself.' His voice carried a dangerous tone, making Lis want to take a step backwards.

'In this trying time, the young prince, Rei Remi, must step into his brother's place as heir. He will be of age to be announced in three years. Your youngest daughter would have been offered for selection if he had been the eldest.'

'Tradition dictates that the future empress is chosen as a child. We presented our eldest daughter for the Choosing twelve years ago,' he said, and although he did his best to keep his voice level, Lis heard the strain. 'She is too old,' he said.

'There is little choice, General Long. The Empire has decreed that the new crown prince will be treated as the former was, and a bride must be chosen from amongst the daughters of the Empire's best men.'

Her father bowed slowly before the little man, and Lis's heart stopped.

'But I am to marry Peng in the summer,' she said, then looked down as her father turned angry eyes on her.

Her mother slipped a warm hand into Lis's and squeezed gently.

'You are not married yet, child. You will present yourself for the Choosing on the next full moon.'

'Next week?' Lis said too quickly. She chewed on her lip as she looked down again at the polished floor rather than meet her father's disappointed eyes.

The little man bowed and turned on his heel. He shuffled towards the door, the guards only a step behind, and the whole family followed them out to watch them sail away from the small island. The mountains of Fourth, one of the main islands of the Tei-Emi Chain, loomed in the distance and they stood in silence as the little boat moved slowly across the waters towards its shores.

Peng joined them in standing to watch it disappear as he put his arms around Lis and pulled her close.

'You can't let her go,' her mother begged, turning to her father and grabbing at his arm. 'They will find her out.'

'There is no choice,' her father responded, his focus on the disappearing boat.

'What has happened?' Peng asked.

'The crown prince is dead,' Lis's sister, Ting, said. 'Lis must present before the emperor for the Choosing.'

'She is too old,' Peng said quickly, 'and we are to marry.'

'But you are not married yet,' her father said, turning from the water, the tone of his voice making it clear there would be no argument. 'Lis is of age, or at least she would have been when the new crown prince was at the age of the Choosing. I will tell the emperor of the match. She is a country girl; she will not present as well as the daughters of those living on the main islands. We will go as requested and return with stories.'

Lis sighed with relief as Peng nodded against her head.

'Go home now, boy. We must prepare for the journey, and you shall see her again soon enough.'

Peng bowed low to Lis's father and then to her mother. Lis walked with him towards his little boat at the end of the jetty. As she took his hands, she allowed him to kiss her, even though she was sure her family still watched over them.

'See you soon,' he whispered before kissing her forehead and stepping into the boat.

She choked down the threatening tears as she waved him off. His little boat disappeared quickly against the blue-grey waves of the ocean, and yet she continued to wave.

She walked slowly back to the house, thankful that her family weren't watching her. The field of pink flowers was still in full bloom. She wanted to run back through the colour and remain wrapped in Peng's arms, but instead she walked back into the house.

Standing in the doorway, Lis watched her family in silence. Her father sat at the centre of the table as her mother served his evening meal. She poured rice wine into a small cup, and he drank it down, then nodded at the cup without a word. She refilled it and he drained it again before she sat beside him.

Lis stepped forward and dropped to her knees before them. 'Is there no other way?' she asked.

Her father shook his head without looking at her, and her mother put her hand on his arm.

'Do you really think they will not choose me? That I will not present well?'

He sighed then. 'I do not want you to take offence at my words,' he said softly. 'But you have been raised to do as you please. You run free in the fields, working your magic.' As Lis opened her mouth, he put up a hand and looked at her with friendly eyes.

'This is the life I wanted for you,' he said. 'You are the reason I asked for this island, so that you would be safe and free to live. You do not know what I have done in the name of the Rei-Een Empire, nor do I want you to know. This was our chance at freedom, your chance. When you stand before the emperor and empress of Rei-Een, you will be standing amongst young women who have trained their whole lives to make good wives. Peng would be lucky to have you, and he would treat you well, but these other girls were bred for different lives in a different world. The empress will look over you to the next in line. When I talk with the emperor about your connection, it may be that he will excuse you from the line before it is formed.'

'Thank you, Father,' Lis said. Holding her arms out before her, fingertips to elbows, she bowed low and touched the floor.

'We will go together, to offer our condolences for the lost prince and congratulate the family of the next hidden princess.'

'Yes, Father,' Lis said, bowing again.

'I do not need to tell you that you must be very careful with your magic. If there is even a hint of it, they will kill you. Without a thought as to who you are or your connection to me. Do you understand?'

She nodded quickly.

'The law is to kill everyone with magic. Everyone.'

2

Prince Remi paced the balcony outside his room and tried not to think of his brother, Ta-Sho. But he couldn't do anything without thinking of him. He stopped, leaned on the thick rail and looked across the Palace Isle towards the neighbouring island. The second island of the Empire was much closer to the palace than he had realised before. Despite the number of times he had stood on this balcony, looking across at the trees and red-tiled rooves of the large houses that covered its slopes. Many of the nobles who spent their days at the palace had homes and estates on Second.

Remi preferred Third and Fifth, perhaps because they were further away from the Palace Isle. He wouldn't have the same chance to travel now that he was the crown prince. He had sometimes looked out from his ship to the tiny islands further from the main islands with a sense of envy. Most of them were uninhabited. One was a hospital for the mad, and another had been gifted to a general who had fought in the magic war with his father. Remi had heard many stories of the great General Long, but he had not seen the man since he was a child.

Not that the magic war had really been won, despite what his father told him. Remi felt the magic in the Empire every day. He always tried to seek it out, to do his father's bidding. When he had found Ta-Sho, bent and burnt, the reek of magic hung in the air.

But his father hadn't believed him then. Believing him would mean believing magic had found its way into the royal residence, into the centre of the Empire, and the emperor couldn't have that—or admit it.

All Remi wanted was justice for his brother, and now his mother was insisting on the Choosing. Insisting that, as the new heir, it was imperative he have a bride. He thumped his fist on the railing. He didn't need a bride; he needed his father's men so he could find Ta-Sho's killer.

That was what Ta-Sho would have done, if things had been reversed. If Remi had been killed, his brother would not have waited for his father's approval. But the emperor was hesitating in a way Remi had never before seen.

Remi jumped at the sound of the door, then balled his fists in frustration that he could be so easily spooked. Princess U'shi appeared in the doorway to the balcony dressed in white, her eyes red and her face damp as she wrung her hands before her.

'You shouldn't be here,' he said.

'I have nowhere to go.' She sniffed loudly. 'I am nothing without your brother, and I have heard rumours of another Choosing.'

He nodded once and turned back to the view.

'I am trained,' she whispered, standing beside him. 'I am ready to be his empress and yet he is gone. Why choose another? I could be your empress,' she said softly, placing her hand on his.

He pulled his hand from beneath hers and sighed. 'Traditions must be followed,' he echoed his mother's words. Not that he wanted to follow the traditions himself—but U'shi had been trained to be his brother's wife, hidden away since she was a child. *She should still be hidden*, he thought. He had no preference for his own bride, but he didn't want his brother's. She was beautiful, with a round face, pale skin, light brown eyes and hair blacker than the night. But he didn't like her. He only hoped his mother would choose better for him.

He wondered then, for the first time, if his father had liked his mother.

There was more to worry about for the Empire than whether Remi had a bride he could like. She would be whatever was best for the Empire, he hoped. He glanced again at the woman beside him. Large tears tracked down her cheeks, marking her pale makeup. He wasn't sure what had inspired his mother's choice, but he couldn't picture this woman as Empress.

'You should return to your palace,' he said softly. 'Mother will know what is best.'

'By starting afresh with some girl who has not enough time to become what you need her to be?' She sucked in a breath.

He waved her away without looking up and tried to ignore the sob as she shuffled towards the door. What did she hope he would be able to do for her? He had no say in any of this, and he wanted to be out searching for his brother's killer.

After waiting long enough for the princess to be beyond the residence, Remi headed for his father's throne room in the hope of persuading the man to send him out.

Many of those he passed on the way were dressed in white to honour his brother. As he drew closer to the throne room, he wondered if he should have checked his brother's room first, for his parents might be there praying for his soul. He was almost disappointed to find his father sitting on the throne, giving instructions to soldiers. Remi stepped forward and bowed, then stood to the side while his father continued with his instructions.

'Let me go,' Remi finally said as the last of the men left the throne room.

The emperor shook his head and waved forward another man from behind him. Remi turned to see the short advisor, Gan, his angled hat tied firmly beneath his chin. He bowed low before the emperor.

'Your Excellence, I have informed every family with a daughter of age to present before you on the appointed day.'

'Did you experience any problems?'

'There was one daughter already wed, but we were aware of the match. Another, General Long's younger daughter, is promised to another, but they are not yet wed.'

'If she is promised to another, she is ineligible for the Choosing,' Remi said.

'They are not married,' the little man repeated, 'and she is the daughter of General Long. I think it worth her attending. They have become country folk,' he said. 'She is outspoken and the empress may not approve, but tradition calls for all eligible girls to attend.'

'Indeed,' the emperor said.

'Can this not wait?' Remi asked.

'She is already missing years of training. The sooner your bride is chosen, the sooner we can get on with the business of discovering the cause of your brother's death.'

'We already know,' Remi muttered under his breath, and his father stood tall.

Remi dropped to his knees, crossing his arms and holding them out, he bowed his head.

'The whole Empire cannot fall apart as we search for one man,' the emperor said. 'Traditions must be maintained. The killer cannot get far; the whole world is watching for him.'

'And if it is more than one man?'

'Magic has been destroyed in the Empire,' Advisor Gan said. 'Your father has seen to it.'

'Many years ago. What if it has returned?'

'When you have your bride hidden,' his father said sternly, 'you may use your gifts to find the killer. But not until she is hidden. One more week is all you must wait.'

Remi bowed low before his father and stood slowly. A week might as well be a lifetime. He strode out from the throne room, too angry to think of where to go or what to do. He would have to wait as his father instructed, and then he might get the freedom to do what was needed.

As he strode through the palace, he found his mother standing by a channel of water that flowed across the island. Large golden fish swam in the murky water, between the lilies and beneath the red painted-bridges that crossed the many channels. She stared unseeing into the water, and he took her hand as he stepped up slowly beside her.

'You will be present for the Choosing, my love?' she asked, her gaze still on the water, and he nodded as he squeezed her hand. 'It is important.'

'I will,' he said.

'She must be to your liking.'

'Must she? Did Ta-Sho have a say?'

'He did, although he was a child. Traditions are turned around, and I worry she will not have the time to train as required. But you are a man, and you must find in her what a man wants.'

He gulped down his surprise, staring at the usually distant woman and what she was offering him. She turned slowly and lifted a hand to his face. Her eyes were wet although she did not appear to have been crying, and she left her hand on his face as she stared into his eyes.

'Your brother chose a beautiful girl because he thought she would be beautiful on the inside as well as the out. She may not have been best for the Empire, but she was the best of what was offered in the Choosing. You may consider differently, for they will not be girls standing before you, but women.'

'I thought it was your choice,' he whispered, placing his hand over hers.

'It is, although I may take your choice into consideration. It is you who must live with her.'

'Did father have a say in your Choosing?'

'I do not know.' She pulled her hand from beneath his and turned back to the water. 'He has never told me, and it is something I cannot ask. I miss Ta-Sho,' she said.

'Would you like me to pray with you?' Remi asked.

She shook her head. 'I have prayed all night and no peace has found me yet.'

'What will happen to U'shi?'

She turned back to him with a questioning look. 'You cannot have her.'

'I do not want her,' he said quickly. 'But I want to know what will become of her.'

'She will assist with the training of the next hidden princess. She will watch over her, serve her.'

'I don't think she'll like that,' he said quietly.

'She was trained to be of use to the future emperor. That man is now you,' his mother said softly, her voice catching in her throat. 'Her use to you will be to watch over your bride.'

He nodded and kissed her quickly on the cheek before turning back towards his room. Only a week, and he had no idea how many women of the Empire he would have the chance to choose from. Advisor Gan had only mentioned the two out of the running, one already wed and the other promised.

He didn't care for the bride, but the sooner she was hidden away to train, the sooner he could hunt out the magic he was sure still survived within the Empire.

3

Lis stepped into the boat and, as it swayed beneath her feet, she stretched out a hand to her father to steady her. It had been some time since she had left their island home, and a nervousness crawled over her skin, making her shiver. She took the bag handed to her by her sister and then her sister's bag, and despite the sick feeling welling in her stomach, she moved slowly to the front of the boat to add the bags to those already there.

She straightened, looking over the world around them, and wondered just how long they would be away. Her mother gently ran a hand over Lis's cheek as she passed her to stand beside her father. Lis tried to prepare herself for the hours they would be spending on the small boat, her father at the helm.

'It will be nice to see the palace again,' her mother said softly, but her father only nodded.

'You are going to love it,' Ting said. 'It is so beautiful.'

Lis looked out across the ocean, so vast and empty. She longed to remain at home, waiting for Peng and news of someone else being chosen. The sound of the wind hitting the sail made her jump, and suddenly they were moving through the water.

'Can we pass Peng's home?' she asked.

When there was no response, she turned to her serious father staring out beyond her, across the water. The red family seal shimmered in the morning light as wind pushed against the sail. Lis's hand tightened around the railing. Their little island was already disappearing into the distance behind them, and Fourth seemed larger than she remembered as they drew closer. Fifth was hazy in the distance to the east, with the sun rising behind it. Lis was sure she could see other sails moving towards them on their way to the Palace Isle.

As a child, she had been so scared that her sister wouldn't return from the Palace Isle. That she would be chosen for the young prince and become the Hidden Princess of Rei-Een. It would be a great honour, she had been told by her mother, but they had returned home in silent relief that they had kept her for themselves. The girl chosen had been quiet and very beautiful, Ting had said, and despite the relief that she could keep her sister, Lis was sure Ting would have been a much better choice.

'What has happened to the hidden princess?' Lis asked. Her mother shook her head and returned her gaze to the water. 'But she was trained to be the wife of one prince; surely she could marry the other.'

'There are strict traditions,' her father reminded her.

'What if something happens to this prince?'

'Lis, enough,' her father scolded, and she turned to look across the boat at Fourth. She wanted to ask again about passing Peng's home, somewhere amongst the tall trees, steep hills and red-tile rooves. But they wouldn't. They would skirt past the island on the way to the palace.

It took much longer to sail beyond the island than she imagined. The steep hills smoothed out to rolling plains, and a beach stretched along the shoreline with people lining the sands. When a child amongst the group waved, Lis held her hand up high and waved back. They were too far away to see faces. Lis wondered if she would ever get the chance to know these people once she married and lived with Peng's family on the large island.

Tradition dictated that she would move to his home, although her father had made promises of his land and that Peng should live with them. The adventure would be exciting. But as they passed the shore and Lis tried to count the number of people watching the boats carry possible princesses towards the capital, she longed for the quiet isolation of their little island.

The Palace Isle, when it came into view, took her breath away. Long, high, grey walls grew out of the rocks along the island, covering the entire shoreline. Soldiers lined the tops of the walls, their silver armour glinting in the fading sunlight. Lis wasn't tempted to wave at them.

More boats than she imagined sailed slowly along the wall, looking for a place they could dock. Her father seemed to know what he was doing, but he had said very little on the journey. Several men pointed towards them from the wall, some saluting, and she remembered her father hadn't always been the man she knew at home. She tried to visualise him in the armour of the Empire, but she couldn't.

As they rounded the Palace Isle, a large dock came into view with many more boats than Lis had anticipated already tied up, bobbing slowly in the water as people disembarked. With so many visitors, so many potential princesses, her chances of going home again were increasing every moment.

'You must be careful,' her father whispered in her ear.

She took a deep breath and nodded as their boat joined the many others at the dock.

Lis and her sister stood with their bags in hand while her father tied up the boat. A soldier marched quickly towards them, determined in his step, and a sudden fear grabbed Lis. The man stopped, pulled her father into a rough embrace and then slapped him on the back.

'Do you not bring servants?' he asked, waving a young man onto the boat. 'You leave your wife to carry her own luggage,' he chastised, holding out his hand for Lis's mother, who smiled at him and took it. He led her down the plank and then bowed low before her. 'If you had married me, dear woman, you would be waited on hand and foot.'

She laughed easily with the soldier, and Ting was quick to hand over her bag to the young man and follow their mother to shore. A shiver ran through Lis before she too handed her bag to the young man, but she couldn't quite bring herself to leave the boat. Her family stood talking and laughing on the dock, yet she couldn't make her legs move.

'Do you need assistance?' the young man asked.

Lis shook her head, but she remained where she was until her father caught her eye and nodded slowly. 'No, thank you,' she said, stepping off the boat. She had the strangest feeling when she stood on the dock, swaying slightly from the hours on the boat as she watched the people and sails around her.

'The Emperor has prepared the Kai Palace for you and your family,' the soldier was saying to her father. 'I will show you the way.' He clapped and a number of young men appeared, taking their luggage and then disappearing again.

'It is exciting,' Ting said as she took Lis's arm and pulled her along behind their parents.

'I wish Peng were here,' Lis murmured when they passed beneath a huge, shiny red gateway. 'The Empire of Rei-Een' and 'Emperor Rei Shoashu' were painted in golden symbols above it. Thick, studded doors stood open for them to enter, but Lis was sure they would be secured of a night as she took in the number of people and soldiers around her.

Although the sun was starting to dip low in the sky, the city before her was alight with lanterns and torches. The white stone of the temple reflected the orange lights, making the world around it glow. She stopped and smiled. It was just as beautiful as her mother had described. High rooves dominated the space, with flags of the Empire fluttering in the wind from towers along the wall and against the pillars of some of the larger buildings. She had no idea what any of them were, or what business went on within them.

'There are so many people,' she murmured.

'There aren't usually this many,' the soldier with them said kindly, and she turned to him. 'Many have come to the Palace Isle to see who the next hidden princess will be.'

'Will we have a chance to visit the baths?' Lis asked.

Her mother smiled but shook her head. 'There will be much to do,' she said, following after her husband. Lis tried not to sigh as she allowed the soldier to lead them towards where they were to stay. It was further from the main buildings of the palace, and she wondered if there was any greenery at all amongst all the stone and tiles.

When they entered a walled section, Lis realised just how vast this island was. But as they walked, she thought it didn't look quite as shiny as her mother had described; many of the walls were simple grey stone, and the rooves she could make out were faded.

Despite the tired appearance of the palace and the fact that she was wearing her best skirt, Lis felt like the country girl she was. They had seen so many people, yet she couldn't tell who was here to look and who was here to present a daughter. She could understand just what her father had meant more and more with every girl they saw—how much more presentable they were. But no matter what her father said, this was not going to be as easy as she'd hoped.

They stopped at an old wooden gate, its red lacquer even more faded than other parts of the palace.

'This is perfect,' her father said. He pushed it open with a squeak to reveal a small building with the prettiest garden Lis had ever seen.

Every flower was pink, blossoms on the trees, flowers in pots and between the perfect lawn. She disappeared for a moment between the trees and found a small pond, smiling when large white fish appeared from its depths. Perhaps this visit wouldn't be so bad after all. She worked her way back through the garden to find a soldier standing outside the house. She nodded once, but he didn't move.

The house had been described as a palace, yet it still appeared to Lis to be a house. A small, covered veranda ran the front of the small dwelling. Two simple chairs sat side by side and Ting stood beside them, taking in the garden. Lis entered the house to find it light and bright. A maid waiting by the door bowed to her, and she found a simple room with a low table and cushions, her father already sitting at it with the soldier, raising a cup of rice wine.

'Lis?' her mother called, and Lis followed her voice through to a smaller room beyond. A bed was built into the far wall of the room, the pulled-back curtains revealing exquisite silk bedding in the same pinks as the garden. 'We will not be here long, but let's enjoy the comfort.'

Lis nodded. 'Shall I prepare the meal? I feel as though we have been travelling all day.'

'There is no need,' her mother said. 'We have a maid to assist, and the food will be...'

A small bell sounded, and Lis and her mother entered the main space to find several maids placing food on the table. The soldier made to stand up, but her father took his arm. 'Join us,' he said, and the other man sat quickly.

Her mother sat slowly beside her father, and Lis found herself beside the soldier.

'Lis, this is an old friend, General Zho-Hou. Although he wasn't so highly ranked last time I saw him.'

The man laughed comfortably. 'I hear you are promised to another,' he said to her.

She nodded slowly as she looked over the plates before her. A maid poured wine into a cup for her, and she felt surrounded.

'Peng,' she managed, wondering where to start.

'May I?' the small maid behind her asked, reaching beyond her with chopsticks to place meats and an unknown vegetable in her bowl.

'Thank you,' she whispered.

'It is a shock for you to be off your island,' General Zho-Hou said as Ting joined them. 'The old general should bring you girls to visit more often. The Palace Isle is not what it was. Not as many visit from the other islands, unless they need to. I fear once the Choosing is complete, he will take you away again.'

Lis smiled then. Feeling a little more relaxed, she picked up her chopsticks and started to eat. It was very good, and she lost herself for a moment in the simple joy of good food.

'How long will we be here?' Ting asked.

'Do you not like it?' he asked her.

'Oh yes, I am happy to stay as long as we can, with food such as this.'

Lis smiled in agreement and gulped at the wine, which made her head buzz.

'It depends on the Choosing. If it is an easy choice, it may be over in a day. If not, it may take weeks.'

'How long were we here before?' Ting asked.

'Five days,' her father answered.

'There will be some small variations from tradition,' the general said.

'What kind of variations?' her mother asked. Lis could hear the fear in her voice.

'Given the age and smaller number of girls to choose from, as well as the lack of time for training, the empress wishes to talk with each girl in private to ensure the correct choice is made.'

Lis gulped again at her wine. 'How many girls will line up?'

'Fifteen,' he said, his voice solemn.

'So few?' Ting asked.

'It is an honour to be selected, and many families would have tried to produce a daughter for the crown prince.'

'Only he died, and no one was prepared for this one,' Lis whispered.

The general smiled kindly. 'No, they weren't.'

'Fifteen is not many,' she said, looking at her father, and he nodded slowly.

She would need to be careful. But then, she was already promised to Peng; hopefully she would be out of the running before the race started.

General Long knew before he had even opened his mouth to ask that the emperor would deny his request. It had been twelve years since he had stood in this throne room, and nothing but the colour of the emperor's hair had changed. Emperor Rei Shoashu sat before him on the wide, low, golden throne; bright yellow fabrics highlighting the opulence of it. The emperor himself was dressed in the deepest blue robes with silver trim. The general looked down over his own attire and brushed absently at the rough cloth of his sleeve. It was much finer material than he would have worn as a soldier, yet he felt inadequate before his emperor.

The emperor, his hair greying by his temples, glanced across at the general but did not speak nor beckon him forth. The others in regal dress were all seen to first, and for a moment the general was tempted to step back out into the courtyard and check the sun. It would not be long before their daughters would be called to stand before the royal family. He had hoped for a quiet word, to have his daughter excused before the proceedings began. Once she was lined up with the others, he wasn't sure what he would be able to do.

'General Long,' the emperor finally called, and the general knelt quickly on the floor before him, bowing low. 'It has been so long, old friend. Tell me, how is your island?'

'It is perfect, Your Eminence,' General Long said softly, his eyes still focused on the highly polished boards before him.

'Do not stand on ceremony,' the emperor said. 'Let me look you over and see which of us has aged better.'

'That is certainly your luck,' the general said, standing slowly, his knees creaking. *Has it been so long since I have knelt before the emperor?*

'You have a daughter to present to me,' the emperor said.

'As honoured as I am, Eminence, I hope to excuse her from the Choosing.'

'Truly?' The emperor drew out the word in a way that made the general cringe.

'She is promised to another,' he said, trying to sound apologetic.

'She is of age?'

'Eighteen.'

'Did she visit for the last Choosing?'

He shook his head once, but said nothing. It had been too dangerous then to bring her with them. She had developed her magic so young and so clearly that he'd been sure she would have given herself away—or worse, and he would have lost two daughters. They had claimed she was ill.

'Your eldest would have been of age for Crown Prince Ta-Sho.'

He nodded once.

'It may be well that she was not chosen then. But I will see the youngest.'

'On her own?' he asked, unsure what that would mean and whether he should be relieved or more concerned.

'In the line. She is not married yet. She should have the option of the other girls.'

General Long bent low before the emperor. When he looked up, the emperor was already talking with one of his advisors.

He moved quickly out into the sunshine of the courtyard and sucked in a deep breath. He didn't want Lis here. The risk was too great. But he had no choice; if he were to hide her away or try to return home, it would be taken as a personal insult to the Empire and he would lose more than his daughter.

The Empire from his vantage point didn't look nor feel any

different. All those years of hunting and killing during the magic war, and the world still went on. He shook his head to dispel the images starting to take form in his mind, images of what he had seen and what he had done in the name of his Empire. He had been released from service with the only gift he wanted, somewhere safe for his family, somewhere safe for Lis to grow without being discovered.

'General Long,' a deep voice said behind him, and he turned to find a fit, handsome young man bowing. Unlike his father, he wore white, his jet-black hair tied neatly on top of his head with a small, simple crown pinned in place over the bun. 'I could not wait until the Choosing to meet you, for I have heard much of you and what the Empire owes you.'

'Your Highness,' the general said, returning the young prince's bow. 'It is an honour.'

'I was not sure if I would see you,' the young man went on, and the general waited for an explanation. 'Your daughter may not be lining up with the others.'

'Your father has declared she will, so you will see us all.'

The young man's face clouded. 'I thought her promised to another.'

'She is not yet wed, Your Highness, and so she is eligible for the Choosing.'

'Do you know how many have come?'

The general shook his head just as the young man continued, 'It matters not. My mother will make the choice she thinks best for the Empire.'

'I hope your hidden princess is all that you need her to be.' The general bowed before the prince.

He was not the boy the general remembered, he was already a man. If he had been the eldest son, the general guessed he would have considered differently when the hidden princess was chosen at eight. Now he was choosing a woman of eighteen. It would be a very different prince looking at very different prospective princesses. The crown prince bowed again to the general and then turned and walked away.

The general watched after him. He probably wanted to be focused on different tasks, such as finding out what had happened to his brother, for there was very little information about the death or what was being done. He had been cremated the same day he was found, and although the prince wore white, the general was sure he would be dressed as his father was by the time the girls lined up to be viewed.

He hurried down the steps towards the little palace he shared with his family. He still thought she would be going home with them when the time came, but he was nervous to tell her she would have to line up with the others in the afternoon sun.

4

Despite her father's calm assurances, and the number of people standing in the large open courtyard that led to the throne room of the palace, Lis felt nervous. When her father grabbed her arm, his fingers biting into the skin, she felt even more so.

'Why is *she* here?' he asked, so quietly Lis wasn't sure if he had spoken.

'Who?' she asked as she looked around.

'The high priestess,' he said, motioning towards the top of the steps.

The royal family stood together, all in matching deep-blue robes with silver trim. Lis noticed, even with the distance, that the trim was different for each, the pattern varying enough to differentiate the three.

The empress was perfect. She should have been a similar age to Lis's mother, but she appeared years younger. Her slim figure accentuated the size of the men beside her, and her hair was pulled back perfectly into a number of curved shapes. Her crown shone brightly in the sunlight, as did the golden pins that showed just how powerful this woman was and the wealth of the Empire.

The woman beside her was simple in comparison. Her robes were white and, although they crossed at the neck in the same style as worn by everyone else in the Empire, that was where the similarity ended. They fell almost straight to her feet from her armpits, her arms covered in fitted sleeves rather than the wide, flowing sleeves everyone else wore. Thick bands of gold surrounded each wrist, almost reaching her elbows. She was marked as a priestess of the gods, the size of the armbands noting her as High Priestess, and Lis wondered why she was present for such a day. She had thought someone of this woman's station would remain on the Sacred Isle.

Lis remembered vague stories of their involvement in the magic war, although she wasn't sure where she had heard them, nor could she remember any detail of their involvement. She wondered for a moment if that was why her father had reacted so.

Lis tried to slow her breathing and pull her magic deep inside, where this woman couldn't read her, but she was sure the high priestess's eyes were already focused on her through the crowd. A deep gong sounded and the girls around her started to move forward, Lis's father's hand still tight around her arm. Her mother murmured something in his ear and he released her. As she stepped forward slowly to take her place in the line, Lis only hoped that her long silk sleeves hid the mark she was sure her father's grip had left.

Despite the different coloured gowns, embroidered flowers, fantastical hair styles and beautiful pins, Lis thought they all looked the same. As she looked between the girls being directed into the line by various advisors, all with strange angled hats like that of the man who had visited their island, she found some looked more confident than others. One girl looked so nervous, Lis worried she would faint. Some held themselves still; others fiddled with hair pins or sleeves.

Lis had selected pale colours. Her dress was white with tiny embroidered blossoms in the palest pink. She had thought they should all be dressed in mourning, but as the emperor himself was not, she was sure it would not go against any one of them. She cleared her throat, clenched her hands before her and then looked up at the priestess watching her.

The advisors moved back, and the royal family stepped forward. The line of girls raised their arms before them and bowed as one. Lis tried to contain her smile. They had actually managed, without practice, to be synchronised.

The prince was a tall, broad man who looked older than Peng, and it surprised Lis how much more like a man he appeared to be. In some ways she had expected a boy, thinking of the usual traditions associated with such a day, but he was far from such. He was similar in his features to his father, and he rolled his shoulders with a glance at the line of women before him as the empress slowly walked down the stairs.

Lis didn't want to focus on the girls beside her, instead watching the priestess follow the empress towards them. The empress walked slowly along the line, the priestess a step behind. All they did was look, and the longer it took the more uncomfortable Lis felt. She chanced a glance at the emperor and his son standing watch over the proceedings and found the prince watching her. She shifted her gaze back to the front.

The empress moved back to the front of the line. 'A beautiful group of girls,' she said softly, but her voice carried across the expanse of the yard. Lis gulped down her growing unease. 'My son will look,' she said, waving her hand along the line.

As the emperor walked down the stairs with the prince, Lis wondered if they would eventually choose a bride as they might choose a horse. Would she be expected to show her teeth?

Again, the viewing seemed to take an age, given the number of girls. She tried to maintain a downward gaze as the two men stopped before her. The emperor looked over her too long, and she raised her eyes a little to find the prince studying her seriously. She wanted desperately to cough as her throat closed and the saliva in her mouth dried up instantly. She wanted to turn and see what her father was doing, whether he understood what they might think of her. She could feel her magic pushing its way to the surface, and she thought she would burst.

The emperor and the prince joined the empress to discuss each girl, quite clearly. At times one would turn and point to a place in the line. Lis felt ill. They might as well be horses, she thought as anger grew in her chest and pushed aside her previous fear. Several girls were described as pretty, and one girl gasped out loud. Lis couldn't see her face but assumed she was the one the emperor referred to as chubby.

They talked amongst themselves for some time whilst the sun grew hotter in the sky, and Lis regretted wearing all that she had. She longed for a cool breeze. The emperor was becoming more animated, whilst the prince looked mostly at the ground, occasionally glancing up. Lis caught his dark eyes more than once. The empress was quite forceful with her words, and the priestess whispered in her ear.

Eventually, the empress held out her hand and silenced her husband. Then she turned to the line. 'We shall review the line one more time,' she said in her quiet way. 'If you are told yes, you will enter the next round of investigations.'

Lis looked at the woman seriously. 'Investigations' was an odd word to use, and she wondered what they would do to these girls to see who was fit to be Empress. The current empress wore a serene face and perfect hair, but Lis wondered what trials she had undergone to become the woman she was now.

She tried not to flinch as the group drew nearer and the priestess still watched her closely. Lis tried to look beyond her, out across the stones, and count the steps that led to the throne room. She must have distracted herself well, for suddenly the group stood before her and the priestess was placing a hand on her forehead. Her first thought was that she hoped it didn't damage the hours of work her mother had put into her hair. The woman nodded and the empress said, 'Yes.' And Lis found she couldn't form a single thought.

The emperor smiled again and, as they focused on the next in line, Lis turned and looked for her parents in the crowd. She wished Peng was here.

The girl beside her lifted her hands to her chest as she was told 'yes,' and Lis was sure she was pleased. Whoever was chosen from this group to represent them as the future empress would spend the next three years in isolation, learning all there was to know about being Empress and pleasing the emperor.

It could have been worse. She might have been chosen as a child to spend thirteen years in training. Locked away somewhere in the palace, hidden from the world and the prince. The current hidden princess had spent twelve years hidden, so close to becoming the wife of the crown prince, yet now she had no place in the world she had trained for.

Lis wondered again what would become of her, but now was not the time to ask. She closed her eyes, listening half-heartedly to the empress tell each girl yes or no. There appeared to be far more yeses than noes. *Still not enough of a crowd to disappear into*, Lis thought. Then she remembered her father's words, that the empress would talk with each of them individually.

Lis was sure the sun had started to dip when the empress resumed her place before the line. Despite some of the crying, the woman's voice carried clear. 'If you were told no, you may enjoy the rest of the festivities with your families or return to your homes. The girls to continue in the line will be sent for.' With that, they turned and walked slowly up the stairs to disappear into the throne room.

Lis let out a breath and turned to the girl next to her, who narrowed her eyes. A girl a little down the line started to sob, but Lis only wanted her family, so she searched the crowd until she found her father's serious face. As she drew closer, her sister gave her a half smile and her mother just stood in stunned silence.

They stood as they were for a moment, and then her father pulled them into an embrace that locked them all together.

The next day, Lis sat in the pink light of the morning sun, enjoying the crisp, cool air and the silence that surrounded her as she dipped her fingers into the pond. Large, white coy appeared from nowhere and kissed her fingers. When she sprinkled food across the surface, they followed it back into the depths.

She wanted to push her bare feet into the cool water and wake herself from the strange dream she seemed caught in. She could still feel the priestess's hand on her forehead, and she wondered just what the woman had found or felt that made her choose to keep her.

She couldn't picture remaining here, as beautiful as it was. She missed her home, and she wondered whether the prince actually wanted a bride. But then, he had seemed to study her for far longer than was polite. Had he looked at them all in the same way? she wondered. He was a handsome man with an intense look, she thought with a blush, and she was sure he would find someone to match him within the small group on offer. Her memory of the priestess was clearer, and she wondered if the woman's piercing eyes only concerned her because of her father's reaction. Lis ran her hand through the water again.

What if they know what I am and it is a trap?

She shook her head. She didn't think they would be so subtle. If she'd been discovered, she would have been dispatched, and the viewing of the line would have continued as though she had never been there.

She ran her damp fingers through her hair, thankful it was free. Her mother had wanted her to sleep in it so she would be ready if she was called the following day. But the pins had hurt her head and her hair had been so tight. She stood slowly, stretching her arms high over her head and closing her eyes, thankful for the cold stones beneath her feet. With the sky starting to turn orange, Lis headed for the house, where she was sure her mother would soon appear demanding that she dress.

It would take time to talk to each in the line, if they were to be spoken to individually. It could take days to work through them all. Just as Lis's foot found the first step, a loud banging started on the gate, and the maid raced from the house to open it before anyone could stop her.

'Long Lisabet is requested to attend the empress,' an older man called in a singsong voice.

Lis's mother appeared at the front door with a look of horror. 'We shall dress immediately.'

'You are required to attend the empress,' the man said again, turning his back and waiting by the gate. 'Now.'

'Hurry,' her mother whispered.

'There is no time,' he said, his voice losing the patience it had held so briefly. 'The Empress of Rei-Een waits for no one.'

Lis squeezed her mother's hand and followed the man out into the narrow laneway that ran beside the wall of their palace. Men waited at other gates and girls appeared in similar states to Lis. Most looked tired, and some had their hair still done. One even had a pin sticking neatly from the side, small jewels hanging from the end of it. Lis wondered if she had slept in that too, or if her mother had managed to secure it as she left.

When they arrived in the courtyard, they continued through to a part of the palace that Lis had not visited, and she was in awe at the size of it. The girls' journey ended with a large group in a small room. Lis discovered that despite their differences, she was the only one with bare feet.

The advisors appeared and worked their way through the girls, looking over them with disapproval. They organised the girls into a short line and then stood at the doorway. The silence was overwhelming. Lis looked around and discovered she was similarly placed as the previous day, though the girl behind her looked far less friendly. Lis realised she would be seen as competition. She had just opened her mouth to reassure the girl when the advisor at the door 'shushed' the room, so she closed it again without speaking.

Lis leaned carefully to the side and counted four in front of her. The advisor at the door glared at her again, and then the door opened. The first in line was ushered through before the door quickly closed again. Lis listened, but she could hear nothing. They all remained in line, waiting their turn for whatever might lie on the other side of the door. Glancing around, Lis was finally able to count the girls behind her. Six. Who knew there were so few eligible girls within the Empire? There would have been at least three times that number when her sister was called.

It was half an hour before the door opened again and the next in line was ushered through. Lis wondered what had happened to the first one. Had she been shown home, shown to another room, given back to her family? Would they open the door and announce the hidden princess had been chosen and they could all go home?

Lis wasn't sure she could endure the waiting. But when the door opened again and the next was moved through, it had barely been five minutes. Lis wondered why the girl had been dismissed so quickly.

Will I be sent away? Can I tell them of Peng?

The waiting was becoming unbearable when the fourth in line was shown in. Lis wondered what she might be asked—and how she could answer in a way that would not embarrass her father but also would do her no favours. She smiled to herself then. There was no way they would choose a country girl, particularly one with bare feet and free hair.

When the door opened, she jumped, and the advisor indicated that she step forward. The door closed behind her and then another opened in front of her. The room she stood at one end of was long and narrow. The empress sat on a wide throne at the far end, the high priestess behind her. Just to the side, an advisor or the like stood at a desk. There were silk screens just out from the wall along both sides of the room, and with barely any effort she could sense someone behind one of them. The prince, she imagined, but she didn't acknowledge him. Instead, she walked the length of the room and knelt before the empress.

'Lisabet,' the empress said softly. 'Such an unusual name.' She waved at the man standing at the desk, and he picked up a brush.

'Your Eminence,' Lis said softly. 'My father discovered it on his travels whilst serving the emperor.'

The empress waved her words away, and Lis waited while the woman stood and walked around her slowly. 'Stand up,' she said.

Lis lifted herself to her feet and tried to stand still as she was surveyed.

'Quite pretty,' the empress said.

'Thank you, Your...'

'Shh,' the empress snapped. 'She has lovely hair, a good face.'

Lis bit her lip, hoping she wasn't going to be asked to show her teeth, for she feared she wouldn't be able to remain polite.

'Her father is a good man. Can you count?' the empress asked, and Lis nodded. 'Can you write?'

Lis nodded again.

The empress sat back down with a nod, then waved the other woman forward.

'Do you pray often to the gods and ancestors?' the high priestess asked, her eyes burning into Lis's skin.

Lis nodded again.

She moved her hand over Lis's head but didn't touch her. Then she nodded once and moved back behind the empress. They both stared at Lis silently for a time, then looked at each other.

Unsure if the audience was over or not, Lis bowed low and made to walk towards a door she could see to the side with an advisor standing in front of it.

'Sing,' the empress said.

'Pardon?' Lis asked, stopping in her tracks.

'Sing,' the empress instructed.

'What would you like me to sing?'

'Anything.' The empress smoothed out her dress, folded her hands in her lap and waited.

Lis cleared her throat as she took her place back before the two women. Then gripped her hands before her and thought of Peng. She sang soft and high, a song she had heard her mother sing, one she would sometimes sing to Peng when they were alone, one that brought tears to her eyes.

When she finished, the empress nodded once. And Lis chanced to glance at the doorway.

'You are promised to another,' the high priestess said.

'Wu Peng,' Lis whispered.

'Is he a good man?' the empress asked, and Lis nodded, willing the tears that were starting to spill over to stop.

'If you could say one thing and one thing only to Crown Prince Remi before you leave for your little island home, what would it be?'

'I am sorry for your loss,' she said quickly, wiping at her face. 'I cannot imagine how hard it would be to live without my sister; I'm sure it is unbearable to lose such a brother.' Lis chewed her lip as she thought the empress's own lip trembled. 'And I am sorry for you too,' she added, 'for a parent should not outlive a child.'

The empress opened her mouth to say something, although Lis didn't think she had taken the words exactly as they were meant, because her brows drew together. She shooed Lis from the room instead.

5

'I don't think she liked me,' Lis said, playing with her collar and lifting her hand to her hair. Her mother slapped it away before she could disrupt the smoothness she had created, or dislodge the pins delicately protruding from the side. She wore one of her mother's combs, one she had marvelled at the beauty of.

'The phoenix is luck,' her mother had said as she had pushed it into place. 'And it shows that we are not as poor as some think we are.'

'I am only here to show our standing in the Empire?' Lis asked mockingly.

'Of course,' her father said with a wry smile. 'Now finish dressing so you do not embarrass us.'

He was joking, but Lis's eyes fell to her lap and her heart thumped in her throat. 'I hope I have not,' she said softly.

He took her chin and lifted her face. 'I do not think it is possible.'

Lis nodded slowly, and he left them to finish.

It hadn't taken as long as Lis expected for the royal family to select a bride, and she was relieved they would be going home. She missed Peng, and it itched trying to contain her magic. Not only could she not use it, she had to ensure that no one could sense it, so she had pulled it tight within her. She longed for the moment when she could step back onto her little island and be herself again.

The room was hushed when they arrived, a nervousness heavy in the air. The empress and crown prince stood stiff beside the emperor, who sat on his throne. *There is room enough for the three of them to sit*, Lis thought as she tried to contain her own growing nerves. She was unsure if the feeling was because of her own situation, or if it had grown of what she could feel in the air.

She reached again for her hair, but her mother took her hand before it made the distance. Lis tried not to sigh as she looked over the group before her. The high priestess was not amongst them, and the prince himself looked directly at Lis. She gulped down a sudden fear.

'Lis,' her father said softly, 'it will be over soon enough.'

Lis nodded absently, watching the prince turn to his mother as she said something to him, her voice not carrying in the chamber as it had before. That was a skill Lis would like to have, and she wondered what the woman's secret was.

As the last of the families arrived, Lis realised just how many people had come. For the first time, she felt overwhelmed by the crowd and close proximity of so many people. She closed her eyes, thinking of the open spaces of the fields, and then someone tapped her on the arm and she reluctantly looked up to see the girls move forward to take their place in the line once more.

'Last time,' her father whispered.

She nodded as she moved carefully forward to take her place. As the empress stepped forward, another woman appeared behind her. Lis thought she had probably been standing there before, but had gone unnoticed. Her dress was simple but stunning, mostly white with a deep blue beneath it. Although it was a similar colour to that worn by the royal family, it was not the same, and Lis wondered if this was the former hidden princess revealed.

'Tradition is important to the Empire,' the empress said, her voice carrying through the room, and Lis tried to calm her nerves by blowing out a long, slow breath. 'Part of being an empress of such a world is to know these traditions, and so we spend thirteen years training her to be everything the world needs her to be.' She paused, and Lis could see the calm façade crack a little. 'When my eldest son and your crown prince, Rei Ta-Sho died, our traditions were disrupted. Not only was the heir to our Empire gone, but we had wasted twelve years training an empress who would never be.'

Lis noticed the woman in white open her mouth and then close it again. She wiped quickly at the corner of her eye and then looked down at the floor. Lis wondered if she was sad for her lost prince or her lost opportunity.

The empress didn't look away from the crowd or indicate the woman in any way. Still standing tall, her hands before her, she took a breath and then held out a hand to the right. The girl looked up again. 'My son, your Crown Prince Rei Remi, is now heir to the Empire.'

The prince took a step forward and bowed his head to the people. Lis wasn't sure whether they should clap, but the room remained silent.

'As Crown Prince Remi prepares for his place in the world, so shall his bride. Tradition dictates that she must be two years younger, and that she will be hidden away from the world to prevent distraction from her task for thirteen years. When she emerges at the age of twenty-one, they shall marry before all the world.'

Thirteen years is a long time, Lis thought, her heart pounding. There would be no contact with family, but she wondered how many other people the hidden princess could interact with. *Would they change tradition for the new hidden princess? Will she be an old woman once she is free?*

'We must do what we can with what is left of the tradition,' the empress said. 'The hidden princess chosen today will be hidden until she is twenty-one. She will only be hidden for three years.'

The room remained still, and Lis realised she was holding her breath. It made no difference to the outcome of today. Hidden was hidden. She glanced at the young woman standing at the back of the group and thought she looked a little lost. No one acknowledged her; no one looked at her. Although Lis was sure that every other girl in the line was hoping to become her.

The prince stepped forward and smiled at the line, somewhat nervously, but Lis thought it improved him greatly.

'We have chosen,' the empress said softly, stepping down to join her son. He glanced at her and she nodded. 'When the choice is announced, all but the new hidden princess and her family will leave the room immediately.'

Lis wanted to look around then, to find her family and the nearest exit. Would they run, or would they walk in an orderly fashion? Would the other girls move slowly to take the time to look over the one who could have been them?

She closed her eyes, drew in a deep breath and tried to settle the prickling feeling that was moving over her skin. It was not long now and she would be leaving with her family. Running for the little boat, as her father had already ordered the bags packed. And they would be home, Peng waiting on the jetty. She smiled at the idea, opening her eyes just as the prince stepped forward, bowed low before her and said her name.

'No,' she whispered, stepping back as the room emptied around her.

He stood slowly, his eyes a little hard, the friendly smiling prince dissolving.

'I am promised,' she said quickly. 'To Peng. I am to marry Peng.'

'You are to marry my son, Crown Prince Remi, in three years,' the emperor said, his voice hoarse as he stood from the throne. Lis dropped to her knees, bowing low before him.

'Forgive her shock,' her father said beside her.

'There was much deliberation,' the empress said. 'You should be honoured.'

Her father knelt beside her, bowing low to the empress. 'We are very honoured by your choice,' he said.

'Thank you,' her mother whispered, kneeling on the other side of her and bowing low.

'She is bright and beautiful,' the empress said. 'She will make an excellent empress, or at least my son is sure that she will.'

Lis chanced to look up at the man who now seemed somewhat disappointed in his choice.

'Your words to my mother,' he said. Then he turned on his heel and left the room, the unknown woman a step behind.

'Say your goodbyes, child,' the empress said, taking her hands and helping her to her feet. 'For we have much to cover and only three years to do it.'

Lis nodded slowly and then turned to her parents, who pulled her into a tight embrace.

'You must be careful,' her father whispered. 'Please be careful.'

She nodded against him, unable to find her voice as the lump in her throat seemed to close over it. She tried to swallow, reaching up and grabbing at her neck.

Her mother pulled her hand away and smiled through the tears. 'Breathe,' she said softly, putting her hand to her cheek. 'You are clever and beautiful; you will make a wonderful empress.'

The tears rolled away as Lis nodded. 'Peng,' she sobbed.

'I will talk with him,' her father said. 'He will understand. There is nothing that can be done that would undo this. There are strange rumours in the palace,' her father said softly, leaning in close. 'You must not use it. Ever.'

She nodded once.

'Promise me,' he said sternly. 'For it will mean more than your death.'

Lis stared at him as the meaning of his words sank in, and she dragged in a ragged breath. 'Tell Peng I love him.'

Her mother shook her head. 'It is not a good idea.' She opened her mouth to protest, but her mother held up her hand. 'You are the hidden princess.' She bowed a little. 'You are linked to the crown prince and will become our next empress. You cannot love another.'

Lis felt the world heavy on her shoulders, and she nodded through the tears. Ting pulled her into a tight embrace and then ran from the room. Her parents dropped to their knees and bowed low before her. And then they too silently left the open room and Lis started to fall, her knees giving way beneath the sorrow that filled her. A strong hand caught her arm and kept her standing.

'Your Highness,' the deep voice of the owner of the support said, and she turned to the serious face of the prince. 'It is time for you to be hidden away.'

She nodded slowly as he led her towards the throne and then through a door in the screen behind it, his hand still tight around her arm. When she tried to pull from his grip, he held her tighter.

'I will not run away,' she said, her voice still thick with tears. 'For where would I go?'

He nodded once, but kept his hold.

'You are hurting me,' she said softly, her voice cracking, and he let her go instantly. She rubbed at her arm.

'It is my place to take you to your new home. For we shall not see very much of each other...' He looked at her seriously. 'You will not see very much of anyone. But it is my place.'

She nodded, and when he held out his arm, she put her hand on it and allowed him to lead her. They moved in silence through the passageways, and she was surprised by how simple and quiet they were. They passed no one.

'If you know where I shall be hidden, then you can find me at any time.'

He nodded. 'Everyone knows where you shall be hidden, and that is why no one will visit.'

'Oh,' she said.

They stopped in the middle of a passageway, and the prince listened for a moment before opening a door she hadn't seen. They entered a large room with a desk covered in books, scrolls and wooden slips. One whole wall was covered in shelves filled to overflowing with more of the same, while another wall contained a smaller shelf with a beautiful, simple jade pot, a dragon carved into the front of it.

Lis stopped, taking in the room.

'My father's study,' the prince said, pulling her forward.

'How did we get here?'

'Secret tunnels only for the family.'

'But now I know,' she said, looking up at him, and he gave her a tight smile.

'You are now family.'

'Oh.' She allowed him to lead her out of the study and across a smaller courtyard. A long pond ran along its edge, and she could see the large golden fish in the dark water as they passed over a small bridge. The stone was perfectly smooth and the red lacquered railing somehow calming as she slowly moved her hand over it.

'My mother likes this bridge,' he said. 'They all look alike to me, but she often finds her way here.'

Lis smiled at the idea of standing at the top of it and watching the fish swim beneath her, and then she remembered this wasn't a visit. She wouldn't be sailing home again. She coughed, trying to remove the lump that had quickly formed in her throat again.

The palace covered the biggest island in the Ti-Emi Chain, and it appeared that every inch of it had been covered. There was not a soul to be seen, and the further they walked the more nervous Lis became.

'The main residence,' the prince said, pointing to a large building, and she stopped.

'Is there another building on the top?'

'Another storey, yes. It looks out onto the hills of Second.'

'It must be like being up high in the temple.'

'Similar. Have you climbed the temple?' he asked.

She nodded absently as she took in the building. 'When I was a child, on Fourth.'

When he said nothing, she turned and found him smiling. It unnerved her more than she thought it could.

'Will I be hidden in there?' she asked.

He shook his head and led them past the building, over more ponds and bridges, through little gardens, and eventually they arrived at a wall similar to the one behind which she had stayed with her family. The gate was bright red with the symbol for 'hidden' painted in black on it.

As she made to run her hand over it, the gate opened and a large soldier—who towered even over the prince—stepped forward. Lis stepped back, bumping into the prince. The soldier, with a long, narrow sword in his belt, bowed low and then stepped through the gate to stand to the side of it.

The prince nodded at him once and then directed Lis forward. Above the door of the palace, similar to the one in which she had stayed with her family, hung a sign denoting the hidden princess, painted in gold. Lis stopped at the doorway and looked over the garden. It was much larger than the one she had been in; it contained a pond, trees in blossom and flowers that bloomed along one wall. She smelled something sweet and then discovered a tree with fruit. 'How?' she asked.

'They come from different parts of the world and so flower and fruit at different times.'

She looked at him seriously, but he shrugged.

Then the empress was standing in the doorway, and Lis bowed.

'You may go, Remi,' she said kindly.

He bowed low before his mother. 'Your Highness, I present Hidden Princess Lisabet.'

'Lis, please,' she murmured, and the empress frowned.

He bowed to Lis, then turned and disappeared through the gate.

Lis took a deep breath and walked up the steps to meet the empress, who indicated inside the house with an outstretched hand. Following it, Lis stepped into her new life.

6

Lis found the palace was smaller than she'd expected when she stepped inside. Smaller than the other palace they had stayed in, and much smaller than her home on the island. She bit back any comment. They stood in a small foyer with a narrow door directly before her and two larger doors to each side.

'Welcome to the hidden princess's palace,' the maid said, giving an uncertain bow, then clasped her hands before her and looked down.

It was only when the empress coughed that she looked up, and Lis found herself eye to eye with the former hidden princess.

'Thank you,' Lis said, trying to keep the wobble from her voice.

'This is your classroom.' The empress indicated a door to the left, and the maid slid it open. Beyond was a simple room, cabinets with various sized drawers lined one wall. In the centre of the room, two desks sat facing each other, one with a map across its surface. Lis stepped forward and ran her fingers over the old parchment.

'Do you recognise your Empire?' the empress asked.

Lis nodded, looking over the five main islands and then tracing outward with her finger to find her little island home.

When she looked up, the empress was staring at her with hard eyes.

'Yes, Your Eminence,' she said softly. She looked back at the map and ran her hand over the palace. 'This is the centre of the Rei-Een Empire, the Great Palace, also referred to as the Palace Isle. Second, Third, Fourth,' she said slowly, running her finger along the beach line where she had waved at so many. 'And Fifth.'

The empress selected a scroll from beside the map and unrolled it over the top. It was another map, a detailed one of the Great Palace. 'This one you must learn first,' she said.

Lis bent down over the paper and noticed it was newer than the other one, the ink brighter and the parchment not as brittle. 'The main residence,' she said, then looked up at the empress. 'Such a glorious building. The golden roof in the sun was incredible.'

'Yes,' the empress said. 'It sits at the centre of the island.'

Lis nodded and traced over the rivulets that moved through the grounds. 'The bridge,' she said, holding her finger where she hoped the bright red bridge was. 'It was very beautiful. I could stand there all day and watch the fish.'

The empress nodded, and then her face darkened. 'You will have much to learn. Three years is not enough time, not nearly enough,' she added quietly, turning away from Lis and clapping her hands. The sharp sound filled the room.

Two men and a woman appeared from a doorway at the back of the room. Each wore the golden yellow colours of an advisor, but only one of them wore the little angled hat tied beneath his chin with black ribbon. Lis glanced back at the empress, who was waving her forward, then closed her mouth, stepped around the table and bowed to the group.

'These are your tutors,' the empress said. 'They will watch over every aspect of your training. Although they will surely be tested.'

'Three years,' the eldest of the men muttered.

'Yes, thank you, Tutor Jichun. I understand the issues, but traditions must be upheld.'

'Of course, Your Highness,' he said with a bow.

'Tutor Jichun and Tutor Nizen will ensure that you know all

you need of the Empire, and that you can read and write and know your numbers. They will advise what to read and ensure your understanding. They will teach the history of the Empire and its emperors so that you understand why we rule the world as we do.'

Both men bowed, and Lis chewed at her lip. The younger of the advisors glanced towards the maid, but she kept her eyes down.

'Tutor Na,' the empress said, indicating the older woman, 'will ensure that you are a groomed and polished princess.'

Lis looked at her closely.

'That you know how to behave,' the empress snapped, and Lis nodded quickly. 'Your dress, your hair and makeup, as well as your food and general needs shall be met by U'shi.' The young maid looked up at her sharply. 'She will be your sister.'

Lis smiled at the woman, but she scowled and looked back at the ground.

'I thank you for your help,' Lis said.

'We start at dawn,' Tutor Jichun said. He turned and bowed to the empress before turning for the door, and the younger man followed. Lis felt the fear grow again in her chest.

'We shall start this afternoon,' Tutor Na said, a little more friendly in her tone. 'I think you should find a more appropriate dress and take the time to eat. I will join you here.'

Lis bowed her head and wondered what could be more appropriate to wear.

Left alone with the empress and the maid, Lis looked between them.

'Tradition is very important,' the empress said. 'Life is what the gods determine, and they have determined that U'shi shall not be empress.'

U'shi sniffed, and Lis stepped forward but stopped short of her. 'You are the hidden princess,' Lis said softly.

'No,' the empress said sharply. '*You* are the hidden princess. U'shi is here to help you.'

'Would she not want to return to her family?'

U'shi lifted angry eyes to Lis.

'I'm sorry,' Lis said quickly. 'Would you?'

'I cannot,' she snapped.

Lis looked to the empress. 'She knows the secrets of the palace and the family; she must remain here. And her family would be shamed by the loss of status.'

'Surely you would like to see them again.'

'My place is here,' U'shi said, somewhat begrudgingly. 'With you,' she added through gritted teeth.

The empress smiled despite the heavy feeling in the air. 'Good,' she said. 'the high priestess will see you once a month.'

Lis bowed her head, and the empress left them. U'shi stood for a moment, still looking at the floor.

'Can you show me the rest of the house?'

'Palace,' U'shi corrected and, without looking at Lis, led her back through the entrance and a door opposite the class room to a large room—larger than her parents'—with a huge bed built against the far wall. The most exquisite pink silk curtains hung down over perfectly carved lattice work. The quilt had been folded back, and a step ran the length of the opening. The floor was covered with a large woven mat, deep red and gold thread marking out the outline of a dragon.

At the opposite end of the room sat a long and low table, larger than the one in the Kai Palace where Lis had stayed with her family. Cushions in the same silk that covered her bed ran down either side of the table. A kettle sat atop a burner at one end, one cup set out beside it. It struck Lis as strange that there was only one, because there were usually at least four in her father's house at all times.

'Do you not drink with me?' she asked.

U'shi shook her head. 'I have prepared your clothes. I shall bring your meal.'

Lis nodded, unsure whether to sit at the table or check the clothes.

'Come,' U'shi said, her voice harsh. She indicated the clothes and then waited as Lis stepped forward.

Lis was unsure what she was waiting for, but then the woman sighed, walked around behind her and started to untie her sash.

'I think I can change,' Lis said.

'You are a princess now; there is no need for you to do such things for yourself. I am here to assist with all your needs.'

'Do I not get any time to myself?'

'There is time of an evening before you sleep. Why would you need time alone?'

'Did you study of a night?'

When there was no answer, Lis turned.

'I am not to talk of my time as the hidden princess. I am no longer in such a position, and the records will not hold my name.'

'But you have given so much.'

'Not enough to count.' U'shi's voice gave away her frustrations if her words didn't. 'The honour will be yours, if the gods are willing.'

Lis nodded slowly and turned back to allow U'shi to help her out of her clothes. 'Should I wear white for the prince?'

'This is what you wear for classes. You will only dress as your station dictates when you go to the temple.'

'How often can I go to the temple?'

'The empress told you,' U'shi said with a sigh. 'You would do well to listen.'

'Once a month?'

'Exactly.'

Lis looked over the grey tunic. Even the lavender of U'shi's maid uniform was more appealing. The material was thick and stiff, and Lis shifted uncomfortably beneath it. 'I don't feel like a princess,' she muttered.

'You have a long way to go. I don't think three years will be enough.'

Lis sucked in a large breath as U'shi continued to stare at her.

Then she shook out her arms and walked quickly towards the table. 'I'm ready,' she said, sitting carefully and pouring water into the single cup.

U'shi nodded and left the room.

Lis rolled her neck and tried to dispel some of the tension building in her shoulders. It already felt like the longest day of her life, and the midday sun was barely above them. It would be hours before her family was home again, likely after dark, and she wondered if Peng would still be waiting on the jetty as he had promised. How would her father break the news?

U'shi re-entered the room with a tray of bowls of various sizes. She sat one with rice directly in front of Lis and then the others around her. She poured more water into her cup and stood back. Lis glanced at her before peering into each bowl. The food was not as special as the first night at the palace, but it was all different to what she would have eaten at home. She spent her time picking through the bowls and trying not focus on the woman watching her who occasionally coughed or cleared her throat. But Lis had been eating on her own for some time, and she didn't dribble any of it down her chin. She pushed the empty bowl away from her and leaned to the side.

A bell rang in the distance, and U'shi was grinning when Lis looked up. The bell grew louder as U'shi poured more water.

'Do you hear that?' she asked.

And then it stopped. Maybe there was someone passing the wall. Then the door slid open to reveal a furious Tutor Na.

'I know that you are new, Your Highness,' she said sharply, 'but you will need to put in some effort if you are to be the empress the Empire expects you to be.'

Confused, Lis looked from the tutor to the still grinning U'shi. She sat the cup down, stood slowly and bowed low to the tutor. 'I beg your forgiveness for my tardiness,' she said softly. 'I have no excuse, but I do have a question.'

The old woman nodded once.

'Who was the former hidden princess's maid?'

'Shigi,' Tutor Na said softly.

'Was she good to the hidden princess? Did she assist her?'

'She was excellent in her position, Your Highness. Why do you ask?'

'I fear that U'shi has had others direct her movements for so long that she finds it difficult in her new position. I do not want her to suffer further because of this. Perhaps another role would be more appropriate, and Shigi returns here to assist me? Three years is not long in the life of the Empire, and I must utilise all the time I have.'

'U'shi knows well enough what the call of the bell means, and the requirements of you. She is best placed to assist you.'

'Perhaps you can explain the bell to me, so I can be sure not to anger you again.'

The tutor looked at U'shi with an angry glare, and the woman hung her head.

'The bell is for your training time. It is rung at the beginning of each lesson and at the end. Between the bells you will be in the classroom.'

Lis bowed again and walked past the woman through to the classroom. She sat at the desk and looked over the tea set in the centre of it. She sat her hands in her lap and waited for the tutor, who was only a few steps behind. As U'shi appeared in the doorway, Tutor Na slid the door closed, keeping her out.

'She should have told you what would be expected,' the tutor said softly, indicating that Lis stand with an upward motion of her hand. 'Today you will show me what skills you have with tea.'

Lis bowed her head in acknowledgement.

'There may be times you will have to serve your husband. Tea is an important skill.'

'I have made tea for Peng and his parents,' Lis said softly, then bit her lip.

'I understand the hardship,' the tutor offered. 'It is difficult for you both,' she said, looking back at the door. 'But this is your life and we have much to cover. Whether you have the skills or not, you must learn to do it as an empress would.'

Lis nodded slowly.

'Now, make tea.'

Lis stood at the desk and moved through the ceremony she had learnt from her mother, trying hard to maintain smooth arm movements and steady hands. She was careful and deliberate with her folding of the napkin, and despite her stiff sleeves she held them as though they were the softest, longest silk. She imagined the gown she had put away for her wedding day that would never come.

She swallowed back the sadness that was building in her chest. It would come, but not as she'd pictured it, and she would be wearing red for another, a gown far more elaborate than the one she would have worn for Peng.

When she finished and presented the tea, the tutor only said, 'Hmm.'

'How can I improve?' Lis asked quickly.

'I don't know that you can,' Tutor Na said, and Lis stood back with her hands clenched in front of her. 'It was perfect.'

Lis smiled at the compliment. 'Thank you.'

'There is so much more.'

Lis nodded and looked back to the ground. 'Is there no other way?' she asked quickly. 'Could U'shi not remain the hidden princess?'

'Prince Remi chose you. Tradition dictates that the empress must be two years younger.'

'Why?' she asked, sitting on the floor beside the desk.

'Traditions are the realm of Tutor Jichun.'

'I am to spend the next three years trapped in this palace,' she said softly.

'You will travel to the temple regularly.'

Lis sighed. 'Out, but not out,' she said.

The tutor indicated she sit down and then clapped her hands. U'shi appeared, collected the tea things and then disappeared.

Tutor Na laid out a large sheet of paper and placed small, round weights at its edges. Then she opened a drawer and pulled out several round brushes. She laid them down on the desk just as U'shi reappeared with ink.

'Now, show me your writing skills, and then we shall look at your painting. Prepare silk,' she said to U'shi as she ushered her from the room. 'I want to see your embroidery.'

Lis nodded slowly, wondering how she was going to make it through this first day without her magic.

'The character for your name, please, Your Highness,' she instructed, and Lis picked up a brush and dipped it into the ink.

7

Remi looked out over the view of the world from his balcony and waited. He had asked for an audience with his father, but the call was yet to come. It had already been days, and his mother had been silent on every subject except his bride, wondering if they had made the right decision.

It was too late, for she was already installed within the palace and the others had been sent away. Remi didn't think there was much of a choice; they were all very similar when he had first looked over the line. Lisabet had intrigued him with her bare feet, and she was beautiful. He had guessed by his mother's questions that she was not entirely convinced Lisabet was the best choice, but when the girl had mentioned his brother as she had, Remi couldn't remember any of the others.

His chest tightened at the memory of kneeling before her, and her look of horror rather than the excitement he had been expecting. His grandmother had fainted when she was chosen. He realised in that moment who she was and that she was in love with another.

But life wasn't about fairness or equality, and love was not part of the agreement. If it were, he would have been given the chance to find his own bride during his travels. That hadn't been allowed either, despite his being the second son.

His brother's death was where his focus should be, the issue of magic and the Empire. For if they were to continue as they were, if his father was to continue as Emperor, all magic had to be destroyed.

'He will see you,' a voice said quietly behind Remi, and when he turned, the advisor was already on his way out the door.

Remi strode quickly behind him to catch him up and then slowed to a reasonable pace, trying to look like the prince his mother expected him to be. He nodded to several men he passed along the way, one of them a high-ranking soldier, and thought he would have liked to spend some more time with General Long. He wanted to learn from the great man what he had done during the magic war and how he had managed to be instrumental in stamping out the magic in the Empire.

But as they reached his father's study, he thought of his brother's burnt, twisted body and remembered that magic hadn't been expelled from the Empire at all. That was exactly the point he needed his father to admit so they could find his killer.

The emperor beamed at Remi as he moved quickly into the room and dropped to his knees.

'I trust you are content with your choice of bride,' he said.

Remi looked up and nodded once.

'She is very beautiful, and your mother tells me she sings like an angel.'

Remi nodded mutely, remembering the soft, sweet voice that had unexpectedly tugged at emotions he rarely showed.

'Well, you only have three years to wait until she is ready to stand beside you, and then you can learn all you wish of her. Your brother had to wait so much longer, and I'm sure there were times he tried to sneak into the hidden princess's palace just to remind himself what she looked like.' He smiled wistfully.

'I want to speak to you of Ta-Sho.'

The emperor sighed.

'We cannot let his killer go free.'

'I agree,' he said, standing from behind the desk, 'but we can make no announcements in regard to his death. We cannot publicly seek out one with magic.'

'We don't need to publicly announce anything, but I'm sure the people wonder why nothing has been done to capture his killer.'

'The people know nothing of his death,' the emperor said sternly.

'They know he died unexpectedly, in a way that rattled the palace and closed the gates.'

'You have other tasks now.'

'But this is what I do. This is what I can do, Father. I can seek them out.'

'You are heir to the Empire,' his father said sternly.

'I am a hunter first,' Remi pushed, despite his father's tone.

'No, you are not,' the man said sharply, stepping forward, and Remi held his breath. 'You are the crown prince of the Rei-Een Empire, first and foremost. Your preparation to become Emperor is more important than anything else, more important than the girl locked away preparing to be your bride, and more important than whoever was responsible for your brother's death.'

'But if we do not find them, they could kill again. Magic is back in the Empire.'

'Never,' his father said, swinging around and stepping back to his desk. He sat slowly, smoothed out his tunic and looked seriously at his son. 'Magic cannot find its way back into the Empire, and it hasn't. I promise you.'

Remi bowed his head once, knowing he would get no further in relation to any discussions of magic in the Empire. He turned for the door and tried to maintain an air of calm, for it would do him no good to lose his temper.

'You keep any investigations discrete,' his father called after him, and he nodded again without turning back.

'There is too much for you to learn,' U'shi snapped, 'and you aren't doing very well.'

'I am,' Lis threw back sharply, despite promising herself that she wouldn't bite. It didn't matter what she did or how well she did it; no one in the palace seemed to think she would make it.

It had only been a few days in the hidden princess's palace, and she'd sat at the desk learning all she could for hours at a time. After the evening meal was cleared away and U'shi left her alone, Lis continued with her studies or practiced what she had been taught that day, but it was never enough.

'I am only a year away,' U'shi continued.

'You *were* only a year away,' Lis said before she could stop herself and regretted it instantly, particularly as she was trying to agree with U'shi.

'You will never be Empress,' U'shi said.

'I don't want to be,' Lis said, sitting at the table and clenching her hands before her. She was so tempted to allow the magic to build and push her out of the palace. Although there was very little her magic could do. *I could hide myself*, she thought, *and then they would never find me.*

'It does not matter what you want,' the empress said, and Lis jumped at the sound of her voice. 'You have been chosen.'

'But I will never be ready,' she said too quickly. 'U'shi is correct; it should be her. She should be Empress.'

'Tradition dictates that the empress must be two years younger than her emperor. U'shi is the same age as the crown prince.'

'I'm sure she wouldn't be the first to lie about her age,' Lis said quietly, an idea forming in her mind. 'She could marry the prince and be the perfect empress.'

'She was not the prince's choice.'

'Then let him father his children via his concubines.'

Silence followed and, by the stern look on the empress's face, Lis knew she had gone too far.

'I will never be good enough for him,' she said with a sigh.

'We must make you so.'

'Why did you select me?' she asked. 'I am clearly not the best daughter of the Empire.'

'Your father was a strong man, instrumental in our win during the magic war. You are beautiful, caring, bright, and my son chose you.'

Lis hung her head and dragged in a deep breath.

'Your previous life is nothing now. Who you were before, where you lived, what you might have planned as your future. It no longer matters. You are the hidden princess.'

Lis nodded slowly.

'U'shi,' the empress said softly, and Lis glanced up at the expectant look on the young woman's face. 'You have no place now except to serve the hidden princess, and you would do well to remember that.'

U'shi bowed deeply before the empress and remained so as the empress left the room, waiting for a release that would never come. She turned a dark, cruel look at Lis and then left the room. As the door opened, Lis could hear the empress talking with the tutors. She stood slowly and waited by the door as U'shi closed it behind her.

She struggled to make out what they were saying. She thought she heard longer classes, or was it longer time? She wasn't sure, and she didn't have any longer than the three years allocated. Once the prince reached the required age, she would be announced whether she was ready or not.

8

After four long weeks, Lis had finally started to accept that she would remain on the Palace Isle forever. There was no chance for someone else to step in. She was exhausted, working long, hard hours to prove herself capable of being what they wanted her to be.

She had seen no one other than U'shi and her tutors, with the exception of one visit from the empress. At times she hoped for the prince to visit, if only to gauge a better idea of him as a man. He had almost seemed friendly when he had escorted her to the palace, but Lis was desperate for her family and her own home and Peng—and she knew she would never see any of them again.

When the clothing laid out on the end of the bed was different from her usual uniform, Lis baulked, thinking it a new test she wasn't sure how to face. As U'shi silently helped her into the flowing silk, she couldn't help but run it between her fingers. It made her feel even more homesick than she had.

She would not let them see her tears, though. As Tutor Na entered the room, she bowed her head while U'shi tied the sash tight between her shoulder blades.

'You are called to see the high priestess,' Tutor Na said.

'I thought she would come here.'

The tutor raised her eyebrows, and Lis bit her lip. She would never remember that she was not to speak until given permission. She had always been free to speak her mind at home. And if she was to be empress, after all, surely she would speak freely then.

'You are to go to the temple in the centre of the Palace Isle.'

Lis felt a sudden nervousness at being seen by the rest of the world. She had opened her mouth to say so when the tutor held up her hand.

'You shall not walk through the palace,' she said quickly. 'You will be carried, and the temple will be empty except for the high priestess and her attendants.'

Lis bowed her head.

'Come,' Tutor Na said, waving her towards the door.

In the laneway outside her new home, there was a carriage with a single horse, a driver and four guards. All of them faced away from the gate so as not to lay eyes on the princess, and she felt a moment of isolation. Even the horse looked away.

U'shi moved to the steps leading up to the carriage and held out her hand. Lis moved forward slowly, taking U'shi's hand and stepping up to the front of the carriage behind the driver, where she moved through the heavy red curtain into a comfortable space. She sat on the large cushions, pulled her legs beneath her and leaned back. The curtains were the same deep red on all sides of the carriage, and she couldn't see through them.

The steps slid loudly into place against the thick wall of the carriage. Lis waited, but U'shi didn't enter the space with her. Instead they lurched forward, the horse's hooves clopping over the stone streets and the guards' boots keeping time. Nothing else, only silence. Lis tried to feel the movement of the carriage to determine which way they might be going through the Great Palace, but she didn't know it well enough to guess where they might be.

The Palace Isle was so much larger than she thought it could be. It took longer than she had expected to reach their destination, and she waited, eventually listening to the sound of wood against wood as the steps were pulled down.

'The hidden princess,' U'shi announced. Lis took a deep breath and pulled the curtain back.

They were outside the temple, and again the guards had their backs to her, the horse and driver looking away. U'shi stood at the bottom of the steps holding out her hand. Lis moved quickly to take it and step down.

The priestess stood in the temple doorway and, although she didn't dare glance around, Lis knew there was no one else within the vicinity who might see her. The high priestess turned her back and stepped inside the temple, and Lis followed. She thought U'shi might join her, but she didn't.

The quiet whispering inside the temple died as she entered. She looked around her then at the wonder of the space, the bright white stone. The smell of incense, blossom and fruit filled her senses. Statues of the gods lined the walls, with small bowls of offerings at their feet. They only had a small shrine within their home and, other than when they visited Fourth, Lis rarely had the chance to visit any temple.

Her mother made offerings and prayers to the gods every day. Her father would pause at the table, but he rarely offered more than a nod.

Lis felt somewhat overwhelmed. The space was big enough to hold hundreds of worshipers at a time, and there must have been thirty gods lining the walls, each of them different.

'You will have many questions,' the high priestess offered kindly.

Lis nodded slowly, looking up at the high ceiling and trying to take it in.

'You are familiar with the gods?'

'Not all of them,' Lis murmured.

'Do not worry; we shall ensure you learn all you need.'

Lis bowed to the woman before her.

'Today we shall just familiarise ourselves with the temple, the offerings and each other.'

She held out her hand, and Lis stepped to the feet of the god across from her. The statue was carved from the white stone in the wall, as though she were stepping from the wall itself. Each panel met with the next to form the circle in which they stood. It was only broken by the entrance and another doorway two thirds of the way around.

At the feet of this goddess were several bowls, each holding oranges, lemons and limes. Lis allowed herself a smile, as she knew what they were. Oranges had been new to her when she had first arrived, and she had been learning about a lot of fruit and foods she had never seen before. Growing up, if they didn't grow it, she didn't know it.

'Aga, goddess of the people. She ensures the royal family continue strong in their hold over the Empire. That they are good to the people and make sound decisions for the continuation of the Empire.'

Lis feared another attack, that the priestess would be yet another voice to tell her she wasn't what they needed her to be.

'You are here. It is your turn, whether others want that or not. There is always doubt,' she said softly, raising her hand towards Lis's forehead, but then she pointed at the fruit at Aga's feet. 'Citrus fruits are thought to please her, and so her guidance will be thoughtful.'

'You mean that people have left oranges at her feet so she will guide the royal family to choose a hidden princess who will help the family continue in strength?'

The high priestess nodded, and a broad smile lit up her face.

'What would happen if they chose incorrectly?'

'I know this is not your choice, Your Highness, but you are the princess.'

'You wanted them to choose me,' Lis said, looking into the dark eyes that had stared at her so often during the Choosing.

'She may whisper in my ear. I am a priestess of the gods, after all. I am to be of use to gods and man.'

Lis waited, and when the high priestess said nothing else, she moved to the next statue and looked over the rice left at his feet. Not only was it a simple dish, the bowls in which it sat were simple wooden bowls. Lis doubted there were any like them at the palace, except maybe in servants' quarters.

'I have seen something in you,' the priestess whispered in her ear, taking Lis by surprise. 'Something special.'

Lis turned to her seriously.

'There is much for you to learn. You will learn to pray.'

'My mother prayed over the shrine in our home,' Lis said.

'I want you to listen first. Listen for the voices of the gods within the temple.'

Lis nodded and, turning back to the statue of Aga, she found herself alone. She walked slowly around the temple, looking over the statues of the various gods. From the offerings at their feet, she wondered what aspects of their lives they ruled over. Leaning forward, she ran her hands over the smooth stone. It was cool beneath her fingers, and she traced the patterns etched into the gods. At the feet of some gods were small bells, yet she left those alone. She listened, but she heard nothing. No whispers, no voices, no gods. She wondered if she would ever hear them, if she should hear them, yet she wasn't sure if she wanted to hear what they had to say.

She could sense U'shi before she saw her appear in the doorway to indicate they leave. She took a deep breath, hoping that she wasn't pushing her magic out as she had before, and she pulled it tight within her before she followed U'shi out. Lis found the sunlight startling when she stood atop the steps. As she adjusted to the light, she found the world looking away from her just as they had before. She glanced around, looking for a sign of something familiar or another living soul. In the distance, she could make out the tall royal residence, and she wondered if the prince stood at one of the windows.

She climbed back inside her carriage. Then they were moving back towards her little palace, and it appeared to take too little time before they were there.

The high priestess watched the hidden princess's carriage disappear into the growing crowd. She knew what she was and what she would become, yet she had been unable to sense it on her. There was magic there, she was certain of it, but she had felt nothing as they had walked in the temple. She longed to touch the princess and see if she could sense it. Perhaps there had been a mistake, a misunderstanding of what she had been shown.

Perhaps the girl was able to supress it or hide it away, but then she hadn't met anyone who could manage such with their magic— at least not from a priestess.

The girl had been so disappointed when she had been chosen, not at all the reaction she had expected. Every other girl in the line had been hoping it was her. If she had magic, it would have flared then. Even the prince would have seen it. But he appeared to have seen something else in her.

The high priestess needed to pray, to sit with her sisters and allow the gods to tell her what they planned. They had waited a long time for this moment. Too long. She tried to remain calm as she headed into the chamber to kneel with her sisters and listen to what the gods might tell her.

The empress had given her full access to the princess, so she could work with her in private. She would be back at the next full moon, and she had until then to prepare the next lesson.

9

Lis stood at the gate and waited. It was such a beautiful garden, but she had no time to spend in it. She couldn't remember the last time she had been able to sit in the sun. Now she was waiting for the second outing in a week, and she didn't know what this one involved or where she was going. When she heard the horse shuffle and snort on the other side of the gate, she wondered just how far she would be able to travel.

And when U'shi appeared with a basket, she was even more intrigued.

The lane outside the palace was silent and empty as the soldiers looked away. Lis noticed two soldiers by the gate who turned as she walked by so that their backs were to her at all times. She wondered if they had been there before, as she couldn't remember them.

Would she get used to the idea that no one could look at her? It would only be another three years of this until the crown prince was of age, but that felt like an eternity.

U'shi gave the driver the instruction to move on, and Lis wondered if she found the change in people's reaction to her unsettling. She had endured years of no one looking at her, of limited contact with people, and now she was seeing more and being seen by more.

The smell of steam and soap penetrated the curtains of the

carriage long before they stopped, and Lis felt her heart jump. Her mother had told her stories of the baths, the women all washing together, the steam, the chatter, the peace. She had hoped they could experience it together during their time together on the Palace Isle, but there hadn't been enough time. The baths were fed by a natural hot spring, and her mother's eyes misted over when she talked about them.

Lis smiled for the first time. She might actually get the chance to meet with others.

At an impatient cough from U'shi, Lis pulled back the curtain, lifted her skirt and descended from the carriage to come face to face with Tutor Na. This was not going to be the freedom she had hoped it would be.

She followed the tutor beneath the red gate into a beautiful garden. Bamboo lined its edges, hiding the wall and giving the impression that they could be in a forest somewhere. A pebbled path wound its way through short-clipped grass, and flowers she had never seen before grew in small pots. She longed to reach out to them, but she held her hands tight before her.

A small bridge ahead of her led into a warm steamy mist, and she felt as though she were walking through a veil to another world. In the large space they entered, several baths were sunk into the stone floor.

'The baths are open to all,' the tutor said. 'But they can only be used on certain days by certain people.'

'I'm here alone,' Lis said.

'Of course you are,' the tutor said softly. 'And you will use the royal bath.'

Lis nodded, disappointed that she was alone, but thankful for the time to relax a little, and to not spend her day trying to learn everything.

A door stood at the far end of the steamy room, the symbol of the Empire over it, and Lis followed the tutor through it. The room on the other side was almost as large as the one they had just passed through. A single bath was set in the middle of the space, larger than any of the others, and Lis wondered for a moment how many people used it.

Several stools sat around the stone floor, which was more pink than grey. Although the floor was far more even than anything she had seen before, she was surprised that it hadn't been polished to the same shine as every other floor in the palace.

'This is the private bath of the royal household. It is closed to all on such a day that the household wishes to use it. Although this day is for you alone. U'shi will assist you with washing, including your hair.'

Lis chanced a glance at U'shi then, who didn't seem very comfortable with her new role.

'You may remain here as long as you wish, provided you return to the palace before the evening meal.'

Lis looked tentatively back towards the door. The freedom sounded blissful.

'U'shi will tell the guard when you are ready. As you dress, they will clear the streets. That way, they shall be ready for you when you appear at the gate.'

Lis nodded and stepped closer to the steaming pool. She couldn't see the bottom, but it seemed inviting. She had swum off the shores of her island home her whole life.

'I shall see you in the morning for class, Your Highness,' the tutor said with a low nod of her head.

Lis bowed before her and tried to contain her excitement.

As the door closed behind her, U'shi was already pulling at her sash, loosening the ties and helping her from her uniform. It was a relief to stand in her undergarments as the heat of the room had already started to peel her skin.

'All of it,' U'shi muttered.

But rather than help, she watched as Lis removed the last of her clothes to stand naked at the edge of the water. U'shi looked her up and down, all but rolling her eyes. Lis looked back at the pool and then sat gingerly on the warm tiles at the edge of the water.

'A princess would have stepped in,' U'shi muttered.

'A decent servant would have assisted,' Lis snapped back.

U'shi hmphed as Lis lowered herself to the first step and then carefully walked down into the water, which was surprisingly deep and very warm. Much warmer than any bath her mother had drawn for her growing up. She breathed in the steam, allowing the hot water to pull the tension from her muscles, and her worries faded momentarily. U'shi glared down at her from the edge of the bath.

'How can you wash my hair from there?'

U'shi turned her back and walked away, returning with a small stool and several bottles covering it. 'Hold out your hand,' she said, then poured a creamy liquid from one directly onto it.

Lis lifted it carefully to her nose. It had a hint of cherry blossom and something else she couldn't place.

'It is for your skin,' U'shi said, stoppering the bottle and mimicking washing herself.

Lis lathered the cream over herself, amazed at how it bubbled and foamed. Then she stepped into the centre of the pool, dropping beneath the surface and rinsing it from her skin. She emerged, running her fingers through her hair and smiling easily, to see U'shi looking more disgruntled than usual.

'The red one is for your hair,' she said.

'You are to help,' Lis said.

'Not today,' U'shi said, swinging around and marching away from the pool.

Lis lost her in the steam, unsure if she had left the room or not. It wasn't worth the fight, she decided. U'shi might pull her hair from her head. Lis had been washing herself since she was a small child, after all. She leant forward, pulled the stopper from the small spherical bottle and screwed up her nose. It was not the sweet smell of the soap, but if anyone questioned what she had done in the baths, the punishments would belong to U'shi.

The dark liquid ran out of the bottle with surprising speed, and she rubbed it through her thick, long hair. It also foamed, and she ducked under the water to rinse once she had rubbed it through all of her hair. When she emerged, she didn't think her hair smelt too bad. Once clean, she found a step to sit on that kept her shoulders below the water line.

She settled back with her head against the smooth tiles at the edge of the pool, her legs floating freely before her, then closed her eyes and tried to clear her mind.

Memories of home invaded her quiet time. Images of her mother sitting at the table telling tales of their life on the Palace Isle before the war, the excitement at moving to their own little island afterward. But there was something in her voice, something longing, as though she could have stayed in the palace and been happy.

One of those happy memories was of the pools, chatting with her friends. Despite the sadness creeping into her heart, Lis could understand the joy her mother felt here. The quiet, peaceful harmony. It was the only place on all the islands where hot springs came to the surface. She had wondered whether they could find some if they dug deep enough on their own island, but her father had simply laughed.

He always seemed happier on their island home, and Lis worried that it was her fault they couldn't return—her magic, and what that might mean. For all of them, not just her.

The splash was a surprise, and she sat up expecting to find U'shi throwing her shoes into the water. The face of a man broke the surface as he stood before her, still clothed. His black hair was plastered down over his face, his eyes were wild, and his strange, scraggy moustache hung limp over his lip, which curved up in a strange grin.

Lis screamed, unsure what else to do, and he leapt forward pushing his hand over her mouth. She felt her magic build, but she had never used it for self-defence before, so she wasn't sure how it would act or what the man, far too close, might do.

'I know what you are,' he whispered hoarsely, gently lifting his hand.

But as soon as he did, she started screaming again.

He was quick to clamp his hand back over her mouth, pushing her head back into the tiles. She blinked as the spots before her blurred the assailant.

'I know what you are,' he said again.

She shoved back at him, but he didn't move.

'I know what you are to become, and I cannot allow it.' He continued to push her back, and she could feel the tiles pressing into the back of her head.

'You must help us,' he said.

She lifted her feet up between them and pushed against his chest with everything she had. He was thrown back, and Lis clambered out of the pool, trying desperately to get her footing. Now she understood why the tiles weren't polished.

'Someone help me,' she cried as he came out of the water after her.

She threw out her hands in a feeble attempt to prevent him reaching her again, and he slipped on the wet tiles. The panic made it hard to breathe as she shivered at the idea of what could happen. He climbed up onto his hands and knees, and she wondered if she could push him into the water with her magic when he stood slowly. The door banged open behind her, causing the steam to move around the room. In the dim light, she didn't know how many were at the door.

'Help,' she screamed, doing what she could to raise her voice above her fear. 'Help.'

The man at the door stepped forward, and Lis recognised the prince. 'I am here to help,' he said, drawing a straight, shiny sword. 'Are you hurt?'

Lis shook her head and then raised a hand to it. The prince was focused on the man before him. The intruder grinned and raised his hands, but before he could do anything the prince stepped forward and ran him through the heart with his sword, which seemed so much like her father's.

He made a fizzle sound as he dropped to the tiles, his blood spilling across them and into the water.

'Did he hurt you?' the prince asked without looking from the body at his feet.

She shook her head.

'Where are your clothes?' he asked, glancing at her face.

Lis looked around wildly but could see nothing. She shook her head. 'U'shi,' she muttered.

'Where is U'shi?'

'I don't know,' she said too loudly. 'You are asking the wrong questions. Who was he? What did he want? How did he get in?'

'Magic,' the prince whispered.

'What?'

'Don't fear. He is dead now.'

Lis's heart stopped. 'How did you know?' she asked quietly, fear closing her throat.

'I sensed him, and you scream very loudly.'

'I was very scared,' she said, willing the tears to stay away, but she could only shiver.

He pulled at the belt around his waist, removing his coat from around his shoulders. He stepped purposefully towards her, and she backed away. Then he stopped and held the coat out, and she nodded slowly as he stepped forward and wrapped it around her shoulders.

The sob escaped before she could stop it, and he pulled her into his arms, holding her close, rubbing his hands up and down her back. 'You are safe now,' he said softly. She nodded against him, thankful for his strong arms as she thought of Peng.

'You're a hunter,' she whispered, pulling back from him.

He nodded once. 'We aren't spoken of so much now.'

'But you sense the magic and kill them,' she said, looking across at the man still leaking into the pool.

'It felt very strong as I passed. I was worried it was back in the palace.'

'I thought magic was stamped out.'

'So my father claims.'

He turned away then, leaving her dripping in his coat and trying hard to hold it tight in front of her. She took a deep breath and pushed her arms out through the sleeves. As she pulled it across herself, he turned back to her with the belt in his hands. Once he had tied the coat securely, it almost reached the floor. It managed to cover most of her, although the long slits up each side exposed her legs.

'I want to leave,' she whispered.

'I will see if it is safe; wait here,' he said, heading through the doorway.

'No way,' she said quickly, racing after him. Her feet slipped on the tiles, and she only just managed to stay standing. 'No,' she said more quietly once she had regained her composure.

He walked her through to the front garden where a soldier stood waiting, his sword drawn. The soldier bowed to them both and then turned his back quickly.

'Tell the carriage she is ready,' the crown prince said. 'And there is a problem inside I need you and another to deal with.'

'That will leave only two guards for the hidden princess,' the soldier said, his back still turned.

'I will travel with her.' He looked at Lis, and she nodded once.

The man ducked through the gate, spoke to those outside and then knocked on the gate. The prince stepped forward and looked out before he motioned her forward. Lis sucked in a deep breath, wanting desperately to check behind her, but she was too scared. She was thankful that no one was watching her as she climbed awkwardly up the steps into the carriage, very aware of her own nakedness and her exposed legs.

She almost squealed as she settled into the cushions and the curtain opened. She nodded slowly, and the prince settled in beside her, knocking on the carriage wall. She heard the steps sliding into place, and then the carriage lurched forward.

She wanted to cry. A lump had formed in her throat and seemed to be growing. She stared towards the window, unable to see anything, her hand trying to hold the material across her legs as they folded beneath her. She closed her eyes, but the toothless grin reappeared before her, followed by his life leaking into the pool.

She jumped as the prince rested his hand on hers.

'It is safe now,' he said softly.

She nodded mutely. When she looked around at him, he gave her a small smile, but it was fleeting.

'Where is U'shi?' he asked.

She shook her head. *What if U'shi set me up?*

'She must learn her place,' he muttered under his breath, and Lis heard a hardness there that scared her.

'Are there others?' she asked.

'Do you mean servants, or possible threats in the bath house?'

'Both,' she said quickly.

He laughed then, and she chewed her lip, unsure how she should be interacting with the prince. 'I will talk with my mother,' he said, the seriousness returning. 'I will ensure more guards when you leave your palace.'

She nodded her thanks as the carriage rocked to a stop.

'I'll go first,' he said softly, releasing her hand.

She was surprised by the feeling of loss as he stepped through the curtain, and how quickly her fear returned when she was left alone.

'Princess,' he called softly, and she looked out of the curtain. The two guards stood with their backs to her, their long swords drawn and pointing outward. Prince Remi stood at the bottom of the steps with his hand out, but she clutched at the sides of the coat with both hands to prevent it exposing her any further. As she stepped, he reached up and took her elbow.

With an arm around her shoulders, he guided her through the

gate and closed it behind him. The pebbled path dug into her feet and she winced, finding it harder to keep the tears at bay. Then he had her in his arms, her bare legs exposed as he carried her into the palace.

Tutor Na was in the classroom and appeared with a smile, saying, 'I expected you to take the day…' She stopped, her mouth agape as she took them in, and Lis squeezed her eyes closed as she buried her head in the prince's shoulder.

He pushed his way into her chamber and sat her gently on the edge of the bed.

'Send word to my mother and General Zho-Hou that I will meet with them before my father,' he said, and the older woman rushed away.

He squatted down before Lis and sighed.

She looked into his dark eyes and bit her lip.

'I will not allow this to happen again,' he said, more gently than she expected. 'I tried to tell my father that the Palace Isle was not as safe as he thought,' he said, and Lis swallowed hard. 'Now for U'shi.'

'She doesn't want me here,' she whispered.

'It doesn't matter what she wants. This is the way it is.' He stood quickly, and Lis flinched before she could stop herself.

He looked at the coat rather than her and sighed again.

'I'll return for that another time,' he said, turning for the door. Lis nodded at his back.

10

The prince entered his father's study to find General Zho-Hou present, but not his mother.

'She does not appreciate being summoned,' his father said before he could comment on her absence. 'Not even by you.'

'I understand you have been filled in on what has happened,' Remi said to the general, ignoring his father's comment. 'The hidden princess and her education are my mother's domain. She also insisted on placing U'shi with there. The princess was in serious danger, and neither U'shi nor my mother appear to be able to explain this. Is it that this hidden princess is not of the same importance as those who came before her?'

'It may be that she will never be ready to be crowned as your wife,' his mother said, entering the room behind him.

'Then release the girl to the world she lived in before and allow me to choose my own bride when I am ready.'

'That is not the way it is done,' she said.

'If you insist that she is the only option, why not prepare and protect her? If I had not been in the area, had not felt the magic, we may be trying to explain to her father how she ended up drowned in the royal bath.'

The empress pursed her lips and glared at her son.

'We have doubled the guards on the carriage and on the palace,' the general said. 'We have included a hunter amongst their number, hidden from the others so that it is not obvious what we do.'

The prince nodded his thanks and turned back to his mother. 'U'shi,' he said.

His mother sighed and shook her head. 'The girl is having trouble adjusting to her new position.'

'She left the princess unattended. And when I arrived, there was no sign even of the princess's clothes.'

'Her clothes?' his mother asked.

'I wrapped her in my coat,' he said softly.

'You do realise what you have done, don't you?' she asked.

'Do you suggest that because of her nakedness, I should have left her to die rather than see her?'

The empress paused, opened her mouth and then shut it. He took a deep breath.

'It isn't right,' she murmured.

'Neither was the chance for a scoundrel with magic to drown her in the waters of the private royal bath. It could just as well have been her blood running into the hot springs, rather than his.'

The empress sighed again.

'What is to be done with U'shi?' he asked, stepping closer to his mother.

'She is to remain where she is,' the emperor interrupted. 'She shall be punished for her negligence of duty. Perhaps that will remind her of her new place. Twenty paddles,' he said with a nod to the general.

The general bowed in return and left.

'That seems somewhat extreme,' the empress said.

'She abandoned her post and her princess,' the emperor said, looking at his son rather than his wife. 'She left her exposed and she shall be punished accordingly. Especially in light of a lack of explanation, for the girl hasn't offered any reasonable excuse for her lapse.'

His mother shook her head more reluctantly.

'Then let that be the end of it.'

'What of the magic in the palace?' Remi pressed.

The emperor glared at him, and he knew that if he said any more, the investigations he had undertaken would be stopped.

He bowed low before the emperor and then his mother. 'I thank you for your wisdom,' he said and then backed out of the room.

Lis sat at the desk in the classroom early the next morning trying to focus on her lesson rather than what had happened in the bath house the day before. She had heard U'shi return in the night, but she was yet to see her. The maid hadn't appeared with her breakfast and hadn't helped her dress. Lis was thankful for the peace, but she wondered just what U'shi had been up to and what it meant for her future. She wondered if the prince had spoken to his mother about the event, and whether there was a chance of another servant being sent.

Lis had instructed that the coat be laundered and returned to the prince as soon as possible. She didn't want to give him an excuse to visit again just yet. She had wrapped herself up in it during the night and allowed herself to cry. She had imagined Peng lying beside her, his warm body pressed against her, his lips against her skin as she drifted off to sleep, only to be woken by U'shi returning.

The cane smacking the desk made her jump, and she focused on the angry face of the tutor. 'This will never do,' he snapped. 'There is not enough time in all the world for you to learn what you must, and you waste the time we have.'

'I am sorry,' Lis said softly. 'I was thinking about...'

Tutor Jichun smacked the desk again. 'I do not care what you were thinking about unless it was the start of the magic war, as I was discussing.'

'It was the visitors,' she said.

He glared at her. 'What visitors?'

'The travellers who came from a faraway land and asked to stay. Then they talked with those who had magic, twisting them and training them to work against the Empire.'

He stared at her for a moment as she chewed her lip. She was sure her mother had talked of the visitors, though her father rarely talked of the war and what had happened, despite his position and instrumental part in winning it. She didn't know what that was, but she did know it was the reason behind the gift of their island from the emperor.

Tutor Jichun nodded once.

'My father is General Long,' Lis said softly.

He nodded again. 'Do you know what he did in the war?'

She shook her head.

'It does not matter,' he said. 'Yes, the visitors caused the uprising and then disappeared before it started.'

'Are there still pockets of magic in the Empire?' she asked.

'The magic was vanquished,' he said matter-of-factly.

'What does that mean?'

'All those with magic were driven from the Empire. Those who stayed were killed.'

'Really?' she asked.

'If you were paying attention to my lessons, you would know this.'

'I thought they were all pushed out. Why would they stay if they knew they would be killed?'

'Some were too young or too poor to make the journey to another land, and they chose to fight instead.'

'Too young?'

'Children can show signs of their magic early, and they can be just as dangerous as adult magics. They were all put to death.'

'My father killed children?' Lis asked, her voice catching.

'When he had to, I'm sure. They are not safe,' he insisted, and she realised why her father would never talk of what had happened—why he had moved them so far away and why she had to be so careful now.

'Were they really such a threat?' she asked. 'They had worked with those without magic for generations.'

'It was difficult to see how it could have happened in the beginning,' Tutor Jichun admitted softly. 'I knew those with magic, and they hadn't wanted change or power before the war started.'

'Do you think there are those who still want things the way they were?' she asked.

His face hardened. 'There is no magic in the Empire now. If it were to appear, then it would be stamped out immediately.'

'They would be killed,' she said softly, thinking of the dead man at the baths, his blood spreading across the floor.

'You do not need to worry, Your Highness. I understand the prince has inserted a hunter nearby to ensure your safety.'

She nodded slowly, panic closing her throat. 'Where?' she whispered.

He shook his head. 'The general wouldn't say, only that you were safe.'

She looked down at the desk and the map before her.

The tutor smacked the cane down again, the tip almost hitting her hand. She looked up at his serious face, his thin, pointed beard and his old, tanned, leathery skin. 'You will not have to worry about surviving if you do not learn all you can to prepare yourself. There is too little time and you are too far behind.'

Lis sighed. She was tired of hearing these same words from the tutors. She knew more than they gave her credit for. If they spent less time lamenting what she couldn't learn in the next few years and taught more, she might actually learn what she needed.

11

The time was getting closer for Lis to leave her palace again, and although she had been assured she wouldn't be left alone again, she didn't want to go. She regretted sending the prince's coat back, wondered if it would not have been better for him to visit and tell her himself what he had put in place.

It was only when she looked over the dress that morning that she realised it wasn't her usual uniform and her heart stuck in her throat.

'Temple,' U'shi said quietly. She had been very subdued since the incident in the bath house and also seemed to move more slowly around the palace.

Lis had learnt very little at her last visit to the temple. She wasn't sure about the high priestess, but the idea of getting out of the palace was both exciting and unnerving. As she walked slowly towards the gate, she felt even more nervous. She had been very careful not to allow a hint of her magic to escape, and yet there was a hunter now watching her every move. Or at least watching over her. What could she do if they felt the magic that flowed within her?

When they moved through the gate to find a larger number of alert soldiers, all with their backs to her, she glanced between them to see if she could determine which was the hunter. She couldn't distinguish any of them, and she wondered if the other men in the group knew who he was.

She took U'shi's hand and climbed the steps, the maid climbing up behind her. As she pulled the curtain aside, her heart caught in her chest. The prince held his finger to his lips and motioned her forward.

'Are you settled, Your Highness?'

'Yes,' she said, pulling her legs in beneath her as the carriage lurched forward. 'What are you doing?' she whispered.

'I was concerned for your safety,' he said.

'I thought you had a hunter amongst the soldiers?'

'Who told you that?' he asked a little too loudly, his face hard, and she gulped down her rising fear.

'A tutor,' she whispered, looking down at her hands.

'I wonder who told him,' he said softly.

'Surely you have more important things to do than watch over me,' she said.

'Perhaps watching over you helps me with another problem.'

'What problem?' she asked, but he shook his head.

The carriage stopped, and the steps were pulled into place. Lis was more nervous than she thought she should be. 'Princess,' came the call from U'shi, and she took a deep breath. The prince gave her hand a squeeze. But when she looked up, he was looking away. She pushed through the curtain, relieved to see the same number of soldiers surrounding the carriage and the high priestess standing in the doorway of the temple.

Lis stepped forward without looking back, but she wondered if the prince would wait for her to return, to be with her while she travelled back to the palace. Would he do that for every journey she took? Not that there were many, only the temple and the baths—and she wasn't sure she ever wanted to see the baths again. She smiled at the high priestess and followed her into the temple.

'You have had a difficult time,' the high priestess said as she led the way towards the statues of the gods.

Lis watched her back but didn't say anything.

'You want to go home,' she continued.

Lis stopped. 'It isn't an option,' she said softly. 'I am the hidden princess.'

'You are. But it does not follow that you want to be here. Others before you have shared your apprehension.'

'Have they?' Lis asked too quickly.

'This is not an easy position to hold,' the woman said, turning to her. 'Some may wish for such a thing, but it is a hard life, with no time of your own. Once you are crowned and released from your training, very little will change.'

Lis looked down at the ground.

'Why did he come for you?' the priestess asked softly.

Lis looked up then, trying to read the woman's features, then shook her head once.

'What did he say to you in the bath house?'

Lis shivered. She wanted the high priestess to mean the prince, but she didn't. How did the woman know what had occurred in the bath house?

'He did speak to you,' she whispered.

Lis remained unmoving. She tried not to focus on the scary face that appeared before her every time she blinked. She clenched her fists, remembering the magic building in her veins when he chased her out of the water. She held it back, trying desperately to keep the feeling hidden from the world. The crown prince, a hunter, was just outside in her own carriage.

'You are to teach me of the gods,' Lis said, looking up into the hard eyes of the priestess.

'You are not to tell me what I am to teach,' she said. 'I am to learn from you what I can, to ensure you will be the best empress.'

Lis nodded once. The high priestess swung around, her robes moving smoothly around her. What did the priestess want to know, and what might she do with the information?

As they entered the centre of the temple, Lis again wondered what the space would be like filled with people. Would they make any noise, or would the silence be maintained? The high priestess clapped her hands once loudly over the top of her head, and the lamps around the space lit up.

Lis held her breath as the light played against the statues. She turned slowly, looking over each one and then towards the ceiling where the candles hung. As she turned quicker, the priestess stood smiling in the middle of it all.

'You have...'

The priestess held up her finger, silencing her with more than the motion. Lis put her hand to her throat, feeling the tight band that suddenly kept her silent.

'I know the prince waits outside for you,' the priestess said softly. 'I know his power, even if he does not fully understand it himself.'

The band tightened further.

'Do not fight it. There is no need for us to fight each other. We are the same, are we not?'

Lis shook her head.

'I know what you have. I know what you are. I know that you are the only chance to reunite this Empire.'

Lis shook her head again.

'It is the reason I whispered your name to the empress, and why she raised your name with her son.'

'No,' Lis managed to push out.

'You are much stronger than you realise,' the priestess said, a friendly smile on her face, but the band tightened again around Lis's neck. Lis wondered if she would die as she tried to suck in a breath. 'But you will work with us, or I will expose you for what you are.'

'That would be exposing yourself as well. For how could you know if the crown prince does not?'

The high priestess glowered as Lis sucked in a deep breath.

'How does he not know?' the high priestess asked, but Lis simply shook her head.

'What do you want?' she asked, her voice scratching the inside of her throat.

'I want you to be empress, to bring magic back to the Empire. Allow us the freedoms we had before.'

Lis shook her head. 'How do you think I can do that?'

The older woman shrugged.

'If I am always at threat of discovery and death, how will that change for me to bring magic back?'

The priestess grinned at her.

The prince appeared in the doorway then, a guard directly behind him, but as soon as they hit the main temple, the man turned his back on the room.

'Your Highness,' the high priestess said sweetly. 'This is my time with the princess.' She bowed her head. 'Is there something you need?'

He shook his head and turned for the doorway, tapping the soldier on the shoulder as he went.

When the priestess turned back to Lis, she smiled. 'He senses you.'

'Or is it you?' Lis said, trying to look more confident than she felt. 'I think I have learnt enough today.'

'The empress wants you to learn all you can of the gods.'

'Is that what she thinks you do?'

'It is something you must learn, for you too shall be a priestess of sorts once you are Empress. You must be advisor and confidant to the emperor as well as the mother of his children.'

'Then it can wait until next time,' Lis said, walking towards the door.

'There is not enough time for you to learn what you must,' the high priestess said quickly.

'And yet you waste the time we have. Everyone spends more time telling me that there is no time than they do trying to teach what they think I need to know. This is not my choice,' she said, her voice louder than she intended, and it echoed around the temple. 'This is not the life I wanted, but it is the life I have. You chose me. The empress chose me. And, whether he intended to or not, so did the crown prince. You need to start helping me be what you all chose me to be, or let me go.'

The priestess surprised her by kneeling down before her. 'Forgive me, Your Highness. You have not been treated fairly.'

'I know that I am nothing until I am crowned and connected to the prince. But I cannot get there with the constant reminders that I am not worthy, that I shall not be ready.'

The priestess bent forward, her head touching the floor, and Lis wondered if she had ever made such a show before.

'I cannot be another U'shi,' she said softly.

'You shall not be,' the priestess said, standing slowly. 'Come, let me show you the secrets of the gods.'

Lis nodded once and followed the priestess to one of the statues, taking in her flowing gown and the fruit at her feet. 'Today I shall teach you all you need to know of Goddess Ba.'

When Lis lay down that night, her head was full of yet more information, but she felt she had a stronger grasp on it. The prince had been gone from the carriage when she left the temple, and Lis was sure that one of the many soldiers who walked with her was a hunter.

U'shi was still uncharacteristically quiet, but she seemed to walk taller, more naturally than she had for some time. Lis wondered what her punishment had been, although she had not been replaced as Lis had hoped.

For the first time since she arrived, Lis had the feeling that she might be able to survive this. That despite her hopes for her life and the fear of her magic leaking into the world, she might be able to do as they wanted her to do and bring honour to her family.

12

Lis sat at her desk as the tutor droned on. The sound of the gate made her look up, but the empress coming through the doorway was a surprise. As was Lis's father behind her. Lis leapt up from the desk and threw herself into his arms. There was something about him, something uncomfortable, and it was a new experience for her.

'You are dismissed,' the empress said curtly. The old tutor turned and shuffled from the room.

Lis was so overcome by excitement that she wasn't sure what to do with herself.

'Lis, my darling.' Her father sucked in a deep breath, and she saw how much he had aged since she'd seen him only a few months before. 'I must…'

She indicated the seat she had leapt out of. It seemed an effort for him to lower himself into the chair. When he raised his dark eyes to hers as she stood beside the desk, she saw far more hurt there than she had ever thought possible.

'Your mother has been ill,' he said softly. Lis chewed at her lip, knowing what was to come would be far worse than she had anticipated. She wanted to ask to see her mother. She wanted to return home. But she knew that could never happen.

'She's gone.' The last of his composure slipped as he drew a ragged breath, and large tears rolled down his cheeks. Lis looked to the empress for confirmation or clarity that a mistake had been made, but the usually confident woman only looked at the ground, her hands held too tight before her.

Lis fell heavily into the desk, the ink splashing across the work she had painstakingly done that morning. She worried about the tutor's anger, the swish of his cane at the mess she had made. What would her mother have thought about the life she was living?

Lis sat heavily on the floor as the loss of her mother overwhelmed her. Yet in some ways Lis had already lost her, when she was taken—chosen—to be the hidden princess. Her father's words confirmed that there was no way back. In her mind, she had always felt there was an escape, that despite her hard work and the unrelenting pressure of the Empire's traditions there would somehow be a way for her to return home.

Now, with this terrible news, it was as though more than just her mother's life had ended. Any chance for Lis to end this way of life had gone with her.

Her father's arms closed around her, and she breathed in the scent of him, feeling the familiarity of his embrace. She allowed herself to cry for all that was lost, clinging to his robes and feeling his wet tears on her skin. When he pulled back from her, U'shi stood in the doorway, her face serious. Then she turned away.

'We have provided a shrine for your mother,' the empress said. 'You and your father are welcome to stay as long as you need to.'

'Thank you, Your Eminence.' Lis wiped her sleeve across her face and looked up into her father's devastation.

'I am so sorry,' he said, taking her face in his hands. 'I had hoped you would send her a letter when she was ill.'

Lis shook her head slowly. 'I didn't know.'

'She wrote to you herself,' he said.

Lis looked up at the empress, who turned away. 'U'shi will take you to the shrine,' she said and, before Lis could ask anything further, she left the palace.

'I didn't get any letters,' Lis said, taking her father's hand. 'I think they want to keep me separated from my old life. I'm not allowed to talk to anyone other than the tutors. I rarely leave the palace, and they clear the streets when I do so no one can look at me.'

Her father pulled her into a tight embrace. 'Are you lonely here?' he asked, pulling her even tighter against him.

'I want to go home,' she whispered into his chest. 'I can't be what they want me to be. I don't want to be what they want me to be.'

'I am so sorry, my daughter, that I was not able to stop this, but any sway I had with the emperor is gone.'

'It is not your doing,' Lis said softly. 'The prince seemed to think I was the best fit. And the high priestess seems to have sensed something in me as well.'

Her father tensed, then stepped back to hold her at arm's length. He searched her face, and she could feel the question he couldn't ask aloud. As he raised his eyebrows in question, she shook her head once.

Lis gently wiped her thumbs over his worn, weathered face. She smoothed over the rough material of her uniform and took his hand, then turned for the door. 'You may lead the way, U'shi,' she called, her voice clearer and more confident than she felt. Her father gave her hand a gentle squeeze as they followed the maid through the garden and out of the gate.

The carriage was already waiting for them. General Zho-Hou stood by the steps, bowing low. Then he surprised Lis by stepping up and throwing his arms around her father. When her father was released, he gulped in a breath, stood back and nodded slowly.

The number of soldiers around them had increased again when Lis returned the general's bow, accepted his hand and stepped up into the carriage. She half expected to see the prince sitting within it, but the carriage was empty. And as she made space for her father to join her, she heard the steps being pushed into place. She wanted to pull the curtain aside to be sure that her father walked with her.

She stifled a sob, feeling more alone. Her mother was gone. She looked to the empty cushions beside her, missing the presence of the prince to take her mind from it. She could hear her father talking with the general in hushed tones, and she wondered if it was good for him to walk so far.

'The old town seems much quieter than I remember,' she heard her father say. And she wondered if they had cleared the streets again, even though she was in her carriage.

'The world is not what it was,' the other man said quietly, and Lis leaned towards the opening to hear better. 'People don't visit like they did before the war.'

'You said something similar on my last visit,' her father said.

'Perhaps I did,' the general said. And then there was nothing more.

Lis wondered why people wouldn't come to the capital as they once had. When the carriage stopped, she was jolted back to her reality and the reason they were there.

In the heavy silence of the temple, Lis focused on the tablet on the table in the centre of the space. The black lacquered wood stood out amongst the white stone walls, gold painted symbols marking out her mother's name, birthplace and death. Lis felt an uncertainty as to exactly how old her mother was. It was something she should have had an idea about, but she had none.

Large, slow tears tracked down her father's face again and she bit her lip, holding back the odd question that she suddenly seemed so desperate to know the answer to. He dropped heavily to his knees and bowed low before the memorial. Lis followed. Her own tears ran unchecked. She felt hot and cold and empty.

'Ting,' she whispered.

'She is preparing for your mother's cremation.'

Lis nodded once, taking an incense stick and lighting it. She placed it carefully in the pot beside the plaque, then took another and did the same.

'Once I have prayed with you, I shall return home and light the fires,' her father whispered.

Lis paused with the incense stick held out before her, but she didn't plant it in the pot. Her hand shook with his words, as she knew she could not return with him. He knew the same. Surely, he understood that the letters had not been passed on; if they had been, Lis would have found a way to return, to see her mother one last time.

'We are no longer your family,' her father breathed, and she struggled with the idea. 'It is the way of the hidden princess.'

Lis shook her head. Her hand fell, the stick slipping. A strong hand closed around hers, and she gasped at the shock of it. Prince Remi guided her hand back to the pot and, in her numbed state, helped guide the incense into the sand.

'She will always be your mother,' he said, a sad smile curling one side of his mouth. 'General Long, I am sorry for your loss,' he continued, bowing as he turned to her father, his hand still holding hers.

She looked at it then, realising as though for the first time that he held her. His hand warm and soft and oddly calming. She should be worried that he could be this close, that she might give herself away. Despite the feeling washing over her, she wanted to be anywhere but here, and she gently pulled from his grip and clenched her hands before her.

'I have organised for an offering pot to be set up in your palace when you return. The shrine shall follow.'

'She is not to remain in the temple?' her father asked, his voice loud and echoing through the open space.

Lis reached out a hand for his, but he leapt to his feet.

'Our customs are as they always were,' the prince said quietly, standing and bowing low to her father.

'She deserves to be in the temple,' her father asserted.

'She is,' the prince said carefully, and Lis closed her eyes.

She took a deep breath, overwhelmed by the mixed scents of the temple, the fruit, the incense and the variety of flowers. She wanted a cool breeze to blow over her skin, to wipe away the sick feeling that had settled on her. But even if she could muster such magic, the man beside her would cut her down without a thought. She wondered if she would make the same fizzle sound as the man in the baths, and she shivered. As she remembered his face emerging from the water, she wondered what it was they wanted from her. What he wanted from her. Were there others? He had given the indication that there were others. And that they knew what she was.

She shouldn't be here. She wasn't safe. She opened her eyes and took in the black lacquered plaque. 'It shouldn't be like this,' she murmured.

'If only we could influence the gods,' the prince whispered.

Lis looked slowly around the temple, the offerings and pleas left at the feet of the gods. Wasn't that what the people were trying to do? Asking for—wishing for—a different life?

Without a word, Lis headed out into the too bright sunlight of the day. She stood at the entrance to the temple, looking over the silent world around her and wondering how they had cleared the streets so completely. She expected the sky to be dark and cloudy, to reflect the darkness closing in on her. The carriage waited at the base of the steps, the soldiers looked out over the world and U'shi stood silent, looking at the ground. The carriage steps were already pulled down and ready for her.

As she started down the temple steps, a flash of something caught her eye. She stopped, and a pale, young face peered out at her from the shadows of a laneway that led from the square. Then a roar went up from the nearest soldier, and they were running.

Lis stood as she was, watching the frantic movement and shouts as the soldiers all ran headlong into the darkness of the lane. She heard her father's sword before she saw him, the sound of metal on metal as he drew it from its sheath. He stood to one side, the prince to the other with his own sword drawn, his eyes closed. Lis studied him for a moment as a hum surrounded him.

Lis looked back to U'shi, who was now looking around the square herself, fear evident on her face and in her hurried movements. Lis's father and the prince bundled her down the steps and into the carriage. U'shi dove in with her.

Lis didn't know who led the horse or whether her father and the prince walked with them, but they moved quickly away from the temple. The carriage jolted over the cobbled streets, throwing her around.

'I thought you would spend longer with your mother,' U'shi whispered.

'She is no longer my mother.' Lis again closed her eyes to the world and the serious look on U'shi's face.

'I am sorry,' she whispered.

Lis shook her head, listening to the wheels rattling across the streets. Multiple footsteps ran along beside them, and she was tempted to pull the curtains back and look out at the soldiers. She tried to quiet her breathing, to maintain her calm, fearful her magic would leak out into the world and the prince would leap into the carriage to push his sword into her.

She was sure she could hear the fizzle of dying magic, just as she had in the bath house.

'Four,' she whispered.

'What?' U'shi asked, her voice just as low.

Lis shook her head, but the knowledge that four of her soldiers ran with them gave her some comfort, at least from the idea that the magic ones were trying to hurt her. As well as her father and the general moving swiftly at her side.

U'shi pulled out the edge of the curtain. She stared for a moment, then moved to the other side of the carriage and did the same. 'The general runs beside your father.'

Lis nodded. She understood her father's pain at the loss of her mother, and she didn't want to add to it, but it was too hard for her to think of him returning without her. He and Ting would stand by the pyre as her mother found her way to the gods. How could she have slipped away so quickly?

Perhaps Peng could be of assistance to her father. Although where he was now and what he wanted of the world, Lis didn't know.

The carriage came to an abrupt halt, dragging Lis from her thoughts. Following U'shi hurriedly from the enclosed space, Lis almost pushed her off the carriage as she tried to hand the steps down to the soldier who had appeared from the gate. U'shi rushed ahead, and her father's hand was there to help her down.

They moved as one inside Lis's palace, the classroom becoming a reception room. She stood back against the wall while her father talked with the prince and the general about what had happened.

'Your Highness,' someone called from the gate—another soldier, she guessed—and the prince moved outside. She could make out the man in the garden. His armour was shiny and bright, and again Lis found herself cursing the sunshine.

'What did you find?' the prince asked. Lis wondered why he had allowed this man into her garden.

'Nothing. We saw someone and we gave chase, but he disappeared.'

'Is someone hiding him?'

'No one saw anything. I started to wonder if it was a mirage. That we were just expecting something. It has been too quiet.'

'I saw him,' Lis said, more to herself than anyone else. She looked towards her father. 'I saw someone.'

Her father nodded once.

Too much had happened in a small amount of time, and Lis wanted desperately to sit down. Ink still marked her work and the desktop. She wondered why no one had cleaned up in readiness for her return. There was little time enough for her to learn all she must.

'I need to return to my studies,' she announced, straightening her shoulders. 'I am sure you have much to prepare. Thank you, Father, for taking the time to visit with me.' She gently touched her right hand over her left arm to her elbow. Doing all she could to continue to breathe, she bowed low to her father. 'I am sure you are needed by Ting to assist with the preparations.'

'Peng is there to help,' her father said absently, a confused expression on his face, like he wasn't sure who she was. And then his mouth opened slightly.

Lis tried unsuccessfully to gulp down the pain in her chest. A whimper escaped.

'I cannot visit again,' her father said quickly, reaching her in two strides.

Despite wanting to throw herself into his arms and hold on to him forever, she simply inclined her head.

'Lis,' he said, resting his hands on her shoulders. 'I understand that this is very difficult. And,' he added, glancing over his shoulder to the prince in her garden, 'that you are scared. I believe the prince and your soldiers, do all they can to keep you safe.'

She looked at the prince rather than her father when she inclined her head again. A small noise of agreement hummed against her lips, but she couldn't open them in fear of what she might say. What she might do to beg her father to take her with him.

'I have already explained to the princess the measures I have taken to keep her safe,' the prince said, his voice sharp and clipped as he entered the room. 'You have just lost your mother,' he said more gently. 'Take the time to rest and talk with your father. The empress does not expect you to return to lessons today.'

'But there is too little time,' she blurted.

'You learn quickly,' her father added as she shook her head. 'You can take a day to grieve.' He sounded angry, his deep voice reverberating around the usually quiet walls.

'I shall talk with the men,' the general said quickly, bowing to Lis before racing from the room. She turned back to the window to watch him crunching along the gravel path. As the gate closed behind him, she was relieved her garden had become quiet again.

'There is another quiet space through that doorway,' the prince said quickly, pointing beyond the classroom. Lis wondered if he had been here before.

Her father took her arm and half dragged her beyond the classroom out into a small garden. It was shaded from the sun by tall bamboo that grew thick around the walls, hiding them completely from the outside world. A gazebo sat in the middle of the space, with a small table and three round stools beneath it.

Lis's father deposited her onto a stool and crossed his arms savagely.

Lis looked at her hands, and her father continued to wait.

'How is Peng?' she finally asked.

'He is well enough,' he answered gruffly.

Lis looked up then, taking in the angry man before her.

'I don't want to be here, but I cannot leave. I miss you all, and yet I cannot even read your letters. If you had not come, would they have told me at all of her death?'

'I don't know.' He sighed, sitting at the table with her. 'This is not what I wanted for you.'

'But it is where I am,' she said, 'and there is no choice now.'

'Is it so hard?'

She nodded and tried not to let her tears escape. 'The tutors and the empress are forever telling me there isn't enough time to learn all I need to know. Yet if they focused more on teaching me rather than complaining, I would know so much more.'

He sighed.

She looked into his worried face. 'There was a man,' she murmured, unsure how to continue.

Her father straightened, the soldier in him clear and angry. 'Tell me.'

'He appeared in the bath house. I was alone, and my maid had disappeared. He...'

'Lis,' her father coaxed gently.

'He had magic,' she whispered, leaning forward. 'He said he knew what I was.'

'What happened?' her father asked, a shake to his voice she hadn't heard other than when he had spoken of her mother.

'The prince is a hunter. He felt the magic and saved me.'

'And the man?'

'Dead,' she said. She opened and closed her mouth to say more, but she didn't know how.

'He made a noise when he died,' her father added gently, pulling her to him.

She nodded against him. The strange fizzle sound was still clear in her mind. 'You have killed those with magic.'

When he said nothing, she pulled back and looked up at him. He wore a distant look, but he didn't answer her.

'We are given very little choice in this world,' she whispered, standing and wiping at her dry face, smearing her makeup across her sleeve. 'I must look a sight.' She tried to smile for her father and ran her hand over the mark on the light coloured cloth.

'You sound like an empress,' he said, his voice cracking, and he turned his back on her and walked inside.

13

General Long stepped through the gate, looking distant and sad. Remi bowed low before him.

'Your Highness,' the general stammered.

'I am nervous, General Long, and I would prefer to escort you to where you go next.'

The general looked about for a moment, taking in the number of soldiers. 'Would it be better for you to be stationed by my daughter?'

'As much as I would like to watch over her, I am afraid the customs will not allow it.'

The older man sighed as he looked back at the gate behind him. 'I fear I have lost her,' he murmured.

'She will always be your daughter,' Remi said, bowing again.

The general shook his head. 'She is now Hidden Princess of the Rei-Een Empire, and she will be Empress. As much as I love her, I understand that she is no longer mine.'

Remi suddenly wondered if he was worthy of this girl. He had not thought at all about what she would be leaving behind when he chose her that day. Her look of horror still stung, but she had understood what she was losing.

'Will you see my father?' he asked.

The old man shook his head and walked out into the street. Remi had to race to catch him up. Despite his older appearance, he was strong and quick.

'Sir,' Remi said, trying to keep pace with him, 'it is not safe on the Palace Isle.'

The general stopped and looked at him seriously. 'What has happened?' he asked, his hand closing on his sword. 'Lis,' he murmured, looking back towards her palace.

'I assure you I do all I can to keep the princess safe. But there have been some recent signs of magic.'

'What does your father say?' the general asked. His face was neutral, but Remi sensed a shift in him, a nervousness.

'He does not believe me.'

'You are a hunter,' he whispered.

The prince nodded once.

'The man in the bath house.'

Remi looked back towards the hidden princess's palace. She had told him then. What would this man do with such information?

'Why did he come after my daughter?'

'I don't know, but I am trying to find out.'

'You don't think he was alone?'

Remi shook his head.

'She is stronger than she looks,' General Long murmured. 'Stronger than she realises. She understands her place here, no matter how difficult.'

'I know that she was promised to another,' Remi said.

'That is of no matter now,' the general said with a wave of his hand. 'Her training to become your empress is what matters, and…' He stopped, bowed and started off again.

'Sir,' Remi said, running after him. 'What can I do?'

'Keep her safe,' the man said, striding ahead.

'There is more.'

The general stopped and looked back to him. He took a tentative step, aware of the people starting to fill the streets.

'There is more you wish to tell me,' Remi insisted.

The general sighed and looked around. 'I cannot comment on

how the training is conducted, Your Highness.'

'You don't think they train her appropriately.'

'I cannot say. She is bright and learns fast. If given the chance, she will learn all she must to be the empress you need her to be in three years' time.'

Remi nodded once. The old general bowed before him, then turned and disappeared into the crowd. Remi wondered just what Lis had said to her father. His mother had repeated that there was not enough time, yet she had insisted on following the traditions and hiding the girl away. He hoped she wasn't taking her frustrations out on Lis and making this harder than it already was.

He turned back towards her palace and then stopped. He couldn't keep dropping in, and today had been difficult for her. Her mother's death, and a further risk to her safety. He still had not discovered where the man in the bath house had come from or how he had made it past the soldiers. The idea that the attack on Lis could be connected to his brother's death gave him pause.

His brother had not had a hunter's skills, but he was one of the strongest soldiers Remi knew. His reputation rivalled that of General Long on the battlefields of the magic wars. How was it that someone could have killed him as they had? How could they have gotten close enough to kill him?

Remi stopped amongst the throng of people now moving easily through the streets that had not so long ago been empty. He walked slowly towards the temple. Someone had been watching the hidden princess there, and that was where he needed to start.

The hunter amongst her guard had sensed him but had been unable to follow. Ignoring those around him, Remi walked slowly, reaching out with his senses and touching those who passed him, but there was nothing.

Once standing on the steps of the temple, he looked towards the laneway. There was nothing now. Not even a hint of what had been. Could someone have been playing with them? Trying to lead them away and gain access to the princess again?

The idea made him uncomfortable, and he wondered what else he might need to do to keep her safe. He turned and headed into the temple, which was surprisingly quiet. Two worshipers prayed before one of the gods while another stood across the temple, bent before another god. A priestess hovered around another statue, dusting and tidying.

The hidden princess's mother's shrine remained as it was, alone in the middle of the temple. The cushions before it for her to kneel upon and grieve had been abandoned early. What was it that had spooked her so that she would not stay with her mother?

Remi gently touched the base of the plaque. He took an incense stick and lit it, then bowed low before placing it beside those his princess had placed. 'I am sorry I took her from you,' he whispered.

'It is where she is meant to be,' a soft voice answered behind him, and he turned quickly to find a priestess smiling sadly. 'Whatever the cost.'

He scowled at her, and she bowed slightly before moving away.

The costs would be high on the Palace Isle. She would never be truly free again. But of all the girls who had lined up before them, she was the only one he had seen. Her words to his mother had only endeared her further. She was compassionate and thoughtful as well as beautiful. And now her father spoke of her intelligence. She would be the perfect empress—yet did she want to be?

The incense was thick, and Remi's eyes started to water. He had more important things to worry about than whether his future bride wanted the position or not. There was no choice now. He just had to keep her alive and discover what had happened to his brother.

He stood again at the top of the steps of the temple and closed his eyes. There was no feeling of magic, no inkling of anyone with magic within the vicinity. He headed determinedly down the step and across the square into the laneway. He took his time, but there was no residue here, and he started to wonder just what tricks had been played and why.

Remi stood at the gate to the home of Tutor Na. It was connected by a laneway to the back of the hidden princess's palace. All the tutors were close by, and although all gates of the tutors' homes opened into the laneway, there was no other access to it.

He waited. He was unsure how he could ask her about his concerns, but he remembered hearing his mother talk about how knowledgeable a tutor she was.

General Long's words still rang in his ears. There was something he hadn't said.

The maid bowed low and stood back to allow him into the small courtyard, which led directly into the small house. He waited for her to close the gate and lead the way into the house. He was sure his mother was going to have a lot to say about this. She would see it as interfering, but there was something about Lis that had Remi nervous. Was she just unlucky to be the focus of the changes he had felt around the Palace Isle, or had she brought them with her?

The room he entered was simple and lined with shelves. Each one contained piles of books, scrolls and wooden slips with their tags hanging down. Beautiful teapots and delicate glassware sat nestled amongst them.

He absently looked at the tag of the closest one. 'Etiquette for the marriage night' it read. He let it drop from his fingers, his face hot and his mouth dry. *What does this tutor teach exactly?*

'Your Highness,' she greeted him sharply, making him jump, and he moved away from the shelves.

'Tutor Na,' he said, bowing before her.

'Is there a reason for your visit? I have much to prepare.'

'And not enough time,' he said without thinking.

She pursed her lips. 'Has something happened?'

He nodded once. 'But I wish to talk to you about the hidden princess and her learning.'

'Her learning is of no concern until she becomes your empress, and then she will have all that she needs.'

'Will she?' he asked.

'You fear the lack of time. That instead of thirteen years we have only three.'

'I understand that my hidden princess is more than capable of learning everything she must within that time, but...' He took a moment. 'But I understand she may not be supported to reach that potential.'

'Truly, Your Highness? And who has claimed such a thing? We are here only to serve the crown, to ensure that your empress is all she can be.'

'Do you think she will be?'

She surprised him with a smile. 'Yes, Your Highness.'

The tension left his shoulders.

'I shall talk with the other tutors. You have nothing to fear. I understand that it has been a difficult day for the hidden princess.'

'I thank you, Tutor Na, for your honesty. I fear after the attack in the baths that she is not as safe as I would hope.'

'Her guard is always watching.'

'Where were they at the baths? How did the man make it into such a place?'

Tutor Na sighed. 'What would you like to do?'

'I want to be able to watch more closely. To station someone in the access behind the palace. I would prefer someone in the garden, even in the palace with her. But I am sure you won't allow that.'

'There was a time, long ago, when the hidden princess was hidden from everyone, even those around her.' She turned away from him, walking directly to a shelf and looking through the scrolls. She finally selected one and held it out to him.

Remi stepped forward and took it, unrolling it slowly. A hidden princess, dressed in the same grey tunic his hidden princess wore. Her hair was pulled back from her face, a simple pin holding it back, and the rest hung loose behind her. Across her face she wore a pale veil. It sat below her eyes, across her nose, and it flowed down to her waist.

'The hidden princess was hidden at all times. No one saw her face until the wedding day.'

'But I have seen her face,' he murmured.

'It is an option I could discuss with the empress. That way she could remain hidden and you could place guards in the palace for her protection. I don't want any harm to come to her either.'

He nodded slowly. 'Will my mother support such a change?'

'It is a return to the traditions of old. It might be prudent to reinforce the traditions at this time.'

Remi bowed low before her. 'I thank you.'

'I cannot promise that the empress will allow you into the hidden princess's palace even with this change.'

He smiled and bowed again. She might not, but it was more important to keep Lis safe. If a veil meant he could keep the guards closer, he would do all he could to ensure it happened.

14

Lis looked over the uniform laid out on her bed. The veil was a new addition, and she wondered what it meant. U'shi silently entered the room and helped her change. Other than the day before, every day felt the same.

She stifled a sob, thinking of her father and just how broken he had appeared. She had done very little to comfort him. But she couldn't allow herself to think about it; she had lost her mother when she first entered the palace. Whether her mother was alive or not, Lis would never have seen her again.

U'shi indicated the seat, and Lis tried to push her father from her mind. And Peng. She had lain in bed the previous night wondering just what he was doing with her family, whether he sat and laughed with Ting as easily as he used to with her. She sighed as U'shi pushed new pins into her hair.

'Your Highness?'

Lis waved her away. When she didn't move, Lis looked up and saw her holding the veil. Lis nodded once, and U'shi attached it to the new pins.

'It is to be worn at all times outside this room.'

'Even in the palace?'

U'shi lowered her head.

Lis pushed up from the seat and strode into the classroom. The prince stood with Tutor Nizen and another guard. 'Your Highness,'

Lis said, pulling herself to a stop and bowing before him.

He nodded in return.

She took her place at the desk, despite the bell not having rung, and looked to the tutor. The younger man glanced between everyone in the classroom and coughed.

'I want you in the rear,' the prince said, directing a soldier out into the rear courtyard.

The tutor shook his head.

When the prince reappeared on his own, he said, 'There will be another in the front and the usual on the gate.' Then he bowed to Lis.

'Am I to have no privacy?' she called after him as he started out the door. She could see the glint of the sun on the armour of the soldier already in the front garden.

'Your safety is more important,' he said, striding out.

She pushed up quickly from the desk and followed him into the morning sunlight. 'Did you find the man from yesterday?'

He turned and shook his head. 'It appears there are people watching you too closely.'

She looked pointedly at the soldier, who turned his back to her.

The prince took a step closer. 'The Palace Isle is not as safe as I would hope, Your Highness,' he whispered. 'These are *your* men; they are just closer than they were before.'

Lis nodded once and returned to her classroom, finding the guard still in the garden when she glanced through the window before taking her seat.

'Tutor Na will explain the veil and the history of such,' Tutor Nizen murmured, looking through papers of his own. He glanced up briefly as U'shi coughed in the doorway. Nodding once, he waved her away. She slid the door closed, and Lis's gaze returned to the tutor.

'What do we cover today?' she asked.

'The Empire and its people. I would like to discuss the islands and the changes that occurred after the magic war.'

'I have covered the geography of the islands,' Lis said, trying not to sigh. 'I know each by name, how far it is by boat from the Palace Isle, and the main families that live on each. I know what they did for the Empire during the war; I know who they aligned with and the gifts granted by the emperor for their service. What else can you teach me?'

'You do not know it all. There is much to learn…'

'And not enough time to learn it,' Lis interrupted.

His eyes narrowed as he focused on her.

'So you all say and yet you teach me nothing new. Much of this I have already learnt from my parents as I grew. I don't know how you think you can help me be what the crown prince will need me to be when you teach me nothing. Is it that my poor mother was a better teacher?' The words were harsh, and Lis felt the same overwhelming sadness that she had the day before. She had also been louder than she had meant to be. She heard someone moving by the door.

'Do you know all that your father did in the war? The villages and islands he helped clear of magic? The destruction he waged in the name of the Empire?'

Lis was on her feet. She knew he had done more than he ever wanted her to know about. And she understood that he had killed those with magic. She also knew he had been a soldier with no choice. Just as she had no choice now.

'Do you sympathise with those with magic?' she asked, the words just as harsh as the previous queries, wondering if this was some test or he just wanted to push her. 'What will I learn from *your* stories of *my* father?'

He stared her down and she glanced at the doorway.

'Why not tell me what part the emperor played? How he directed his troops, how he learned to defeat the magic, how they discovered the hunters.' She took a deep breath. 'Or is there not enough time?'

She wanted to be out in the fresh air, but the men in her garden kept her in the classroom. She didn't even have the privacy of her own palace now. 'You would waste my time with stories and knowledge I already have. You forget who I am,' she said, far more confidently than she felt, for she wanted to be anywhere but here.

'And who is that, other than a lowly student?'

'I am the future empress,' she said softly. 'I am the one who will determine who will train the next hidden princess, and how comfortable your life will be.'

'You will have more important things to occupy your time.' He laughed, as though her words were meaningless.

'I don't think so. All I have learnt of being empress is listening to stories and making tea. I will have nothing better to do than return the favours you have done me.' She gave him a short bow and, as she rested her hand on the door, she heard whoever was on the other side scurry away. Was it U'shi or the crown prince?

'I understand the last few days have been difficult,' the tutor said softly.

'The last few months. I am beginning to understand why it takes so long to train a hidden princess.'

'Your mother has died and you are not yourself,' he said, his face still hard. 'With the accident of your island home following so close behind, I wonder how you are able to study at all.'

'What accident?' Lis asked, the air rushing from her lungs as she stepped towards him.

He remained at his desk. An odd grin grew across his face.

'My father?' she whispered.

'He is well enough. It was a visitor for your mother's cremation. It was thought that he had magic, that he had infiltrated your family in an attempt to harm you. The crown prince sent his own men.'

'What?'

'Peng,' he said. 'The crown prince thinks only of you. He has had the traitor fizzled out, and he has considered your hidden status and instituted the veil.'

Lis opened her mouth and then closed it. Her mind couldn't make sense of the man's words. Her chest hurt as though someone had pushed a sharp blade through her heart. 'The crown prince killed Peng?'

'One of his men, I'm sure, for he has hunters everywhere.'

'Peng was not... He didn't have...'

'Tell me, what do *you* think you should learn today, Your Highness?'

Lis walked out of the classroom, across the small foyer and into her room. It was the only safe place she had, and now she wasn't sure just how safe it was. She sat at the table and poured water into the cup. She stared at it, watching the steam rise in strange patterns.

All she had to do was use her magic. Boil the water dry, or change the colour of her tunic. He was just outside, close enough to feel the magic and come running. He would run her through with a fizzle sound, without a second thought.

What danger does this mean for Father? she wondered. To be so close to one considered to have magic. But the prince was a hunter. She looked towards the door. He would have known if Peng had magic or not. But then, so would she. She had known him for so many years, and yet she didn't have any idea of him having magic. There must have been a mistake.

She squeezed her eyes closed and tried to remember Peng's face, but she couldn't. The harder she tried, the dimmer he became in her mind. The prince, on the other hand, appeared all too clearly.

She had mentioned Peng to him when she was chosen. Had he been listening when she raised Peng's name with her father? Was it a strange revenge for her not wanting to be the hidden princess? Was he making sure there would be nothing for her to return to?

The idea of what might happen to her father if she were discovered and killed was only momentary as she stretched out her senses to the soldier by the front door. He didn't move. She stretched out further, feeling the heavy wood of the gate and the two men beyond it. The world remained too quiet around her.

She felt the hum of magic and knew with certainty that she would have known if Peng had carried magic as well. She would have sensed it as the hunters did. Only no one appeared to sense her magic now.

She stood slowly and turned on the spot. Her dress shimmered in the sunlight, the thick grey material shifting into a flowing pink, the colour of the blossoms in her garden. The material changed from heavy linen to a fine silk.

Lis smiled and breathed as though for the first time. She would at least look like herself when the prince burst through the door and ran her through.

But no one came. No one hurried towards her. She could feel the distant hum of magic, but she remained as she was. Then there was a gentle knock at the door.

Lis froze, her heart hammering in her chest. She put her hands together in a quiet clap as the door slid open. U'shi stood smiling in the doorway, and then the smile slipped as she looked around the room.

'The tutor did not dismiss you,' she called into the room, looking through Lis, who held her breath. 'Your Highness?' she asked more uncertainly.

She turned her back and raced out into the garden. Lis followed behind her, trying not to get too close in case she gave herself away. She followed U'shi back into the classroom, where the tutor sat back at the desk, tapping the end of a brush on the blank page before him. Lis scowled at the man, who looked up lazily at U'shi and then sat straighter.

'What is it?' he asked.

U'shi shook her head.

'Has she...?'

'Worse. She has disappeared.'

'She must be hiding.'

'Where would she hide? She is not in her room and not in the garden. The guard has not seen her. What will the empress say?'

'You should have...' He was interrupted by a knock at the door.

They both turned as the prince entered. A servant behind him carried her mother's shrine, and another had a small fire pot for her to make offerings to her mother's memory. She gulped down the threatening tears, wondering if there would be such a shrine for Peng.

'I thought the rear courtyard the best place for this, although I am happy to set it up in the princess's room if she would rather it close.'

Lis breathed out very slowly, worried she would alert the prince to her presence if he wasn't already aware. He didn't even look in her direction, but he did look concerned.

'What has happened?'

U'shi shook her head. 'The hidden princess is resting,' she said softly, bowing to the prince. 'It has been a trying time.'

'I can wait for her,' he murmured, indicating the servant take the fire pot out into the courtyard before following.

U'shi was quick to chase after him, the tutor glancing at her before he too followed the small procession out into the garden. Lis walked slowly behind, wondering what they would tell him. Part of her wondered how long she could keep this up. And why using her magic hadn't alerted the prince to her presence.

He sat the plaque for her mother gently on the table, and the manservant sat the urn beside it. Then they bowed and stood silently before it. The prince smiled at it sadly, and Lis wondered if he thought about his brother. She waved her hand before him, suddenly rash. He didn't flinch, and she wondered if he was the great hunter she had assumed him to be. But then, he had felt something at the baths that day.

Lis looked at her own hands and then back to the prince. She had played this trick on her sister before. And only the once on her father. It was a skill she had never told anyone about. The day

Peng had come to talk to her father of their connection, she had stood nervously in the corner of the room, biting her lip. She had known what he wanted to ask of her father, but she hadn't told Peng she would listen.

She had been so worried that her father would not allow the match. He had spent so long trying to protect her from the world, she had worried that he wouldn't let her go to Fourth with Peng.

She had desperately wanted to go with him. Her heart ached with the idea of him, and she clenched her fists at the thought that it was the man standing before her who had taken him away. She could feel the buzz of the magic around her, and she wondered what other skills she had that she had not tested.

The prince turned slowly and looked around the garden. Lis took a deep breath and tried to calm the pain that burned darker in her chest. She had to keep it hidden. She had a moment of fright as he looked directly at her and she held her breath, fearful she had succeeded too well to hide her magic away and it had disappeared, causing her to reappear.

He turned to the tutor. 'Where is the guard?'

Tutor Nizen shrugged. 'He is your man, not mine.'

The prince scowled, and Lis realised that she wouldn't want to be on the bad side of this man. Although she was about to be, for he had attacked her family and would soon discover her gone.

'I ordered him here.'

'Perhaps he is with the others,' U'shi whispered, and Lis noticed another glance between the maid and the tutor. Did they dislike her so much?

'There is a taint of magic here. I wonder if someone has visited who should not.'

This time the tutor looked directly at U'shi, and the prince followed his gaze.

'There has been no one,' she said hurriedly.

'Where is the hidden princess?'

'Resting,' she said.

Lis was tempted to cough and throw them all into turmoil. When her father had given his blessing to Peng, she had squealed with delight, almost giving herself away.

'Why are you here?' the prince asked the tutor.

'It is my position to be here to help train the hidden princess. It is you who should not be here.'

The prince raised his eyebrows at the open nature of the tutor. 'And yet she is not well enough for classes today.'

'She was in the classroom earlier. We discussed the magic war and the part her father played.'

The prince looked back to the shrine on the table. 'Light the pot,' he murmured to the manservant with him. Then he strode back into the house.

Lis followed him, wondering if he would leave so soon. But he hesitated at her door before he knocked. She wondered whether he would tell the truth if she asked him about Peng. Would he claim he was looking out for his future empress? Or would there be another, simpler reason?

When there was no response, he slid the door back and entered her room uninvited. The room itself felt cold to Lis. He turned slowly, taking in the empty space. He moved towards the table and picked up the cup she had drunk from not so long ago. He put it to his lips, and Lis found her hands moving to her hips. Who did he think he was? Moving around her palace as though it were his own. Touching her things, drinking from her cup.

'Warm,' he murmured.

He walked more quickly towards the bed, then peered behind a screen.

Lis raised her eyebrows.

He turned around the room slowly, looking up towards the ceiling and the windows. He licked his lips as though tasting something, and Lis worried that he might have sensed her magic in the cup of water she had left on the table.

'Your Highness,' a soldier called, tapping on the door as he entered the room.

'Where is she?' the prince asked.

'There is no sign in the garden, and the maid ran out there not long before you arrived.'

'She is missing, then, and the maid was not going to tell me.' His voice carried a dangerous edge, and Lis was reminded that this man could kill her at any moment.

'Did she run away?'

The prince shook his head and then looked around the room one more time, glancing through Lis. She had hidden herself well.

'There is no sign of a disturbance,' the guard continued.

'But there is something,' the prince said. He walked over to the cup one more time and then turned on his heel. 'There is something about the tutor.'

'He taught the previous hidden princess for many years.'

'Hmmm,' was all he said as he moved more slowly back through the palace. He arrived again in the rear courtyard, Lis only a step behind. The tutor and U'shi were talking in hushed tones a little way from the servant who still stood by her mother's shrine.

'What did my mother say?' the prince asked.

'Your Highness?' U'shi said, bowing a little as she spoke.

'About the missing princess.'

'She is not missing; she is resting.'

'Where did you send her to rest? Her little island home?'

They looked at each other again, and Lis had a moment of understanding. They had worked together to upset her. Whether it was by sharing the news or for some other reason, she couldn't be sure.

'She's...'

'Don't lie to me, or it could mean your head.'

U'shi gulped loudly and tears spilled over, running unchecked down her cheeks. 'I have done nothing,' she wailed. 'She is resting in her room.'

'No,' he said, too calm, and Lis could feel the hum of magic around him. She took a step back, wondering if this was connected to his being a hunter or if it was something else.

'She is,' U'shi insisted, stepping forward, and he swung around and took her arm as she tried to pass him.

He shook his head once, and Lis tried to scuttle out of the way.

'I promise you, Your Highness, she must be here.'

He let her go and turned back to the tutor, who looked far too relaxed. The prince moved quickly through the rooms and out into the front garden, where he stopped before the guard. 'Where is the other guard?' he asked.

The man shook his head, and the prince continued down the path and out the gate. It was all Lis could do to keep up, and then she nearly ran into the back of him as he stopped in the gateway to talk with the two guards there. As he took a single step to the side, she sucked in a breath and squeezed past him, hoping her silk didn't brush against his skin. But he turned as she passed, and she wondered if she had given herself away.

'Lis is missing,' he murmured urgently to the second guard as she stepped back and into the middle of the road. 'I think she has been taken by those with magic. There is a taint in the palace.'

The man drew himself up taller. 'I promise you that we have watched every moment. No one has been near.'

'Perhaps they have a way of not being seen,' the prince continued.

'But they would have been sensed—if not by you then by the…' The man stopped and chewed nervously on his lip.

'You knew there was a hunter amongst you?'

The man nodded. 'It is what I would have done after the incident at the bath house. And your brother,' he added softly.

The prince nodded once. 'I want the palace watched,' he said to the guard, and then he turned to the other man. 'And I want the entire island searched until my princess is found.'

'Yes, sir.' He bowed low to the prince before disappearing down the street.

Lis looked from one to the other and then headed in a different direction. There was nowhere for her to go, but she didn't want to be here or around her prince any longer. *How dare he think of me as his princess?* she thought, remembering Peng, the pain in her chest sharp and real. *And why does he think he can call me Lis?*

The street was quiet. Although several people walked beside Lis, none of them saw her. She hadn't travelled this way before, she didn't think. For the carriage had been covered so well and she couldn't look out the windows. They had walked so far that first day, and she wondered just how big this island was. Much bigger than her own home. Or at least what had been her home. It would never be the same without her mother, and now without Peng.

She wiped at the tears that had started to flow and sucked in a sob. Unsure whether those around her could hear her or not, she bit hard on her lip. The street quickly became a quiet, narrow alleyway, and the tall grey walls surrounding other palaces and homes grew taller as the street between them narrowed. Broad, red-lacquered gates were intermittently dispersed along the walls. Lis didn't even glance at the name plates to see what lay beyond each gate.

A sprinkle of rain started. Lis couldn't be out in the rain. Invisible or not, it would give her away, and there was no way off the island from this side. Even though she had nowhere to go afterwards, she had to first go back through the centre of the Palace Isle and out to the docks.

She pressed herself into the nearest gateway. The gate creaked open and Lis stumbled back, hoping she wasn't falling into whoever might have opened the gate. She looked around the silent garden, similar in style to her own, although overgrown. The rain was starting to soak into her dress, and she shivered. She skipped up the path and onto the veranda. When she turned back to look at the open gateway, there was no one there.

The palace was similar to hers, and she wondered if this had once been home to a hidden princess. It didn't appear to be occupied as she carefully opened the heavy door. There was very little furniture, and a cool breeze blew in from somewhere beyond the room in which she stood.

There was no sign of anyone living there. A layer of dust covered the furniture and, although there was a pot over a burner and cups lined up on the table, it was cold. She sat heavily at the table and allowed herself to relax. She had no idea what she would do next or where she would go. She only knew that she had to be away from the hidden palace and the prince.

I would have known if Peng had magic, she told herself again. He couldn't have hidden it from her, even if she had been able to hide herself from the prince. Although how she had managed it, she didn't know. She wondered if something had changed with magic—if that was why there were thought to be few with magic, because those who had it could hide it. And if that was the case, why did her father worry so much that she would be discovered?

Perhaps he didn't know. Perhaps he didn't care to know. All those years he had kept to himself what had happened during the war, what he had done. But she understood it. It must have been so hard for him, and now it would be worse. Her mother was gone, and Lis would bring shame on them all. But she couldn't go back. She wouldn't.

Lis spent a comfortable night in the little palace, despite the lack of food and the dust that covered everything. She was free, but she was hidden away still, far from where she wanted to be. She breathed in the dust and looked at the cold pot. There was a pump in the rear courtyard, so she crept, now visible, out into the fresh morning air. She stood still for a long time listening for anyone else who might be about.

There was nothing other than bird song, and she drew water into the bucket. She swirled it about and threw it over the rough stones before sitting it back and pumping again. It smelled fresh, so she filled the pot and placed it over the base on the table.

She felt a moment's hesitation, wondering if the prince had indeed laid a trap for her and would burst through the door at any moment to run her through with a fizzle. But he hadn't found her yet, and she decided to take the risk. She blew softly onto the coals and they jumped to life.

Sitting at the table, sipping the warm water, Lis continued to wait. Her hunter prince didn't come to kill her. She peeked out at the front gate, still ajar, and wondered if she could summon a gust wind to blow it shut. But then it was pushed wide open as Tutor Nizen strode into the garden.

Lis clapped her hands and disappeared. Had he discovered her? Was he a hunter as well? She certainly hadn't sensed anything around him as she had with the prince. If those with magic could hide it, she may not be the only one, and he may not be there to help her. She remained rooted to the spot, only just remembering to extinguish the flame for the water as he entered the front door.

He barely glanced around the space as he paced back and forth. Then he stopped, and Lis heard footsteps crunching along the path. He moved over to the door and waited behind it. Lis was surprised to see U'shi's face appear.

'Has the empress summoned you?' he asked hurriedly, taking her in his arms. She flinched, and he let her go.

She nodded once, moving over to the table before turning back to him.

'Did it hurt?' he murmured, taking a slow step towards her.

'It doesn't matter. If they cannot find her, it will be worthwhile.'

'But he marked you,' he said, his voice louder, and she indicated with her hands that he lower his voice. 'I worry,' he continued quietly.

'It was worth the punishment.'

He grinned then and, stepping up to her, he took her chin and kissed her.

Lis bit down on her lip to prevent the surprised noise from

leaving her throat. This was not the way a tutor should behave. She wondered whether this was something new that had sparked once the crown prince died, or if it had been going on longer than that.

'She threatened to have me removed,' he said, releasing U'shi and smiling. 'She thinks she has power over us.'

U'shi pulled away. 'She will have once she is empress.'

'There is no chance that she will be now. She has run away, bringing disgrace on her and her family. Even if she is found…'

'The crown prince will take her back,' U'shi interrupted. 'He cares for her,' she spat. Lis could feel the tension in her words, the hatred. She wondered anew if U'shi had been behind the magic man in the baths.

'You are jealous,' the tutor said, the disappointment clear on his face. He sat at the table.

U'shi surprised Lis by sitting in the man's lap. She reached her arms around him, pulling herself close. Lis wondered if she should make her escape, but then U'shi's arm brushed close to the pot. She focused on it and then the cup, which still contained water.

'Who else do you bring here?' she snapped, leaping up.

'No one,' the tutor stammered, turning to look where she had. Then they looked at each other and around the room.

'Could she have chosen our hideaway?' U'shi asked.

The tutor moved quickly out into the rear of the little palace and then back. He shook his head and moved into the other room. 'If she was here, she is gone now,' he said when he reappeared.

'We should tell the crown prince,' U'shi said quickly, turning for the door. The tutor caught her arm and pulled her back to him.

'And what would you tell him? That you found signs of his runaway princess where you secretly meet your lover? Would you add that we were here together when you should have been assisting her in the baths the day she was nearly killed?'

U'shi shook her head. 'I could lie. I could say I thought I saw her enter the gate.'

'You lie so well,' he murmured, pulling her close for another kiss.

Lis couldn't listen to anymore, and she slipped past them into the garden. The gate had been closed, and she cursed her stupidity in staying so close to her palace. She should have run far.

15

Remi paced in his room, then walked out onto the balcony again. The soldier who had failed to bring him any useful news still waited by the door, and Remi had been trying to hold his temper. 'There has to be something,' he growled at the man.

'Not a sign and no word. Do you think they want something?'

'They took her for a reason, I just don't know what it is. Or how,' he added, turning to the soldier. 'You were there, you saw where the soldiers were placed.'

The man nodded.

'How did they get her out of the palace?'

'The man in the back had disappeared,' the soldier offered.

It was soon discovered that he had gone to relieve himself, but he hadn't gone far enough that he wouldn't have noticed the princess being dragged away.

'She would have screamed,' Remi murmured. 'She's not the type to give up without a fight.'

'What if she went willingly?'

'Because they persuaded her it was for the best?'

'She was engaged to another; perhaps she would rather be with him…'

Remi turned angry eyes on the man as he petered to a stop.

'She knew what was required of her,' Remi said with a sigh. 'She would not bring such shame on her family.'

'Could they have gagged her or knocked her out?'

'It is the only thing I can think of,' Remi said with a nod, turning back into the room. 'Although a tutor and maid were present as well. How did this person enter her palace?'

'There are too many questions, Your Highness, and not enough known of just what those with magic can do. Could they become invisible?'

'I would have sensed him.'

'There have been others on this very isle that we did not sense at first.'

Remi looked around his room and then strode for the door, the soldier following behind. He had a sudden vision of Ta-Sho, twisted and burnt. He had no idea of how anyone had gotten so close to him. Anyone within the residence with magic would have been sensed by Remi himself or one of the other hunters.

He raced along the hallway, pushing out his senses before him. Could there be someone hiding right under his nose without him knowing it? He burst into his brother's room. It was just as he had left it, as though Ta-Sho might walk back in at any point. There were still some papers on his desk that Remi had yet to look at closely. They didn't appear to have been disturbed the day he found his brother dead.

He sat at the desk, feeling the loss of his brother, almost fearful that Ta-Sho would enter at any moment and chastise him for sitting there. But this was who he was. The hunter, the investigator—not the crown prince, not the future emperor. Although, that was who he was to become now that his brother was gone.

The reports were piled neatly on the right-hand side of the desk, and Remi reached for the top one. It was a report from a noble on Third. He skimmed through the report; it talked of supplies and the like, and then there was a brief, unclear mention of a boat he had seen.

'Why would he mention such a thing?'

The next was from General Zho-Hou, and Remi realised that he didn't fully understand everything his brother had done. He had been in correspondence with so many. Remi found his own name on a report and read it with more interest. The general had praised his actions and raised concern that there was more magic apparent within the Empire than they had thought.

'Could it be returning?' Remi wondered aloud.

'Your Highness?'

'Magic. Could it be that the magic is increasing? That there continue to be children born with it, despite the deaths during the magic war?' He had thought that magic must be in the family line somewhere for it to manifest, but perhaps it wasn't as easy as that.

The next report he picked up simply read: 'The child is found.'

'What child?' He turned the report around, but it didn't state who it was from, nor any indication as to when it was written.

What had his brother been looking into? And could this child be one of the reasons he had been killed?

Remi pushed himself up slowly from the desk. 'Have these sent to my room,' he said to the soldier, who placed his arms together and bowed to the prince. 'Have all reports stopped since my brother's death?'

'I will find out,' the soldier said.

'Have everything redirected. The world knows me as the crown prince now; I must continue my brother's work.'

The soldier bowed again and disappeared.

There was still a strange mark in the middle of the floor where Remi's brother had been murdered. Why had his father wanted this kept quiet rather than sorted? Someone had killed him. Someone had been brave—or stupid—enough to come into the royal residence, in the middle of the Palace Isle, and kill the crown prince.

He remembered his brother with a sword; he could have defended himself from anyone easily, yet somehow he had been beaten so badly. What had he discovered? Remi could remember his brother always standing and coming around the desk when he visited. Taking him by the arms. They would have stood on this very spot.

Could it have been someone he knew—someone he trusted?

Despite his need to continue what his brother had started in the hope of discovering who or what had killed him, Remi headed out into the square. He watched the people for a little while, wondering who amongst them might know something, who might be hiding something. He was frustrated that there was not enough he could do.

If the princess had run away, as suggested, she might have gone home. Back to her father, for her mother had just died. She might be caught up in her grief, and there was no shame in that. Remi wondered if she wore the veil as he had suggested. It gave her more freedom, although he doubted she saw it as such. For she could travel and remain hidden. He wasn't sure at what point in their history they had started locking girls away, and he was sure there was more to the history of the hidden princess that he wasn't aware of.

But it didn't matter now. He needed to find her; he needed to ensure she was safe. 'Peng,' he murmured to himself, heading for the docks. The man she had loved before she was hidden away. Could she be so desperate to see him that she had run away?

A strange anger built in Remi's veins as he strode forward, only to be jarred back to reality when he noticed the sheer number of soldiers around the Palace Isle. They were stopping everyone, and he veered along a narrow street that led from the main square. Soldiers knocked on gates and entered homes.

They were doing everything they could to find the princess on the Palace Isle. It was up to Remi to see if she was elsewhere.

He strode through the great gates and onto the docks, looking over the few boats that were tied against it. There was no other way off the island. The rocks against the high walls that surrounded them were too sharp to allow a boat to get close enough, and the watchtowers along the wall housed enough soldiers to notice someone trying to scale the wall from either side.

How could she have made it all the way to the dock without someone seeing something? Remi leapt aboard his own boat. It had been used so often to travel between the islands searching out those with magic, but it had sat idle in the dock for too long while he'd done his mother's bidding. His focus should have been on searching out his brother's killer. Perhaps if it had been, he wouldn't now be searching for his lost bride.

His heavy footsteps brought up the captain from below deck, the man about to growl at whomever had jumped aboard the prince's ship, only to find it was the prince himself. He stopped mid-flight and bowed.

'Do you know where General Long's island is?'

The man nodded once, but then looked back towards the shore.

'I need to get there.'

'I shall pull the crew together.'

'Now.'

'Please, Your Highness. I cannot sail a ship this size alone. The men are all within the nearest barracks. A few minutes and we shall be underway.'

Remi relented and nodded. Perhaps he should have told someone where he was going, but they would be back before nightfall. And hopefully, he would have his hidden princess with him.

The captain moved quickly, as promised, and they were sailing away from the Palace Isle within a few minutes of his leaving the prince. With the large ship, it didn't take long before they were out into deep water passing the other islands. Remi wondered if it had taken her so little time to reach him for the Choosing. Would it have taken hours longer with their smaller boat?

One of the crew pointed out the small island, which grew quickly as they sailed towards it. It was quite some distance from the main islands of the chain, and Remi wondered why the general had wanted to be so isolated from the rest of the Empire in his retirement. His father often talked of General Long's great deeds and all he had accomplished in the name of the Rei-Een Empire during the magic war. They had been friends in a way, Remi had sensed listening to the stories. The general could have retired to a large palace within the Palace Isle itself. Perhaps he had wanted to distance himself and his family from all he had done during the war. Remi also had moments himself he wanted to forget. His brother's burnt and twisted body was one of them.

A man stood on the dock waiting for the boat to reach them, but he was slight in build and Remi didn't recognise him. At one point, Remi wasn't sure if the boat would be able to reach the little jetty, but the crew sailed it in without incident and the man took the ropes to tie it up.

As the gangway was pushed out, the man bowed low to the prince.

'General Long waits for you in the house, Your Highness.'

Remi nodded at the man and strode towards the house. It was a simple but large dwelling, well placed to look over the water and the surrounding land. Remi noticed the field beside the house and wondered what it would look like in flower. There were patches of green around the palace isle, but not like the other islands and certainly not like here. He smiled to himself, imagining Lis standing amongst the wilderness, her hair loose and her feet bare. She belonged here. He sucked in a deep breath, remembering why he had come.

'Your Highness.' General Long bowed low as he entered the main room. The man who had met them on the dock entered just behind him, and the general looked up and scowled, waving him from the room.

'Stay,' Remi said. He would want to talk to everyone.

The man moved over and stood beside a young woman just behind the general. His other daughter, Remi guessed. She looked very much like Lis, the family resemblance clear, but she was not nearly as pretty. He shook his head to dispel the image and tried to determine what he should say. He'd had it very clear in his head as they had travelled here. But now that he saw a nervousness on the general's face, he didn't know where to start.

'Is she here?' he asked, instead of what he had planned.

'Who?' The general looked confused.

The prince opened his mouth and then closed it.

'Has something happened?' the other man asked, clearly concerned.

'Peng, hush,'

'Peng,' the prince repeated slowly. 'You were to marry Lis.'

He nodded once.

'She is missing,' he said quickly.

The general stepped forward. His daughter started to cry, and the young man crossed his arms savagely across his chest. 'How could you let this happen?' he asked, his voice carrying the same anger.

'Peng,' the general admonished again. 'I'm sure the crown prince has done all he could to keep her safe. And now all he can to find her.'

'I wondered if she might have come home,' he said softly.

The general's face turned hard. 'You think she would run away from her responsibilities? That she would bring such dishonour on her family when we have just lost her mother?'

The prince found himself shaking his head quickly, and the general took another step forward.

'But that is what you think, or you would not have come.'

'I thought her taken,' he murmured, unsure of himself now in the face of the great General Long. 'But she can't have simply disappeared, and there was no hint of magic, no sign of anyone else around her palace. I was just outside in the street. Talking of security and...'

'And yet you could not keep her safe,' Peng accused loudly.

'I have failed her,' Remi said, looking down at the ground.

'What can you tell me?' the general asked, stepping forward.

Remi shook his head.

'Why are you here?'

He sucked in a breath and looked at the general levelly. 'She is not happy as the hidden princess. It is not what she hoped for,' he said, looking past the older man at Peng. 'She tries her best, but my mother is hard and the tutors are difficult. When I could find no sign of magic, I feared she may have run away. Returning home in desperation and grief at the loss of her mother. To Peng,' he added almost inaudibly.

The general sighed then. 'Please sit, Your Highness. It has been a long journey from the Palace Isle. Drink with me.' He indicated the table and waved his daughter from the room. He looked pointedly at Peng, who waited before he followed her out.

'He is a great help to your family,' Remi said, watching him go.

'He is part of the family, even though Lis is gone.'

'I did not mean any disrespect,' he said.

The old man shook his head as his daughter reappeared with rice wine and cups on a tray. 'I know your motives,' he said softly as the girl laid out the cups.

She appeared younger than Lis, and Remi studied her a moment. 'Were you at the palace for the Choosing for my brother?'

She nodded once and took a step back.

'Thank you, Ting,' the general said.

She bowed once to the prince and disappeared.

'She is a good girl. This has all been very hard on her.'

'I am so sorry for your loss,' Remi said sincerely.

The general poured wine and held his cup up to the prince before downing its contents.

'What do you think my motives are?' Remi asked after doing the same.

'To find my daughter. Although she is no longer mine. She belongs to you and the Empire.'

'She will always be General Long's daughter.'

The old man smiled a little and poured more wine. 'She is not here,' he said. 'She has not run away. Who would have taken her?'

'I fear there is magic in the palace. I have seen more signs of it than I would like, although my father will not trust my skills as he should. But although I believe magic was involved with Lis… I mean, the disappearance of the hidden princess… I have not been able to detect it.'

'At all?' the general asked, downing another cup.

'I could feel a taint of it, but there was no sign of magic, no scent of it.'

The general nodded once. 'You will find her.' It was a command, not a question.

Remi got quickly to his feet, bowing low to the man. 'I will return now. Soldiers cover every inch of the Palace Isle. They search every home. She will be found.'

The general bowed low to him and he walked unaccompanied back to the boat.

16

Lis stood on the bridge and watched the fish swim lazily beneath it. As desperate as she had been to get home, her newfound invisibility was a welcome relief. Like this, she could take the time to study the island and all its beautiful buildings, although not as many were in use as she had imagined, and there were not as many people as she had expected from her mother's stories.

She had been wandering for hours, enjoying the fact that no one could see her, when she discovered the bridge and the pond she had admired with the prince on her way to the hidden palace.

At the idea of him, she scowled. He had done so much for her, and yet he so easily took the life of someone so dear to her. The only explanation was that he knew what Peng was to her and had killed him anyway. There was no magic involved, not with Peng, and she was certain he had been killed for a very different reason.

The prince himself had seemed so kind. He had certainly appeared to put her safety first, and she could still remember the fizzing sound as the man in the bath house had been run through. She shivered with the idea, then looked up from the calm water and the fish to find a young woman on the other side of the channel watching her.

Lis looked at her carefully, then back to the lacquered bridge rail. She could certainly see her own hands, the faint haze around them indicating no one else could see her. She looked more closely at the young woman, who had a similar haze surrounding her as she watched Lis.

Lis walked down the small bridge and in front of two women deep in conversation. Neither one of them looked at her. She smiled to herself and looked back across at the other woman, but she was gone. Lis hurried along the water's edge, watching the fish. They ignored her, unlike on her first visit, when they had come towards her expectant of something. She leaned over the water and reassured herself that she was invisible, as she found no shadow or reflection. She looked up again, but the other woman was still nowhere to be seen.

Sighing, Lis moved away from the fish and towards the port. She soon realised that there was no way she could take a boat without being discovered. Someone would try to stop a boat drifting away on its own, and it would be obvious if she put the sails up or got wet.

She glanced back at the city within the gate, and her eye was drawn to the royal residence. She chewed her lip and headed back into the main square, where the flags snapped back and forth in the breeze. She managed to walk through the people moving through the city without knocking against anyone. Amongst the people, she was sure she saw the same girl she had seen by the bridge, but once she made it through the crowd to where she had been, the girl was gone.

The residence loomed above her. Taking a deep breath, she headed between the two soldiers standing guard and inside. The walls were covered in beautiful paintings. Golden pillars held up the level above, and the shiny, smooth, dark floorboards echoed her footsteps.

A door to a room ahead was ajar, and Lis pushed it open to look inside. The room was far more beautiful than anything she had in her own palace. Rich red fabrics covered the bed and the cushions that surrounded the smooth, large, square table. She took another step inside and then stopped. The thick rug that covered the floor contained a strange burn in the middle of it. Lis looked around for a sign of fire, but there was none. In fact, the room was quite cool. She moved carefully to the table and put her hand on the pot. Cold.

A large desk stood in the middle against one wall, reports and papers piled neatly to one side. She wondered who had lived here as she moved around, running her hand across the pale wood. Then she sat carefully in the chair.

There were several reports open on the desk before her. She lifted the top one, which simply stated: 'The child is found.'

She wondered absently if it was about her, but didn't think so. They had known perfectly well her status and who she was before she came to the island, and it was for the empress to select. The ink was dry in the well and a brush leaned on the stand beside it, the bristles hard with dried ink. It was as though the owner of this room had simply stood here, expecting to return to what he was doing, but had disappeared instead.

Was it her prince, who had been called away to deal with the magic on her family island? *Or another prince*, she thought, looking again at the mark on the carpet.

She stood, took a deep breath and stepped forward. The death of the former crown prince had been announced, but no details of his illness or the reason for his death had been disclosed. Lis now understood why.

She could taste the faint residue of magic in the air. She squatted down and put her fingers to the burnt mark in the rug. A hot pain ran through her body, and it was all she could do to stop herself from calling out.

She heard footsteps in the hallway, she leapt up and stood by the door to see who it might be. The crown prince strode by, a manservant racing to keep up. He looked angry, and she slipped out of the door and followed along behind them, hoping his heavy footsteps would help mask the sound of hers. She followed him up wide stairs and into another corridor just as decorative as the one below.

He pushed open a door and she followed along quickly, just making it inside before the manservant closed the door behind them. She wasn't sure what she wanted to do, or why she was here, but her own anger at the man before her clouded her thinking.

'Where have you been?' the manservant asked, although she expected his tone should have been more respectful. 'The empress demanded to see you hours ago. Apparently as well as a missing princess, the maid has disappeared.'

'U'shi?' he asked, turning to the man.

He nodded once as the prince shook his head.

'I saw her. Maybe she is involved in this mess,' he murmured, sitting heavily. 'She did leave the princess alone at the baths, and for some reason took her clothes.'

'Her clothes?' the other man asked, his voice rising to an odd octave. Lis thought a tinge of colour touched his cheeks.

'I told you I had to lend her my cloak,' the prince said, more distracted.

'I thought it because she was cold or in shock. Not...' The prince looked up then as the man gulped. 'Naked,' he added in a barely audible whisper.

Lis could feel her own cheeks burning at the memory, but then the prince had hardly looked at her. *Was he disinterested or protecting my honour?*

'I needed to be sure she hadn't run away,' he said, standing again and moving out to the balcony, which Lis only noticed as he stepped onto it.

'Shall I tell the empress you are coming?'

He shook his head, looking out over the view, and Lis moved silently to stand beside him. He had mentioned that he could see across to the next island, and she smiled at the world before her. The red-tile rooves poked through the thick green trees. A whole world so close and yet so far. She closed her eyes for a moment, straining to listen, and then she looked at the man beside her, wondering if he was lonely in this world.

She shook her head. She didn't care about him—she couldn't. He was responsible for Peng's death. And if Lis's disappearing could cause some trouble for U'shi at the same time, she wasn't going to pass it up. She wondered if there was a way to tell the prince about the maid and the tutor. If she could give it away somehow without giving herself away.

'Your Highness?' the man behind him asked, and he turned slowly.

'No, tell her I'm busy looking for Lis…' He closed his eyes and sighed. 'The hidden princess,' he continued. 'I will see the empress when I have found her.'

'What if you can't find her?'

'They have already taken my brother. They can't take her too.'

Lis looked at him closely as he waved the other man from the room and then buried his face in his hands. Did he really care for her so much?

She felt somewhat confused, but then Peng came to mind, and her chest burned with renewed anger at this man who professed to care for her. He was only interested in his own traditions. Her hand went to the veil that still covered the lower part of her face. Why had he done such a thing? Made such a suggestion?

She sighed, and he looked up suddenly. She bit on her lip and hoped he hadn't heard her, but she could sense the magic grow around him as he reached out with his hunter senses. She didn't move and, although he looked around the room, his gaze passed directly through her. She wondered just how long she could maintain this, whether the magic to maintain it would start to leak into the world soon. Then he might sense her as she did him.

She smiled then. They were more alike than he realised, him using skills like those she possessed just to find the same. She had the same sense, but not as strong as a hunter. Her father had never explained exactly what they were, only that they should be feared. Given that her father didn't have any magic of his own, she guessed that he had no idea how they were able to do what they did.

The prince sat at his own desk and picked up a report. Lis was about to step up behind him to see what he read when the door slipped open and the other invisible woman stood in the doorway.

She motioned to Lis, who looked around for a moment and then back to the woman as she motioned again. When Lis stepped closer to her, she nodded and moved back from the door. Lis stepped through and came face to face with the woman, who took her hand, put a finger to her lips—as though Lis needed reminding to stay silent—and led her towards the stairs. Lis pulled against her, but the woman turned back with a smile and gave her a gentle tug.

Lis was desperate to ask who she was and what she wanted, but she allowed herself to be pulled along and out of the residence.

17

Lis sat quietly in the little room and studied the woman across from her, who poured tea and smiled, but as yet hadn't said a word. Nor had Lis. She had been led by the hand from the prince's rooms, out into the sunshine and then along so many streets she had lost track of where she was. Although at one stage she had thought she smelt the baths.

They had come across a small gate, faded and weathered. Once through it, the other woman had pushed a bolt across before continuing into a small house, still holding Lis by the hand. Now they were looking across a table at each other while the woman sipped tea. Lis lifted it to her nose and sniffed, then put it back down without taking a sip.

'I haven't poisoned it,' the woman said lightly.

Lis looked back into the cup. She lifted her veil and brought the cup up beneath it to take one sip, then another. She hadn't had anything since the morning, and she hadn't eaten since the day before. Her stomach growled.

'Why can you see me?' she asked.

'I have a similar magic to you,' the woman said, sitting her own cup down. 'I didn't realise at first that you were even hidden from the world until I noticed those around you didn't even glance at you.'

'Why should they?'

'The way you are dressed, and your face is covered. No one wears a veil. There is something about you, something that shouts to the world that you are different, yet no one looked.'

'Why are you hiding?' Lis asked, trying to deflect the woman's words.

She shrugged then and leaned back, pouring more tea into her cup. 'Why were you with the prince?'

Lis cleared her throat. 'I just wanted to see.'

'You wanted to see the new crown prince because you had heard stories of how handsome he is?' the woman asked quietly, a grin pulling up only one side of her mouth.

Lis shook her head. She didn't want to explain herself to this woman; she didn't know who she was or what her plans were. She clearly had magic. What if she was behind the damage in the former crown prince's room?

'Who are you?' Lis asked instead of answering her question.

'I am a just a girl. Wei-Song.'

Lis opened her mouth and then closed it.

'You are more than just a girl; you are a princess.'

Lis nodded once.

'A long time ago, many hundreds of years ago, they used to hide away many princesses.'

'Many?'

'The Choosing that they do in our time used to be completed at the end of the princesses' training.'

'I don't understand.'

'You can't tell if a child will make a good empress; you can't tell what skills or bad habits may come to the fore.'

Lis thought of U'shi and nodded.

'All of the eligible girls were trained the same, all hidden from the world. When they travelled outside of their palaces, they were covered with veils. No one knew which was which and, in a way, it didn't matter. They were all interchangeable. All insignificant until they came of age and proved themselves.'

'Why did the tradition change?' Lis asked, leaning forward.

'Too many children hidden away. What were they to do with them once they were trained and ready to be empresses, when only one could be?'

Lis shook her head slowly, and the other woman raised her eyebrows. Lis shook her head again, in disbelief, and the other woman nodded.

'Noble families began to hide children who were of age. Girls were dressed as boys, or hidden away until they could be claimed to be younger. The number of eligible girls grew smaller until there were only one or two families willing to give their daughters over in the hope that she would be the next empress.'

Lis sighed.

'It takes many to create change,' the woman said. 'Although I see your prince is interested in the old ways.'

Lis put her hand to her veil. 'I think, in his way, he is trying to keep me safe.'

'You want to be his wife.'

'I have no choice.'

'You have hidden yourself. You could continue to run.'

'I have nowhere and no one to run to.'

'Your family?'

'My mother died. I would bring great shame to my father. I was... There was...'

'Another man?' We-Song asked.

'The prince had him killed. He thought he had magic, but I don't think he did.'

'How do you know?' she asked, tilting her head a little to the side.

'I would have felt it,' Lis said, looking at the other woman. 'Like I felt it on you.'

She drew her eyes together and looked at Lis closely. 'Like a hunter.'

Lis shook her head, but maybe the woman was right.

135

'You can feel magic?' Wei-Song asked.

Lis nodded again. 'You can't?'

'In some ways, but we are all different.'

Lis thought of the man in the baths again. 'How many people do you know with magic?'

Wei-Song shook her head and stood from the table. 'I don't know you,' she said, looking out of the window into the overgrown garden.

'I don't know you either, but you dragged me here. For all I know, it is a trap like those my father warned me of. Or you are trying to hurt me, like the man in the bath house.' Lis stood slowly and straightened out her dress. She put her hands together and felt more solid. The other woman could see her, but who else might be lurking around? If she was discovered, she could claim they had taken her, as the prince feared.

'What man?' Wei-Song asked, turning back to Lis with concern.

Lis looked her up and down. 'You haven't told me everything. I'm not sure I can tell you anything else.'

'We are safe here,' Wei-Song said, stepping forward.

'Until the soldiers come knocking, looking for a hidden princess.'

'This palace hasn't been used in many years. There are lots of them.'

'I know. I spent last night in one, only to discover that others were using it as well. The only way I could escape was when the soldier opened the gate.'

Wei-Song looked at Lis seriously. 'Who was using it?'

Lis shook her head.

She had opened her mouth to say something when the gate swung open. The squeak was loud and clear, and Lis clapped her hands together softly. Wei-Song waved her hands over the table and Lis felt the heat leave the room, a fine layer of dust settled over everything and hid where they had been. The woman took

Lis's arm and pulled her against the wall.

Lis could still see her, but she hoped they were both as invisible as she thought they were.

Two soldiers strolled into the house, glanced around and then turned back for the gate. Lis breathed a sigh of relief as they reached it, but then she heard a familiar voice and sighed in frustration.

'You were asked to search for the princess.'

'There is no one here, nor has there been for some time,' the soldier whinged.

'Your prince has asked you.'

'Yes, General,' he said, bowed and reluctantly headed back into the room.

'She could be bound somewhere in a chest or cupboard. Even if a palace has been abandoned, we cannot assume it still is,' the general said.

Lis wondered if he would let her live for her father's sake if he found her like this.

'So it was discovered,' the other soldier laughed from the veranda as he lifted the lid of a basket. Lis looked at it seriously. Were they looking for clues or for her? There was no way she would fit into that basket. She wondered if U'shi had been discovered, or if she had managed to escape. Could that be what the man was talking about, or had they discovered something else?

Lis glanced at the woman next to her, who was watching the men move around the house, and she wondered if this was Wei-Song's home or simply a place she had brought Lis to learn more about her. Lis needed to know more about who this woman was.

After too long looking at empty spaces, the three men left, pulling the gate closed behind them with a bang. Lis stepped out onto the veranda.

'I thought you bolted the gate,' she said, looking at it. It appeared to be bolted. She pulled away from the other woman and walked down to the gate. How could it have been so easy for the soldiers to push it open? Then she reached forward and lifted the catch the bolt had moved through. It had done them no good.

'What do you want from me?' Lis asked.

'I want to know you. I want to know what you can do and what you are willing to do.'

'Willing to do?' Lis repeated.

Wei-Song nodded once.

'Like the man in the bath house.'

'I don't know who that was,' she said, looking away, and Lis wondered if she was lying.

'Is this where you live?' Lis asked instead.

She shook her head.

'Will you tell me who you really are?'

'What do you want, Lisabet, Hidden Princess of the Rei-Een Empire?'

'Right now, I want to go home. Apologise to my father, hold my sister and mourn my mother.'

'And then?'

Lis shook her head.

'I will take you to your island. If you do not stay, maybe you could come to mine.'

'Are there others?'

She nodded once.

'You do not fear the hunters?'

'He hasn't sensed you yet?'

Lis shook her head. She didn't want to think about it anymore, or him. She just wanted to be far away. Far away from the pain and the hurt and the frustration this island contained.

They moved together, hidden from the world rather than each other. A couple of times Lis thought she saw someone look towards them, or watch them walk, but when she turned she couldn't find them again.

The dock was more crowded than the last time Lis had been on it, and she glanced around wondering how they could take a boat amongst this noise and movement without anyone noticing.

A man sat alone on a small boat, smaller than her family vessel, something more like Peng would sail from his island to hers. Lis felt the lump rise in her throat. The woman took her hand, and the man looked up.

Lis wasn't sure if he could see them or sense them. He didn't look directly at them, only in their direction, as he stood and readied the boat for departure. Without hesitation, the other woman dragged her forward. Lis was sure she bumped into someone, but the dock was crowded enough that the person thought it was someone else and grumbled at them for their ineptitude.

As they reached the little boat, the man pulled it a bit closer with the rope. It looked like he was untying it, but he was in fact helping them in. He subtly pointed to the back of the small vessel, and Lis sat down thankfully. Although as he quickly untied the boat and the wind caught the sail, she started to regret it, feeling somewhat queasy.

'She hasn't eaten,' Wei-Song said to the boatman as they sailed out from the dock.

He picked up a bag from near his feet and held it out as the other woman became visible, taking the bag and holding it out to Lis.

She shook her head.

'You need something in your stomach.'

Lis touched her hands together, and the man sat back. She took an offered biscuit and slipped her hand under the veil to eat it.

'Your Highness, what have you done?' the man asked, trying to gather himself as he looked back towards the dock.

'How do you know...' Lis started.

'Hold your tongue,' Wei-Song snapped.

The man nodded, then pulled a rope attached to the sail and they were off at a faster pace.

Lis looked from one to the other, but she said nothing.

After an hour in the boat, she looked up at the man, who was watching them more closely than the waters ahead. She stretched out her magic, but she could sense very little around him. A slight energy, but very weak. She squinted.

'He can sense us,' Wei-Song answered her unasked question, her voice sounding loud after so long in silence. 'Like you sense the magic, but only just. He knows where we are without seeing us.'

'But the hunters can't sense me.'

She shrugged.

'Could there be others out there that can sense us too?'

'Not that I have found. He waits by the dock in case we need him.'

'How many are you?'

'You're…' the man started, but Wei-Song shook her head. Lis turned back to the water and wondered how long it would take them to reach her father in this little boat and what she would do when they did.

18

'This is the reason she left the hidden princess alone at the bath house,' Remi said. He wanted to be angry, but he was too shocked.

His mother looked disappointed, and he wondered if U'shi had been more of his mother's choice than his brother's all those years ago. In a strange way, he felt a little vindicated. He had never liked the woman, the little he knew of her, and now she had been discovered hiding away in an abandoned building with a tutor.

'There needs to be more protection within the hidden princess's palace,' he said. 'I have been trying to tell you this.'

'She disappeared with several of your soldiers already on the grounds,' his father said softly. 'You have taken on too much with this girl.'

He opened his mouth and then closed it, unsure how he could explain why he needed to be involved in her protection. He knew he was supposed to stay away, that she was his mother's domain. Yet she was to be his wife and, despite her initial refusal of him, he felt a connection to her. He wanted to know her better than tradition dictated. 'Yes, Your Eminence,' he said, bowing before his father.

'Bring the girl in,' the emperor said, standing from his throne, and Remi stepped up to stand behind his father.

He expected U'shi to be sobbing and begging, like she had the day she had come to his room to ask for a better life after his brother died. But the woman before him held her head high as she entered the room. She stopped before them, put her arms together and bowed low.

'You have embarrassed this house,' the empress said, her voice catching, and Remi realised that she cared for the girl. She had spent more time with her than he had, putting much into her training. He wondered if she could care for Lis in the same way.

'Do not get sentimental,' the emperor said, stepping forward. 'This woman has risked our Empire. She has risked our future empress and abandoned her position.'

U'shi looked up then, as though a little confused.

'You have damaged the memory of my son,' he said firmly. 'If you were willing to allow harm to come to the Hidden Princess of Rei-Een, I wonder, did you also allow harm to come to him?'

She shook her head vigorously and dropped to her knees. 'I loved the crown prince. I would never put him in danger.'

'And yet.'

'I was distracted in my grief,' she blubbed, and Remi saw the girl who had visited him, hoping her tears would sway the emperor.

'Distracted?' the emperor boomed. 'You took her clothes and left her to die.'

U'shi gulped down her tears and shook her head again.

'Explain yourself, when you would not before.'

'I was lonely,' she whined, and he glared at her. 'It is a difficult life as the hidden princess, but there is a reason for such a life. I understood such things, but then the prince died and I was trapped with no future.'

'And so, you took it out on the new hidden princess?' Remi asked, and his father gently shook his head.

'Tutor Nizen has always been kind to me. He has helped me become the woman I am, trained and ready to be Empress.'

The emperor actually growled, and the empress glanced at him nervously.

'I am ready, Your Eminence, whether I am needed to be or not.' The confidence had returned to her voice, and her tears dried quickly.

'This does not explain your behaviour.'

'I know little of the world outside of the hidden princess's palace.'

'You have just told me you are trained and ready to be Empress.'

'I know of the world, Your Eminence, but I have not experienced it. In my grief, he comforted me, and I found something in that comfort I did not think I could ever have.'

'You took her clothes to give you time to spend with the tutor,' Remi said.

She nodded.

'What did you think could happen?' he asked before the emperor could say anything further.

'The tutor could take a wife. He could continue to teach, and he has a small house by the hidden princess's palace. We would have continued to serve.'

'A tutor with an empress as a wife?' the empress whispered.

U'shi gave her a small smile.

'You are no empress,' the emperor roared, and she pushed back from him on her knees. 'Does the man want you for a wife?'

U'shi chewed on her lip then. 'I carry his child,' she whispered.

Remi blew out a long, slow breath.

'I should have you beheaded for what you have done,' the emperor said in a low, angry tone. 'The disgrace.'

She bowed low, touching her forehead to the floor. 'Please spare my child,' she begged.

He pointed to the door, and the guards stepped forward. They lifted her to her feet and dragged her from the room. She wailed as they dragged her away, her voice carrying back through the doorway. 'Please, sire.'

He glared at the empress, who looked at the floor. 'I do hope you have chosen better this time,' he said, and Remi felt the threat behind the words.

His mother remained unmoving.

A soldier appeared in the doorway and the emperor nodded. He moved back and settled into his throne before two more soldiers entered, the tutor pressed between them.

They pushed him forward, where he knelt and bowed low before them.

'Tell me the history of the veiled hidden princess,' Remi demanded, and the man before him looked a little confused. His mother raised her eyes and gave him a questioning look.

'In a time when more than one princess was hidden away, they wore veils to ensure they were all hidden,' the tutor murmured, looking between the three of them.

'How many were hidden?'

'All the girls of the Empire of age and eligibility.'

'All hidden and all trained?'

He nodded once.

'How was the future empress chosen from amongst these empresses?'

'A Choosing was held. They were tested, and the crown prince would view each one.'

'They weren't hidden to him?' Remi asked, surprised.

'Not for the Choosing. He would select the brightest, calmest, and most talented of them. Some stories claim the most beautiful was chosen at times, but it depended on the prince.'

'And the others?'

'Your Highness?'

'The others trained to be Empress who could not be—what happened to them? I can't imagine we could have an Empire full of empresses?'

He shook his head and glanced at the current empress.

'Well?'

'They were put to death. Poison is the kindest method, arsenic or the like in their wine at night.'

'Do you think U'shi should be...' the empress stammered.

'Do you think we should have two women trained to be empress?' the emperor asked.

'We have, in our more recent past, had a similar situation to what we have here,' the tutor continued. Remi raised his eyebrows, and the man coughed. 'Where a crown prince has been lost and we have had to choose another hidden princess. In those instances, the first hidden princess has continued in service to the royal family.'

'I don't think it is us she has been serving,' Remi murmured, and the man, to his credit, blushed.

'Is this where the focus of the royal family should be?' the tutor asked.

'You would question us?' the emperor asked, the sharp edge evident in his voice.

The man actually gulped. 'Should you not be looking for your current hidden princess, or is she lost? Would it not be a notion to use the other hidden princess?'

'And raise your child as my own, perhaps?' Remi said.

The man slipped to the side then, surprise covering his features, and then a small smile lit up his face.

Remi scowled. 'She lied,' he murmured.

'She would not dare,' the empress said quickly.

'You continue to defend her,' the emperor said, clearly angry and forgetting their audience.

'She would have told you,' Remi said to the tutor. 'If she carried your child, she would have told you so. She has used the idea of it to save her own skin.'

'You cannot be so sure,' the empress said.

'I can,' he murmured. 'Go for the Imperial Healer and ask him to examine her before she is returned to the cell,' Remi said clearly to the soldier by the door, who bent in a bow to the prince before disappearing. 'How long has this been going on?' he asked, turning back to the tutor.

He shook his head, clearly uncertain how to answer.

'You are a well-trained man yourself. You have studied for many years to be in the position you are and, although young for such a position, you are still much older than the maid.'

'Don't call her that,' he muttered.

'Really? What title should I give her?'

'She is more than a maid,' he whispered.

'She is no more than a common whore,' Remi snapped, the words surprising him as much as his mother, whose eyes grew wide. 'What have you tried with the new hidden princess?'

'That creature is not worth my time,' the tutor said, disdain evident, and Remi stepped forward to find his father's hand across his chest.

'She is the future empress of our Empire.'

'She is a country girl too keen to tell me what I should teach. There is not enough time,' he said, beseeching the empress.

'So she said,' Remi said, more subdued.

'What do you mean?' the emperor asked.

'I think the pressure to train the princess is being put on the princess rather than the tutors.' He looked at his mother. 'She mentioned something about how they lament at the lack of time, telling her she can't learn it all, and yet they do not utilise the time appropriately. This man spends his time bedding the maid rather than training our future empress.'

The emperor nodded slowly and turned again to his wife.

'When she is returned, I shall ensure all is done to assist her,' the empress said.

'If you can find her,' the tutor murmured.

'And do you know who took her?' Remi asked.

He shook his head. 'But U'shi and I may have pushed her a little too far.'

The soldier rushed back into the room, and all eyes moved to him. He stepped forward with a small letter.

The emperor glanced at it and handed it to Remi.

'With child,' it said.

He screwed the letter in his hand and glared at the tutor. How had this man been elevated to such a position?

19

Lis stood silently at the end of the pier watching Wei-Song and the man in the little boat sail away. She held her breath as her father walked towards her. But she wasn't sure how to face him yet, and so she remained hidden from the world.

He sighed and looked after the boat. She hadn't thought of him seeing the boat sail towards the island, and when she looked at him, he looked so sad. The loss of her mother must have been hard on him. He watched until the boat disappeared, and then he walked slowly back to the house. Lis waited before following him, remembering the creaky jetty. She feared the noise would give her away. She wondered if this was a skill her father knew her to have.

As she followed his path back to the house, she breathed in the familiar scent of home and realised just how much she had missed it. In some ways it was no longer her home, and as she watched his slow walk and drooped shoulders, she wondered if he would allow her to stay.

Her father had allowed her to be who she was growing up. She had been able to do anything she wanted with her magic, but it had just been games. She had never thought about what she could really do, and she didn't know how powerful she might be. He had mentioned so many times the need to hide it that she had assumed there was no one, or not many, with magic left in the world. Until the bath house, and then she had met Wei-Song. She had been kind, Lis thought, but there was something beneath the kindness, something she wanted from Lis. Despite their time together, Lis couldn't determine what that might be.

'Who were they?' Ting asked, rushing forward as Lis followed her father into the main room.

He shook his head and sat heavily. Ting knelt beside him and poured tea. It was sad watching them, as though it was only the two of them left and they knew there would never be another. Lis moved as she heard footsteps behind her, and Ting's face lit up with a smile.

'Did they bring word of Lis?' Peng asked.

Lis bit hard on her lip to prevent the strange cry in her throat from escaping. How could he be alive? She moved carefully towards him, taking in his familiar scent. She wanted to throw her arms around him and pull him tight against her body to be sure he was real, but she hesitated, and he was out of her reach.

'They didn't stop. Perhaps they had the wrong island. They pulled up to the jetty and almost immediately left again.' Her father sighed and turned the cup slowly in his hand without drinking from it.

'What could they want with her?' Ting asked, and Peng rushed forward to take her hand.

'They wouldn't hurt her,' he murmured. 'They would only try to send some message to the emperor.'

Lis's heart stopped and the breath left her body. Peng wasn't dead, but he was lost to her.

'If it was those with magic as the crown prince fears, perhaps they do know what she is,' he continued.

'There is no one with magic left,' her father said, his voice hollow.

'Then who and why?' Ting implored.

Her father shook his head. 'Let us eat,' he said. 'The crown prince has promised to inform us the moment she is found.'

Peng huffed, and her father gave him a friendly smile.

'I am glad you have stayed with us,' he said.

Peng nodded and sat at the table. Ting stood slowly and moved from the room, returning soon after with a tray. She set bowls and rice down before her father and Peng, who smiled too much at her. Then she left and returned with another for herself, and they sat to eat in silence, Ting and Peng occasionally looking up across the table at each other.

Lis felt the sharp pain across her chest as her heart broke. They had moved on without her, and there was nothing for her here.

She turned her back and walked carefully from the house, continuing out to the middle of the field, where she sat down. She breathed in the flowers she had hoped would be blooming and then raised her hand, bringing them to life and hiding her further in a sea of pink. Putting her hands together, she came out of hiding. The sun felt warmer on her skin and, with a simple movement of her hand, her hair was loose around her shoulders down her back. A slight breeze picked up and she closed her eyes, pretending she was in another time, a time when the world was easy and she was happy.

She lay back and watched the clouds drift across the sky, slowly changing as they moved, in no hurry to go on their way. She closed her eyes and sighed. It had been so long since she'd had the freedom to simply be, and she tried to focus on the moment rather than where she would go next.

When she opened her eyes, Peng was leaning over her. She smiled, thinking herself transported back to a better time, before the former crown prince died and the new one chose her for a bride.

She reached for him, but he leaned back from her.

'Lis?' he asked.

She sat up slowly and nodded.

'How did you get here?'

She shook her head. 'It doesn't matter.'

'Of course it matters. You are the Hidden Princess of Rei-Een and the whole Empire is searching for you.'

'I can't be what they want me to be.'

'You already are,' he whispered.

She shook her head. He reached out a hand to run through her hair, but then he stopped and pulled his hand back.

'It is just me,' she said. 'Long Lis.'

'You can never be Long Lis again, nor could you be my wife,' he murmured. He looked towards the house then, and Lis turned to see Ting watching them.

'How easily I am replaced,' she said, standing slowly and brushing at her skirt.

'You must return to the Palace Isle.'

She shook her head. She didn't know where she could go, but it couldn't be there. 'Would you take me?' she asked, unsure where the words came from.

He shook his head. 'They will assume we took you back. Think of what it would mean for your father.'

Lis looked down at her hands. Perhaps she could magic herself.

'The boat is returning,' Peng said, indicating the water with a tip of his chin. 'The crown prince feared you had run away, but he was equally convinced you were taken.'

'I was pushed out,' she said, turning for the water. 'Someone told me you were dead.'

'I am,' he said, and she turned back. 'To you, I must be dead, for there is nothing for us, Your Highness. You have to return to the palace and your destiny.'

She laughed then, the sound unnatural and sharp, and it carried on the wind. 'Destiny. You were my destiny.'

He shook his head. 'No more.' He bowed low to her and then gestured towards the jetty.

There was no sign of her father, and Ting had disappeared when Lis looked back towards the house. She had wanted to hold her sister one last time. She wanted to be held by them both, for she felt so empty and alone. The little boat pulled against the jetty, and she stepped carefully into it. She sat beside the woman, who smiled and reached forward to carefully pull a twig from her hair.

Without looking at Peng again, Lis nodded once to the boatman and, with a simple flick of a rope, they were sailing back out to the sea.

'You must be relieved he is alive,' Wei-Song said.

'Not anymore,' Lis whispered, allowing the tears to flow down over her cheeks and across her veil, sticking it to her face.

'Where are we?' Lis asked, focusing for the first time on the shore they sailed towards.

'Somewhere we can be safe.'

The boat pulled up against the little jetty, and Lis accepted help from the boatman to climb ashore. Amongst the trees and up the small slope from the jetty was a large house. Its black tile roof and greying walls made it appear as though it had sat amongst the trees for a long time. It was larger than the one Lis had grown up in, and she wondered just who lived here as she stepped forward.

Wei-Song continued past her on the narrow path. 'There are some people for you to meet.'

Lis followed her into the house and through a long, wide hallway. Several people moved quietly through the space, but none looked up or acknowledged them in any way. Wei-Song rushed ahead as Lis struggled to keep up and look around at the same time. Paintings hung on the walls, and Lis stopped when she realised one was of a man holding fire in his hand.

Why would they have such images on display? she wondered, moving to the next one. It depicted a woman with her hands above her head as she appeared to stand in the rain.

'What is this place?' she asked, pausing in front of one in which a woman was half visible, her hands held together in front of her.

'A school of sorts,' Wei-Song said, moving back to Lis and taking her arm.

'I can do this,' Lis said, looking over the image.

'Did someone teach you?' Wei-Song asked, pulling her along the hallway.

Lis shook her head. 'Who would teach me?'

Wei-Song shrugged.

'I was playing around and then realised my sister couldn't see me standing beside her when I entered her room.'

'Do they know you can do this?'

Lis shook her head. 'Why can't the hunters sense me?' she asked as she hurried to keep up.

'I think you are a Hidden,' Wei-Song murmured, still pulling.

'A what?'

'It will be explained. Come.'

Lis found herself in a room lined with paintings and filled with desks. Three men stood at the front of the room and, as they entered, the men turned, stared for a moment and then bowed towards her.

'Your Highness,' one stammered.

'The hidden princess?' another asked.

'Why did you bring her here?' the third asked, finding his voice and turning on the woman with her.

'She is a Hidden.'

'You are yet to explain what that is,' Lis said firmly, trying to show herself to be what these men thought she was.

'You wear the veil,' the first said, stepping forward.

'There have been a number of incidents, and the crown prince thought it safer.'

'Safer?' the woman scoffed. 'How will a veil keep you safe?'

'It will keep me hidden,' Lis said softly.

The woman laughed loudly, and one of the men grumbled at her. 'You do see the irony,' she said.

'The crown prince is a hunter,' Lis said softly.

The three men nodded. 'His skills are well known,' the first said.

Lis was about to mention that his hunting ability felt like magic, that she could feel it, when she held back. She didn't know who these men were or why she had been brought before them. They could be just as dangerous as the man in the baths. Yet so far, she hadn't sensed any magic on them.

'Your Highness, I would like to introduce you to our tutors: Huichou, Xiamen and Master Yangshing,' Wei-Song said, indicating the three men in turn.

The three men bowed in turn and then stepped forward and looked her over again.

'I still don't understand what you mean by hidden.'

'It means that the hunters cannot detect your magic,' Master Yangshing said.

Lis looked at him seriously. 'The prince mentioned a magic taint in a place I had been.'

'He may have sensed something lingering from another with magic. Or when magic was performed long ago. You can sense magic on others?'

Lis nodded.

'We have one such as this. Call Kei-Bi.'

Wei-Song nodded and disappeared from the room.

'Can you hide yourself?'

Lis put her hands together and disappeared.

The three men looked at each other and then nodded. 'This may seem odd, Your Highness, but would you mind sitting behind the desk?' Huichou asked, bowing a little.

She nodded and moved around behind them, then ducked down behind the desk. She heard Wei-Song come back into the room along with someone else.

'You sent for me?'

'We wish you to test your abilities.'

Lis could feel his searching. She wondered what he was doing, but she stayed where she was.

'There is no one else here,' the young man said.

'You may go,' one of the tutors said. 'Your Highness, you may come out now.'

Lis put her hands together, reappeared and stood up from her place behind the desk to find the other man had gone. 'I can disappear and they cannot detect me. What if I do something else?'

'You are hidden no matter what you do,' Master Yangshing confirmed.

'Are there many with this skill?'

'There are a few of us,' he said.

'The man in the baths.' Lis said it more to herself than anyone in the room, but they looked at her closely. 'When I first arrived, there was a man with magic who attacked me in the baths.'

'Attacked you?'

She nodded and gulped down the feeling that arose when she thought of him, the fear just as real as when he had attacked her. 'I thought he might kill me,' she murmured, her hand at her throat. 'He tried to drown me. He said he knew what I was.'

'What happened?' Wei-Song asked.

'The prince was nearby, felt his magic and...'

'And?' one of the men prompted.

'He killed him,' she whispered, closing her eyes against the memory.

'You heard the magic in him fizzle,' Xiamen said kindly, and he indicated a seat. 'It is hard to know how you might end.'

'I have waited every day for the prince to discover me and run his sword through me in the same way.'

'I thought the prince was to stay away from the hidden princess?' Huichou asked.

'He finds reason; he fears for my safety.'

'He cares for you,' Wei-Song said, a sadness in her voice.

'He does not know me,' Lis said sharply.

'It does not matter,' Wei-Song said, looking to the men. 'He will search for her.'

'Stay with us one day,' Huichou said. 'Eat, rest. We may be able to help you further before returning you to the Palace Isle.'

'I don't want to return,' Lis said quickly.

'There is nowhere else for you to go, and he will turn the world upside down to find you.'

Lis shook her head. 'There are other worlds beyond our Empire, maybe others with magic where I can live alone and quietly.'

Huichou shook his head slowly. 'Rest now, and we can discuss again tomorrow.'

Lis allowed Wei-Song to lead her out of the classroom and through a network of hallways to a small room. The water boiled in the pot on the edge of the table, and the bed looked soft. Lis sat at the table and poured water for herself.

'I will send for food,' Wei-Song said and disappeared, sliding the door shut after her.

Lis felt drained. She wondered if she could move around the complex in her hidden state to learn why she was here. Despite the small room and simple furnishings, she didn't feel like a prisoner.

Wei-Song had brought her for a reason, but the three men appeared to want her to return to the palace. She would just be locked away again in some way or another, and she didn't think she could bear it.

She couldn't spend her life hidden and invisible; it took too much from her. Yet she couldn't return home, for there was nothing for her there. She sighed as the door slid open and a young woman carried a tray in with a bowl of rice and several plates of food. She sat it before Lis, bowed low and then backed out of the room.

She was hardly hidden here; multiple people knew the hidden princess was present. It wouldn't take long for news to reach the crown prince, and he would ride in and rescue her again.

She moved the food around the bowl with the sticks as she thought about him. Could it really be that he cared for her? That he had chosen her from the others because he had liked her? She shook her head and pushed food into her mouth. She couldn't remember the last time she had eaten. She was hungry, but within a few mouthfuls she felt sick. Dropping her chopsticks, she pushed herself up from the table.

With a slow spin, she was in only her undergarments, yet she maintained the veil. Her hair was still loose from her time on the island with her family. The way Peng had spoken to her still cut deep in her chest. She had been so relieved to find him alive, yet he was gone. He was older than her, if only by a few years, and Ting would make a suitable wife.

Lis lay down and pulled the cover across her, staring up at the ceiling. Very much like the one in her childhood bedroom. She squeezed her eyes closed, the tears flowing hot down the sides of her face.

She had nowhere to go.

20

Lis woke to the sound of scratching. She lay in the dark and listened for a moment, wondering where it was coming from. The door?

She crept out of bed and carefully slid the door open, but there was no one there. She looked out into the dimly lit hallway. Silence. She closed her eyes and stretched out her senses to see if she could feel any magic, but there was nothing. She sensed a hint of something, but she wasn't sure what it was.

She put her hands together silently, then headed down the hallway towards the faint feeling of magic. She could hear quiet noises of sleep coming from the rooms she passed, but no one seemed to be awake. There was also no sign of rodents or the like inside the passageways, and she wondered just what might have woken her.

With a single candle in his hand, there was a man in the room she had been in the night before. He looked at the paintings on the wall, then sat the candle on the desk and started to look through papers at the front of the classroom.

He was not someone she recognised from the day before. But then, she was sure there were a lot more people here than she might ever be made aware of. Something made a noise in the distance, and the man extinguished the candle. Lis could feel his magic swell. But she didn't know if he was a threat or if he was searching around him. It felt different from the magic she had felt around the prince, which indicated that the was not a hunter.

Then another man moved through the doorway, just missing her. Lis bit down on her lip to prevent a squeal of surprise. He hadn't seen her, even in her hidden state, and he was different from the others here.

'Are you sure she is here?' he asked the man already in the room.

'There must be something. I saw the boat leave the docks.'

'That man rarely has passengers.'

The other man gave him a dangerous glare that made Lis shiver, even in the dim light entering the room. When the candle sparked back to life, she jumped. The man who had entered the room looked very much like the man from the baths.

Could they work with the people here? They seemed to want to help her, although they wanted her to return to the Palace Isle. Would they want her to do something specific there?

And what could she do? She would be locked away again, either as a hidden princess or in some dark cell somewhere when the prince discovered what she was. He had looked so concerned for her when he had found she was missing. Could he care for her, as Wei-Song thought, or was it only that he cared for his reputation and standing? They had only recently lost a prince. They couldn't be seen to lose a princess as well, or the Empire would start to doubt its leaders.

Lis looked back at the two men now moving through the papers. Was that what they wanted, the Empire to fall? Or just the royal family?

'What is the girl's name?'

'Was she Long?'

'That is why I am asking. What do you think they would record her as?'

'Not by her name. They are trying to keep her from us.'

And who are you? Lis desperately wanted to ask. *What do you want of me?*

'Someone comes,' one of the men said, extinguishing the candle again.

It was all Lis could do to get out of the way of the fireball that lit up the world as it hurled towards the desk. Both men held up their hands, and a gush of water extinguished the flames. It all disappeared with a flash.

'What do you want here?' a voice asked, and then one of the tutors arrived, another not far behind.

'We want what you have taken. The hidden princess. She is ours. You know what she is; we need her to win this war.'

'I know how you think she will help you. Even if she were here, I would not hand her to the likes of you.'

'You will train her for your own purposes then?'

'You tried to kill her. It was one of you in the baths.'

'The prince was closer than we realised, and his skills have grown since the death of his brother.'

'Was that your doing as well?'

'What would we gain from the death of the prince?'

Lis looked between the men, wondering just what it was they thought she had and what they wanted from her. This school, or whatever it was, didn't want to keep her safe; they wanted to use her in some way. She may not have agreed with the magic wars or the devastation they caused, and she didn't pose any threat with her magic. But these people had other ideas.

She slipped from the room, leaving them to their arguments, and she wondered if they would come together in some way. But as she raced down the hallway and out into the garden, she could feel the magic follow her. When she glanced back, she saw a flash of light, and then another.

Everyone wanted something from her.

The jetty was silent when she reached it. She jumped into a small boat, untied it quickly and pushed off. She didn't know where she was, so she had no idea of where to go, but she raised the sail. It caught the wind quickly and pulled her away from the little island. The moonlight stretched across the water as she looked back at the silhouette of the island. A small one, although hillier than her own. Or it could have been one side of another island, she didn't know. There was too much of this Empire she hadn't seen.

The wind pushed her out into the water and away from whatever these people with magic wanted. But she didn't know where to go. She really wanted her father, but the memory of Peng was sharp in her chest, and she knew he would not take her back. She would need to return to the Palace Isle.

It was the last place she wanted to be, but she also didn't know where she was or which direction she was traveling in.

She was tired. It was getting easier to remain invisible, but it was tiring. She could maintain it a while longer, so she leaned back in the boat and closed her eyes, hoping the sea would carry her far away.

21

Remi was sitting at his desk, trying and failing to read through the reports that had continued to pile up. There had been no sign of the hidden princess or those who might have taken her. One of his men rushed through the door and then paused, bowing low and waiting.

'What news do you bring?' Remi asked.

'She has been found.'

He stood quickly from the desk and came around to the man still bent before him.

'Well, tell me,' he snapped.

'We have kept it secret, like you said.'

'You are sure it is her?'

'She was still wearing the veil, which is how she was identified.' He looked nervous.

'What is it?' he asked, fearing the worst.

'She was dressed in her undergarments.'

'She is alive?'

The soldier nodded.

'Then take me to her.'

He followed the soldier out of the room and along the hallway. They travelled out into the city, where no one noticed him. He was somewhat disappointed that life had returned to normalcy so quickly, despite the hidden princess's disappearance.

The old prison stood silent along the wall of the Palace Isle, and the prince faltered before following the soldier inside. He had wanted her hidden from the world if she was found—but to keep her safe, not to lock her away. He wondered how she would react to such a place. She had not been happy about her confinement in the hidden princess's palace, and now she was behind bars.

The section of the prison they entered was deserted and oddly silent as they moved deeper inside. They would need more soldiers, without drawing attention, if they were to keep her here. She had to be safe, but they couldn't alert anyone to that part of the building being used again.

'Could we not make this more comfortable?' he asked, looking through the bars into a large cell. It contained a single cot against one wall, on which the princess slept. A table and four stools sat in the middle of the room, and he realised this was probably the most comfortable cell in the building. It would have been used for a high-ranking political prisoner. He had seen it used in his childhood, but not since. Although he was sure there were those who should be locked away. Any fear of magic, and prisoners were put to death.

She lay still and silent as he carefully lifted a stool from beside the table and sat down beside the cot.

Her face was red and burnt, and she shivered beneath the blanket. He glanced up as Mu-Phi entered carrying a tray. It held a bowl, ointment and a silk cloth. She looked at the prince sternly, and he indicated she sit the tray on the table.

'Where was she found?' he asked in a whisper.

'In a boat that had knocked against the wall of the isle,' the soldier said behind him.

'How long was she exposed?'

'I do not know, Your Highness.'

'Too long,' Mu-Phi mumbled.

Remi chewed his lip and nodded slowly. The girl had served him well over the years. Despite being dressed as a maid, she was a good soldier and a good friend. He waved her away and dipped the cloth into the bowl of cool water. Then he wrung it out and placed it carefully over Lis's forehead. She shivered beneath it. He wondered if he should send for a healer, but then word would be out that she was found, and he didn't know who else might come for her.

It had been his idea for her to go back into the veil, yet he wondered if there was more history to this that he didn't know. Her hair was loose, but she still wore the pins that held the veil in place. He carefully withdrew the closest one and pulled the veil back from her face. She was pink beneath it, for it had done little to keep the sun from her. Reaching across her, he removed the other.

When he turned with the veil in his hand, Mu-Phi stood waiting, her hands held before her.

'Fetch another cloth,' he instructed, handing her the veil and pins.

She bowed before him and disappeared.

'What were you doing?' he whispered to the sleeping princess as he carefully pulled back the covers. Her neck was just as pink as her lower face—partially covered by the veil, he assumed. Her hands were crossed over her stomach, just as bright red as her face.

'Your Highness,' Mu-Phi said with a sharp intake of breath. 'She is only in her undergarments.'

'She is covered,' he said, standing and pulling the cover off completely.

'But you shouldn't,' the girl said.

He held a finger to his lips and waved her out. He had seen far more of Lis. Her bare feet were also red. *How many days had she drifted in that boat?*

Taking the cloth, he dipped it into the water, shook some of the ointment over it and gently wiped at her face and neck. Then he sat back on the stool, took each hand and did the same. And then he squatted at the end of the cot and wiped over her feet.

He noticed the guard on the other side of the bars, his back to them. Remi stood slowly and walked over to him. 'Has she woken at all?'

'No, Your Highness,' the guard said softly without turning. 'I fear she has spent too long in the sun and may perish.'

'She is strong,' Remi said.

He wet the cloth, wrung it out and replaced the one across her forehead with it. He would stay as long as was needed.

He must have drifted off with her hand in his as he wiped cool ointment across it, for he woke to her pulling against him. He cleared his throat as she looked around and sat slowly. He felt a wave of relief as she looked at him, before she burst into tears and threw her arms around his neck. She almost pulled herself from the bed and onto his lap, and he closed his arms around her as he held her close, breathing in the scent of the sea in her hair.

'You are safe now,' he murmured. 'And I promise to keep you safe.'

She released her hold and sat back on the bed, looking around the room, but her eyes had grown wide and her lip quivered. She had seemed so strong, but now he just wanted to hold on to her. He felt the absence of her in his arms.

'You have locked me up,' she whispered, wiping a hand across her face and then wincing. 'I'm on fire,' she said, looking over her hands.

He held out the cloth, and she looked up at him before taking it and pressing it to her face. The cloth that had been over her forehead had fallen into her lap, and she moved away from him when he reached for it.

'Let me wet the cloth for you,' he said, indicating the material. She nodded, allowing him to pick it up and take it.

He stood slowly, feeling the fatigue of sitting on the stool for so long, and dropped the cloth into the water. He noticed it was fresh and clear, so he poured more of the ointment into it. Mu-Phi must have refreshed it. He wondered if he could convince his mother to place her with the princess as a maid. He stretched, rolled his shoulders and turned back to her. She moved the cloth to the other side of her face and watched him as though he might run her through at any point.

He sat down again and held out his hand for her free one. She took a moment before handing it over, and he could feel the tension in her, as though she might run at any moment. When he put the cool cloth down on her skin, she sighed and closed her eyes, allowing her hand to rest in his.

'Can you tell me what happened?' he asked, trying to keep his voice level and calm.

She shook her head.

'You have been gone for some time,' he said softly. She only looked at him, her brow creasing. 'Did you not know how long you were gone?'

She shook her head again and then pulled her hand out from beneath his. She indicated the cloth that he had in his hand, and he handed it to her. She pressed it to her forehead with the hand he had just held and offered him the other cloth. He went back to the table and wrung it out in the water. When he returned, she was lying back with her eyes closed. He sat as quietly as he could on the stool, and she held up the other hand.

He smiled as he took it carefully in his and pressed the cloth to the burnt skin. It was looking less red already.

'Did you take the veil?' she asked.

'I needed to see your face,' he said, and she opened her eyes to look up at him. 'I needed to see how burnt you were.'

'From the boat,' she murmured, closing her eyes again.

'How did you end up in the boat?'

'I ran away. It was dark, and I didn't know where I was or where to go. I just got in the boat.' Her voice cracked a little, and he held tighter to the hand in his.

'Did they have magic?'

'Who?'

'Those who had you. Those you were with.'

'I'm not sure. There was fire and…'

She shuddered again, and he released her hand to pull the covers over her, noticing that her feet were still red. He sighed and moved the stool to the end of the cot. After covering the rest of her, he carefully covered her feet with the damp cloth.

'Thank you,' she murmured.

His mother was going to be furious. But he couldn't leave the princess's care to anyone else. She hadn't been safe where she was. He wondered if there was somewhere she could be truly hidden away, so the tutors could finish their work.

'Your Highness,' another soldier whispered through the bars.

He nodded, covered her feet with the cloth still in place and then moved to the bars.

'The empress wishes to speak with you.'

He tried not to sigh. 'Tell her I'm busy searching for the hidden princess.'

The soldier nodded and disappeared.

Remi turned back to find Lis with her eyes closed. Her hand slipped from the cloth at her brow. He lifted it carefully and turned it over. She looked so peaceful in her sleep, yet he could only wonder what they had done to her, where they might have taken her and who these people were.

He had tried, during the time she was gone, to search out an idea of magic within the Empire, but there was nothing. Until a few nights ago, he had sensed something in the distance, but it had disappeared as quickly as it had flared up. He wondered if that was the fire she had spoken of.

He wanted desperately to close his own eyes, but instead he sat beside the bed and rested his face in his hands with his elbows on his knees. He closed his eyes for just a moment, still remembering her clinging to him as though he were the most important thing in the world. Then he remembered the look on her face when he had chosen her, and the man she loved.

Would she return to the other man if he freed her from her obligation? But he couldn't, even if he wanted to. The choice had been made. She had been named, and it would destroy more than his ego if she left.

Just as he thought it, she sat up, her eyes wide. 'Peng,' she called.

'Lis?' he asked softly, the word causing him more pain than her disappearance.

She looked at him for a moment, as though trying to work out who he was, and then her face crinkled as the tears flowed again. He moved easily to the edge of the cot and closed his arms around her.

'I am sorry,' he said, unsure what he was sorry for. That he had put her in this place to start with, that he had taken her away from Peng.

'You didn't kill him,' she murmured into his shoulder, her hands tight around the front of his shirt.

'Of course I didn't kill him.'

A sob escaped, and she pushed her face into him. Then she pulled back, her fingertips touching the sore skin.

'I'll get you another cloth,' he said, making to get up, but she clung to him.

'They told me you had killed him,' she said, her voice thick with tears, and she sniffed.

'Who?'

'Tutor Nizen,' she said, closing her eyes and leaning into him.

He closed his arms around her again.

'Why would he tell you such a thing?'

'They don't want me here. I'm not good enough, not smart enough. I cannot learn what they want me to learn.'

'Is that what you think?' he asked.

She leaned back from him and sniffed. She studied him, then looked at her hands as though realising she was clinging to him. She let go. 'I am so sorry, Your Highness.' She put her hands together to bow to him and winced as the skin touched.

'You have nothing to be sorry for. Why did you believe the

tutor?' he asked carefully.

'He said Peng had magic, but he didn't, and I thought...' She chewed her lip and looked down. Despite the burn, he gently lifted her chin to look at him.

'What did you think?'

She gulped, clearly unsure how to continue.

'Tell me,' he coaxed.

Her eyes flittered around the space before resting on him again. 'That you killed him to keep me here.'

A shiver crossed his skin, and he tried to smile. There was no way she could return home, whether she wanted to or he deemed it possible. 'You are the hidden princess,' he said instead, and he stood from the edge of the bed.

'They said that you care for me,' she whispered.

'Who did?' he asked, but it sounded harsh and accusatory, as though she had been told a lie. As another large tear rolled away and she brushed quickly at her face, wincing, he regretted his words.

Mu-Phi reappeared with some clothes, and he nodded at her before heading for the door. 'I will give you time to rest,' he said without looking back. 'We need to talk more of those who took you.' As he strode out, he indicated for the guard to move with him.

He stopped just beyond her cell; he couldn't be far away.

'Let me help you, Your Highness,' Mu-Phi said to the princess. 'Here, we must be careful with your face.'

'They all want something I cannot give,' she murmured, and he wondered what it was she couldn't give him.

'The prince only wants you safe, Your Highness.'

'He wants me for his Empire,' she said, 'and I don't know that I am any good for it.'

He closed his eyes and leaned against the wall. What had they done to her in all those days she had been gone?

22

The Empress of Rei-Een looked over the two kneeling before her with bitter disappointment. She had made all the excuses she could for the girl, but the emperor was determined to make an example of her. And Remi was furious. He had always been a serious boy, but there was something angry about him now, something dangerous, and she wondered what he would be like as emperor.

'You said that you pushed her too far.' Remi's voice was level, but she could hear the power behind his words.

U'shi continued to stare at the floor as the tutor huffed.

'Your prince has asked for an explanation. It is only at the grace of the empress that you are both not dead already,' the emperor said.

The empress gulped, despite her best efforts. She had chosen this woman. If her son had remained alive, she would nearly be the crown princess. She understood that the time as hidden princess was hard; she had endured it herself. But it was necessary, and she was a stronger, better empress for it.

'She had mentioned a man from her island,' the tutor said reluctantly, glancing at U'shi as he did.

'Peng,' Remi said clearly.

The empress looked at her son. How did he know? Did he remember her words from the Choosing, or was it something else?

The tutor nodded once.

'That is not the whole story,' the prince continued, and she could feel his strength filling the room. He would make an excellent emperor.

The man at least looked somewhat ashamed before he continued, 'I told her you had killed him. That he was someone with magic who had fizzled as you drove your sword through him.'

The prince actually growled, and even the emperor looked at him.

'After just learning of her mother's death, and the attack in the bath house where she saw such an end to a man. Why would you do this?' Remi stepped forward. For a moment, the empress feared he would kill this man here and now, without waiting for his father's edict.

'She tried to tell me what to teach her,' he said quietly.

'Because you do not teach. You lament at the lack of time rather than helping form the next empress. You are no tutor. You are an imposter, hiding in the palace to get close to a maid.'

Tutor Nizen opened his mouth and then closed it again, clearly realising that no matter what he said, the crown prince was not going to be easy on him.

'You were together when you should have been helping her in the bath house,' Remi said more gently to the girl.

She nodded once, her hands never moving from her stomach.

'Did you send the man to kill her?'

She shook her head vigorously.

'You have already made it known that you thought you should remain as the hidden princess, that you should be my empress,' Remi said, his voice harsh. 'Were you planning on pretending that this man's child was my own?'

She chewed on her lip and closed her eyes. 'The child was unexpected, but I could not have kept it secret from you. It was conceived after the new hidden princess was hidden away.'

'Are there others?'

She looked up at him sharply.

'Other lovers? Other children?' Remi glanced quickly at his mother. 'What might someone do to protect the hidden princess?'

'What do you do to protect this one?' U'shi asked, her voice cracking, her face ugly.

'When she is found, I will do all I can to keep her safe. For she is the next empress.' He said it slowly. The dangerous edge to his voice made the empress shiver. 'Do as you will to them, Father. I have a princess to find.' He strode from the room.

Without looking at his wife, the emperor stood from his throne and stepped forward. 'You have endangered more than the hidden princess. You have brought danger and instability to the Empire.'

Both of them dropped their heads to the floor in a show of respect, but the emperor's eyes were hard and glassy, and the empress knew it would do them no good. They had endangered what he had spent his life building, and the whole Empire was searching for a girl they had treated terribly.

The empress sucked in a breath. She had not done the new hidden princess any favours herself. The princess was needed to ensure this Empire continued, that her son would be the strength of the world and have fine sons to carry on the Empire. When she was found, the empress decided, she would help her become what she needed to be.

'Death,' the emperor said.

'But she is with child,' the empress said quickly, glancing at him as U'shi started to sob.

The emperor glared at her. 'Take him back to the cell. At first light, he shall be beheaded before the people for the disservice he has done the Hidden Princess of Rei-Een.'

The empress gulped down her fears and nodded.

'You, girl, are determined to be in the palace, to be a part of the royal family.' U'shi glanced up at him. 'You shall be locked in your own palace; there are many empty ones near where you were discovered with your lover. You shall be guarded day and night, and a midwife, healer or the like will be with you at all times. They shall eat with you, bathe with you, sleep with you so that you will never be alone.'

U'shi's eyes flashed towards the empress, but she knew he would not allow her a reprieve. She had gone too far.

'The moment your child is born, you shall both be put to death.'

'The child is innocent,' U'shi blurted. 'Please have mercy, Your Eminence.'

'Mercy,' he scoffed. 'A child who would grow to hate me for sentencing his parents to a death they deserved.' He shook his head. 'The child will die. Our customs may not allow for me to put to death a pregnant woman, but there is nothing to stop me once the child is born, and the people will understand. The hidden princess must be protected.'

U'shi burst into sobs, falling from her position to lie on the floor. 'Say something,' she spat at the man beside her.

'You said we would be safe,' he murmured, maintaining his position. 'There is nothing I can say.'

'Guards,' the emperor called, and they appeared to take the prisoners away.

As they lifted the sobbing U'shi from the ground, she gulped down her tears. 'Please,' she begged, her eyes on the empress.

The empress held her head high. She would give her nothing now, for the emperor had decreed it and she would never see the girl again. She only hoped she was not wrong about the current hidden princess. And what would they do if they never found her? Would they choose another? Would there be time to give her son what he needed?

Remi felt something off as soon as he entered the building. It wasn't magic, but it was a sense of something dark. He ran towards Lis's cell to find her standing against the wall, her hand to her throat with the High Priestess standing before her.

'How did you get in?' he asked, looking around for the guards.

'I walked,' the priestess said, turning to him, her face calm and smiling.

Lis gasped as though she could breathe again, and Remi moved quickly through the cell to stand between them.

'Why are you here?' he asked.

'I searched for the hidden princess and found her,' she said softly.

'This building is hardly in use, nor in need of a priestess.'

'It is strange, is it not? The prince looking for the hidden princess has had her locked away. Do you not trust her?' The priestess's voice was sweet and calming, and he blinked away the feeling of darkness he had felt when he entered.

'I am keeping her safe.'

'From what? The whole Rei-Een Empire searches for her, and you have her locked away.'

He could feel Lis's fingers closing around the back of his clothes, as though to keep him between them. 'She is not locked up.'

'The girl was alone in a cell. What was I to think?'

'The door was open,' he said, then silently cursed himself. He didn't need to explain himself to these people. 'Why are you here?' he asked again.

'To talk, to offer my understanding.'

'Your understanding?'

'We have talked before, the princess and I. She has struggled with her position. When I found her, I thought I could assist in the transition back to the hidden palace.'

'I don't think it is safe there,' Remi said quickly.

'So, you will keep her here.' It wasn't a question, and she laughed. 'I think your father might think differently on that. As will your mother. She has just lost one princess; she will not want to lose another.'

'What?' Lis whispered behind him.

'U'shi is no princess. She was a maid who neglected her duty.'

'For that she deserves to die.'

'And she will.'

'What?' Lis asked again.

'After the child is born,' the priestess continued, and he wondered how she could know so much when his father had only just made the announcement. It hadn't even been announced to the public yet. Maybe his mother had talked with her, but then she had been with his father when he had left them. She couldn't have known. 'Will he let the child live?'

Remi shook his head and heard the sharp intake of breath from the woman behind him as she closed her fists tighter around his coat.

'You will leave. I will ensure my parents are told of the princess. I alone am responsible for her safety.'

'Then you should not leave her alone.'

The priestess turned and glided from the cell. Her white robes dragged across the ground and yet appeared to pick up none of the dust. The odd feeling of darkness disappeared with her, and Remi turned to the woman behind him. Her throat was red despite the sunburn fading.

'What happened?' he asked.

'U'shi is to die? She's with child?' the princess asked, looking up at him.

He nodded once.

Anger creased her brow. 'Always telling me I didn't know how to be a princess,' she murmured, moving to the table and sitting down. 'Always so righteous. The tutor is the father,' she said, looking back at him. Then she suddenly dropped from the table and held her arms out, bowing her head in respect. 'Forgive me, Your Highness, that I do not greet you appropriately.'

'Lis,' he said. Stepping forward and taking her by the arms, he lifted her up and back onto the stool.

'Maybe she was right,' Lis murmured, looking at the table.

Mu-Phi appeared, a tray in her hands, and she bowed to the prince before sliding it onto the table.

'Where have you been?' he snapped.

She dropped to her knees on the earthen floor and bowed low. 'The high priestess wanted time alone with the princess,' she said. 'How could I refuse?'

'You are not to leave her alone with anyone.'

Mu-Phi nodded and bowed again.

Lis stood slowly from the table and joined the maid on the floor.

'Please,' Remi said, 'stand up.'

'I am ready to return,' she said softly, a catch in her voice.

'No,' he sighed.

'You want to keep me locked away?' she asked, sitting up.

'I want to keep you safe.'

'I don't think it is as safe here as you think.'

'Clearly, if the priestesses can wander in. Guard,' he called.

The man appeared at the bars.

'I want you watching closer to the entrance.'

The guard nodded and disappeared.

'You,' he said sharply to the maid. 'This is not enough for a princess. Prepare more.'

'I'm not hungry,' Lis said, but he ignored her and waved the girl away.

Lis surprised him by sighing and sitting back at the table. 'Are you to train me yourself?'

He looked up then and shook his head. 'The tutor is gone.'

She nodded once.

'You ran away, didn't you?'

She bit her lip and looked down at the table before nodding again.

'How?'

She shook her head.

He took a deep breath and tried to calm the anger building in him. 'Where did you go?'

'Home,' she whispered. 'But there was nothing there, and I didn't want to bring shame to my father.'

He didn't want to ask the question, but it was formed on his lips before he could stop it. 'Peng?'

'Is with my sister,' she said. 'It does not matter.'

He could see the hurt she tried to hide from him. She had lost everything.

'How did you know?' she asked.

'You were worried that I had killed him, and I knew he lived. I guessed.'

She nodded then. 'I found some people I thought would help me, but they only wanted more from me than I could give.' A large tear tracked down her cheek, and he was tempted to reach out and brush it away. 'This is my life. I must accept it. I do you dishonour by running away, and I am sorry.' She looked up at him then, and he nodded. 'I am ready to return to my studies, although…'

He reached out for her. 'What is it?'

'I am not bright enough to be what you need me to be. I cannot learn all that is needed in three years.'

'Less than three years now,' he reminded her.

She covered her mouth with her hand and the tears spilled freely down her cheeks.

'It will be fine,' he tried to reassure her, but she shook her head.

'What shall you do?' she asked, sucking in another sob.

'Watch over you myself.'

'To ensure I don't run away again.' She wiped the back of her hand across her nose.

He reached out and brushed his thumb over her cheek. How had this woman captivated him so completely? 'To keep you safe,' he said.

23

Lis stood before the emperor and empress and tried not to chew on
her lip. The prince stood at her side, but he had promised not to
mention her running away. They would maintain the story that she
had been taken, and that she was hazy on the details. And she *was*
hazy. She wasn't sure of anything that had occurred while she had
been away, and she tried not to shiver as she held her arms out
before her and bowed low.

She made to kneel on the floor, but the prince took her arm and
shook his head.

'Remi?' the empress asked.

'The princess is not yet well enough to get on the floor. It would
be awkward for her to climb back to her feet. I think, given her
experiences, you would allow this small deviation.'

The empress sighed, and the emperor nodded sagely. He waved
her forward and she took a careful step towards him, noting that
the prince did not step with her.

'I understand you are nervous to enter the hidden palace,' he
said, and then he looked back to his son. 'The crown prince feels
there is someplace more secure where we could house you.'

'I think she should remain at the royal residence.'

Lis tried to remain focused ahead of her. He had told her he had
a plan, but she hadn't realised it was that.

'The royal residence?' the emperor asked, standing from his

throne and walking around her towards his son.

Lis gulped down the fear building in her chest. What was he thinking?

'It has a guard at all times, and everyone passing can see who enters. So if anyone attempts something they should not, we will know of it.'

The empress opened her mouth to speak, but bit quickly on her lip, and Lis was sure that they had the same thought. It hadn't protected the former crown prince, and it was certainly someone with magic who had killed him.

'She will be upstairs, by me.'

'This isn't proper,' the empress snapped.

'She will be in her own room where the tutors can come and visit. I need to know she is safe. It is my duty,' he asserted, and Lis had to turn to see how serious he was. He was face to face with his father. 'She is to be my empress. It is my duty to keep her safe, and as a hunter I am the only one who can.'

'There are other hunters,' the emperor said, turning back to Lis and then climbing to his throne. 'But I know you will not be swayed in this.'

'I have lost my brother, and I will not lose my wife before she has the chance to be what we chose her to be.'

Lis gulped down the threatening tears. She had hardly given him a reason to look after her as he did.

'You have the room prepared?' the empress asked.

The prince came to stand beside Lis and bowed to his mother. 'And you have replaced the tutor more carefully than you selected the last?'

She gave him a dangerous look. Lis wanted to warn him, but instead he took her arm.

'This is too much; I shall escort her back to rest.'

'She cannot stay alone, and you cannot visit her as though she were…'

'I understand that, Mother,' he said quickly, cutting her off. 'I have found a replacement for U'shi I know I can trust.'

Lis looked at him quickly, and he gave her a small smile.

'How do you know she can be trusted?' his mother asked.

'I know.' His tone was just as dangerous as the empress's had been.

He bowed low to both of his parents, and Lis repeated the movement. The prince backed out of the room, his hand tight around her arm, pulling her along behind him.

She looked at him carefully once they were outside the throne room, but she said nothing. She wondered who the maid may be and why the prince was so sure he could trust her. The guards at the doorway bowed to them, and then two of them broke away from the others and followed. She thought one was familiar, but she wasn't sure, and she tried not to look back at them. As they left the throne room, two more men joined them. Lis recognised one as a man who had stood outside her gate. Someone she had walked past invisible not so long ago.

At the idea of the crowd, she stopped, worried that she wasn't as hidden as she had been. The crown prince seemed to be breaking every tradition. He had surprised her by ordering a sedan chair to carry her from the prison to the throne room. He placed his hand over hers, and she looked up into his smiling face.

'It is not far,' he said. 'Do you not want to go back in the sedan? It will keep you from the sun, and I think you have had enough of that.'

She smiled her thanks and nodded.

'Perhaps a hat or the like rather than the veil when you leave the residence.'

'Do I need to leave?'

'To attend the temple or the baths,' he said, and she squeezed her hand closed tightly. 'There are expectations,' he continued, and she could only nod.

Her guards, as the prince had told her they were, carried the sedan chair towards her and set it down. When she climbed aboard, the curtain was dropped across the opening and she was surrounded with red light from the little sun that made it through the curtains. She put her palms together without touching them. She was tempted to disappear, but they carried the weight of her, and she knew it wasn't possible. It would give her away if the prince were to look in on her.

He walked directly beside her and she wondered if he would ever leave her side again. She shook her head as she jostled around. In a strange way, she did feel safer with him watching over her, for he was the only one who appeared to care what might happen to her. And yet he had his reasons, and she wasn't sure if it was simply that she was the hidden princess and destined to be his wife.

He was also the most dangerous person to be around, for he could discover her and kill her without a thought. She remembered waking in the cell, the fear that had thumped in her chest before he had closed his arms around her and held her tight. It had been such a comfort, and she wondered if he might hesitate were something to happen. But she couldn't rely on that, she reminded herself, remembering his reaction when she had mentioned the idea of him caring for her.

She sucked in a deep breath as the chair came to a halt. He was protecting himself and what his Empire would be when he was Emperor and nothing more. The curtain was pulled back, and Lis found herself in the ornate hallway of the royal residence. She was keen to enter her room, but she wanted the chance to look over the place again. She stepped out carefully, taking the prince's offered arm.

'Welcome home,' he said softly.

She bowed to him, unsure what she could say—unsure if this would keep her safe from those who wanted her. She looked around carefully, taking in the beautiful colours, and she paused before the former prince's room. His name and rank above the door.

'You are upstairs,' he said, his voice a little gruffer than it had been. She nodded and turned back towards the stairs to find the maid from the cell standing before her.

The girl bowed low, and Lịs smiled at her. The maid had been a silent member of her time in the cell. She had done much to help, although Lis vaguely remembered her chiding the prince. She looked back at him, and he nodded. Was there something there between these two? Would she care if there was?

She stepped forward, running her hand carefully over the smooth banister as she followed the maid up the stairs. She paused and looked back to find the prince was watching her go, but not following. He nodded again and then turned back to the soldiers.

Lis tried not to look at the other doors and wonder who else may live so close. Would the empress visit with her more? U'shi had been too much like the empress, she realised, and she wondered what she would be by the end of this training, if she survived. Would she too be such a woman?

The room itself was similar to that of the crown prince next door. And she saw his door as she followed the maid into her own room. It was much larger than the hidden princess's palace, with a large bed sitting in the middle of the room. There was a desk to one side, already covered in papers and texts along with beautiful brushes and ink.

Lis sat at the desk and lifted the first document, a history of the Empire. She glanced through it. It was a history she knew well. It detailed the beginning of the Empire, the first emperors of Rei-Een and the world as it had been so many years ago.

The next one she selected was of the magic war, an overview with nothing of the detail she had learnt before. It didn't mention the visitors her mother had told her of, and it didn't mention her father killing children. She sighed as she glanced through it. Her father's name leapt from the page, and she read hungrily.

She sighed. It only mentioned him being the saviour of the war, bringing an end to magic in Rei-Een. She closed it and threw it back onto the pile.

She looked up then and caught the prince standing in the doorway, watching her closely. She made to stand, but he shook his head and instead she bowed to him from where she was.

'I see you are keen to get back to your studies.' He stepped forward and waved at the maid in the corner. She nodded and bowed to the prince before disappearing from the room.

'How do you know you can trust her?'

'She is the daughter of one of my best men.'

Lis nodded once. She too was the daughter of one of his father's best men, yet she wasn't what she appeared to be.

'What were you reading?'

'A history of the Empire, and an account of the magic war.'

'I would have thought your father would have told you all about the magic war.'

She shook her head and climbed to her feet. 'He didn't.'

'Oh,' the prince said.

'I know the history of the Empire, the line of emperors. It is something else the tutors will waste time reteaching,' she said, then turned and bowed to him again. 'I apologise, Your Highness. I do not appear as grateful as I am for this opportunity.'

He opened his mouth and then closed it as the maid reappeared. 'I thought you might be hungry,' she said, sitting the food down on a table Lis had not noticed before.

The prince indicated the table, and she stepped forward. 'Please,' he said, and she sat slowly, surprised to find him joining her. The maid gave him a dark look, and he waved her away.

Lis looked after her as she returned to the corner of the room and stoked the coals beneath the pot. Was she another jealous of Lis's position?

Lis turned back to the prince, who was watching her closely. 'She believes I do not behave appropriately,' he said in a conspiratorial whisper, and Lis smiled at him.

She looked over the bowls before her and realised there was

nothing for the prince. She lifted the empty bowl from in front of her and sat it down before him. He picked it up and sat it back. 'I am to join you, but you need to eat.'

She shook her head. 'I'm not hungry.'

'Do you feel unwell?' he asked, his voice heavy with concern. 'Should I send for a healer?'

She shook her head.

'Then eat a little, if just for me. I need to know you are well after all that has happened.'

'You trust her,' Lis said, moving the food around her bowl without picking any up.

'Completely,' he said, looking across at the girl.

'Is she a hunter?'

'Would it make you feel better if she were?'

Lis studied him across the table and forced a small amount of meat into her mouth. It tasted very good, but it was hard to swallow. She didn't want any of this, but there was nowhere else she could go now. She would have to live her life as the prince deemed best.

Lis jumped at a loud knock on the door, and a manservant entered. He smiled at Lis and bowed to them both. 'Your Highness, I am to remind you of your duty and that you are not to harass the princess.'

'Harass?' he asked the man, then turned back to Lis with a grin. She tried to smile for him, and she put the chopsticks down.

'The empress said you were not to...' He waved his hand in a circular motion. Lis wondered what the empress thought her son was up to.

'I don't think I've been doing any of that,' he said softly, and the maid in the corner coughed.

Lis smiled despite trying to stay out of the conversation. And then she looked seriously at the prince. 'Why does she think you do not behave appropriately?' she asked, looking towards the maid.

'Your Highness,' the manservant grumbled.

'I never,' he said to the man. 'I looked at your feet,' he said quickly.

'My feet?'

'When you were burned.'

'My feet,' she repeated slowly. 'Is it not appropriate to look at someone's feet?' She looked down at the table, feeling the heat of her embarrassment burn through her face. She ran barefoot around the island often, and her father had never once ordered her to put on shoes when Peng visited. She chanced the opportunity to look back at him, but he looked a little pink himself. 'You mean the bath house?'

'Oh my,' the manservant said, bowing hastily and backing out of the room.

'You did not look,' she said, trying to hide the lump that had formed in her throat. She was coming across as the country girl. The harder she tried to understand what she should be doing, the worse she was making the situation. She so desperately wanted to disappear and run. But, she reminded herself, she had nowhere to go.

He shook his head.

'You were only in your undergarments,' the maid said. 'The crown prince looked over you in this state of undress to assess your burns. He is childish and impulsive.'

'And she was injured,' he snapped back at the maid. He sighed and looked back at the table. 'You still have not eaten,' he said.

'I am not hungry; my stomach is unsettled.'

He nodded slowly and waved the girl over. She set a cup down on the table before Lis.

Lis took it and sipped at it. It contained a sweet tea that soothed her somewhat. 'I think I need Tutor Na,' she said, setting the cup on the table. 'She would be best to explain my behaviour.'

'I do not think you have misbehaved,' the prince said, his smile sad, and she looked back at the tea.

'But I do not behave as I should,' she whispered.

'You have been perfect,' he said, anger apparent in his voice. 'It is I who have spent too long pestering you. The girl is right, of course; I do not act as I should.' He stood quickly, and she jumped at the movement, wondering if she would ever settle in this world. Would she always be waiting for him to run her through? 'I am sorry,' he said with a sigh and turned for the door.

'Wait,' she called after him. 'I appreciate what you have done for me,' she said quickly. 'You have saved me, again.' She smiled when he turned back from the door. 'I like your company,' she added. 'Perhaps you could visit soon.'

He grinned and bowed low before he turned back for the door and left.

Lis dropped her head into her hands on the table at the relief. Although she wasn't sure what she was more relieved at, that he had left her alone and alive or that he would be coming back.

'Do you feel up to eating now?' the maid asked, looking over the table, and Lis nodded slowly without lifting her head. 'You are very lucky to have a such a man choose you to be his wife,' she said.

Was she? The one man who could find her out and finish her. But he had not sensed her yet, although she was sure she had sensed something around him. 'Are you a hunter?' she asked the girl, who smiled and shook her head. 'Will you sit with me?'

The maid opened her mouth to protest as Lis nodded.

She smiled then and sat where the prince had.

'I don't have any friends, and there are few who will visit with me,' Lis said carefully. 'I would like someone I can talk with.'

'Of course, Your Highness,' the maid said.

'The tea is very good.'

'It will settle your stomach. My mother is a healer of a type, and I learnt a little from her.'

A strange feeling overwhelmed Lis as she looked over the cup. What if they did something to her?

'He only wants you safe.'

'So he says,' Lis mused.

'You do not trust him?' the girl asked, her eyes wide.

'It is not that,' she said, but the girl was right. 'I'm not sure who to trust,' she said honestly. 'Everyone has their own agenda and their own idea as to where I fit within their world.'

'You are the hidden princess,' the maid said with a broad smile. 'The world revolves around you.'

Lis laughed out loud. 'If only that were true.'

'The prince's world revolves around you,' she said.

'I think the prince has much to worry about without me adding to his woes. You have known him a long time?'

She nodded then. 'He is a good man.'

'You said that,' Lis whispered. 'I hope it is true.'

The door opened, and she jumped despite her best efforts. Tutor Na stood in the doorway, a frustrated look upon her face. The maid was quick to her feet and bowed before her, but would not allow her to enter the room.

'You are to knock, please, Tutor.'

'She is my student.'

'The crown prince insists upon it. She has been through a terrible ordeal, and she is frightened.'

The tutor looked around the girl at Lis and nodded once.

'The princess is eating. She is still weak.'

'The prince himself sent me,' Tutor Na said in a tone that made Lis sit taller.

'The prince himself has placed me here.' The maid's tone carried a similar weight, and Lis knew this girl was far more than she appeared to be.

'I have a need to talk with the empress. Eat and rest, and I shall return.'

Lis nodded, and Tutor Na bowed before leaving.

'I wonder if they have replaced the history tutor with someone nice,' Lis mused aloud.

'I think the prince has thoughts on that as well.'

'It seems that he takes on more than he should.'

The maid sat back at the table, a friendly smile lighting up her face. 'He does,' she said as she indicated the food.

24

Lis woke with a fright to find the empress standing over her. There was no sign of the new maid, and she was yet to find out just why the prince had placed her there. Although, if she could allow the empress to enter without telling her or preparing her, it may be just as it had been with U'shi.

'Are you unwell?' the empress asked harshly. Then she sighed and stood back. 'I have heard too much of your time away from the palace,' she said, a little kinder. 'And my son assures me you have not been treated as someone of your station should be.'

Lis stared openly at the woman before her. Was the empress actually saying she should have treated her better? Lis had not really told anyone what had occurred outside of the palace, so she wondered what the empress had been told.

'You look well enough, although still tanned, and you appear thinner than I remember.'

'Because she does not eat,' the prince said, entering the room behind his mother. Lis looked from one to the other. She still sat in her bed rather than greeting them both as she should, yet she was only in her underclothes. She glanced towards the window and wondered if the sun had even risen.

'We will keep you safe, for the choice is made, but we must act now.'

Lis bit down on her lip. Did they know what she was?

'What are you talking of?' the prince finally asked.

'The baby,' the empress whispered.

'What baby?' Lis asked, feeling even more confused.

The empress opened her mouth and then closed it again. 'There is no need to deny it. We will keep you safe.'

The prince looked just as confused as Lis felt, and Lis looked at the worried face of the empress before she pushed the covers back and threw herself to the floor before the woman. What lies had been told this time?

'I am not with child,' she hissed, bowing low.

'The healer is on the way; he will confirm.'

'Mother,' the prince said. He sounded lost as he looked between the two of them. 'Whose child do you believe it to be?'

'Not yours, or we would find a way to ensure the child survives. He would be heir. Unless it is a girl.'

'There is no child.' Lis could feel the magic burning beneath her skin with her anger. 'Who has told such lies, and why would you believe them?' she asked, and then she sat back on her heels. Who was she to speak to an empress in such a way? She glanced up and saw the woman wore an even darker expression.

Lis sighed. 'I can't continue to do this. No matter what I do or where I go, I am not what you want me to be. And you have made it very clear that I will not be what you want me to be. In fear I may embarrass you as the former hidden princess did, I ask that you take my life now rather than play with it any further. You can claim me an accident, or another victim like the former crown prince.'

'Mother, apologise to the princess.'

The empress turned on her son and glared at him. 'It has come to me from a secure source. I know what she has done.'

'And yet I do not,' Lis said. If she was going down, she might as well go fighting. 'Was this done while I was held against my will, or did I run away with a lover?'

She noticed the pain flash across the prince's face then, before it was replaced with doubt. And then the maid was there, rushing forward with a gown and trying to cover her up. Lis shrugged her off.

'Who told you?' Lis asked again, more forceful and determined than she should be with the empress of the world.

'The high priestess.'

Lis looked at the floor. The priestess was determined that Lis was more than she was willing to say, yet she struggled to find the evidence of it. She had told Lis she would tell the world the truth, or her version of it, when the prince had arrived and interrupted her.

'The same woman who threatened the hidden princess?' the prince asked.

'When you had her hidden away,' the empress said, turning her angry words on her son. 'She is not yours yet. And if she carries the child of another man, it may be that we should do as she suggests and kill her now.'

'I was only gone a few days, and I have only been back a few more. I wouldn't know it myself if I was with child.'

'I knew the moment the prince was conceived,' the empress shot back, then glanced at the maid.

'So how and when was this child conceived?' Lis asked, trying to determine what the priestess thought she was to gain from this.

'Do you not want another empress? Do you want this Empire to end with you?' the prince asked, too loudly. A guard looked in the door and then disappeared again.

Lis wondered if she could disappear before them. Would they notice? Mother and son glared at each other. Lis felt ill, but she knew there was no child. The prince was right; she wasn't eating enough.

The door opened again, and a healer entered. He bowed low to everyone in the room and waited. Lis sat back on the bed, unsure what else she could do or say, although she was certain this man would prove her innocent. She was tired. Tired of the lies and the way of life, and the fact that she had nothing else. If the empress took her head here and now, she would at least have the chance for rest.

The healer stepped forward and sat beside her. He placed a small cushion down across his lap, and she placed her hand on it. Without glancing at the empress, he gently touched his fingers to her wrist.

After a moment, he nodded and Lis took her hand back.

'She is weak and unwell. I recommend rest. No excitement, no lessons and no visitors.'

Lis glanced at the prince, who studied the man rather than her, and she knew any friendship she had thought they might be forming was finished, whether she was with child or not.

'Her condition?' the empress asked, her voice reedy and stretched from the strain.

'She is not with child.'

The crown prince actually sighed with relief, and Lis glared at them both.

'I shall make tea,' the maid said. She had been sitting beside Lis, and Lis hadn't realised it until the girl stood up. She nodded, but she couldn't find a smile. 'A little breakfast is in order, and I have a treat,' the maid whispered, bowing low and then moving over to the little stove in the corner.

'An excellent idea,' the healer said, 'and then you must rest.'

He bowed low to the princess before turning to the prince and the empress. He left the room as quickly as he had entered it.

Lis carefully lifted the covers and lay back down in her bed. She rolled over, with her back to the royal family, not caring that it wasn't how she should behave, how a princess should behave. She wanted nothing more to do with them. She would get her strength back and then she would disappear again, only this time she would go far away from the Empire. Far away from all of them, somewhere she could be herself.

'I thought…' he said quietly.

'I know what you thought,' she said without turning back.

'I thought the priestess could be trusted,' he said, and as she heard the door close, she rolled back with a sigh to find him sitting on the edge of the bed.

'You are the reason these rumours start,' the maid said from the corner.

He sighed and shook his head. 'I did not know she would talk to my mother.'

'You sent her to the cell?' Lis asked.

He shook his head. 'No. Do you not trust that I will keep you safe?'

'You do not trust me,' Lis whispered, turning back again.

'I knew it was a lie,' he said, but his voice wavered a little. Lis sensed something else behind it, although she wasn't sure what.

'I saw your face. You really thought I had returned to Peng, in such a way, when I was promised to you.'

'You did run away.'

'Why would I do such a thing when my life here is so good?' she murmured.

'It will become easier, the more time you are here. One day you will be Empress, and then you shall have all the freedom in the world.'

'Will I?'

'Do you ask about the freedom, or whether you will be Empress?'

Lis squeezed her eyes closed and wished him away.

'Sire, you do not help,' the maid said.

'Where were you?' he asked harshly.

'Sleeping,' she said.

'Your instructions were to never leave her side,' he snapped.

'For the princess cannot be trusted,' Lis murmured.

'You are the only one I know I can trust,' he said, then stepped towards the door.

As the door closed, Lis rolled out of the bed and padded over to sit at the table. The maid sat the cup before her.

'He is hard on you without reason,' she said to the girl.

'He has always been hard on me. He works hard, and he expects the same from those around him.'

'What is your name?'

'Mu-Phi,' she said, bowing to Lis.

'Where have you been sleeping?'

She pointed back to the corner, and Lis frowned.

'I know you would like some space, Your Highness, but he insists that I am close.'

'I would rather you had a proper bed. Let us organise it. We shall be like sisters.'

Mu-Phi smiled and shook her head. 'It is not my place.'

'I would rather you comfortable, or you shall not be able to do your job properly.'

'I shall see what can be done. Now, you must eat, and I have something special.'

Lis watched her skip back to the little corner of the room and return with a small box.

She sat it down in front of Lis and waited, her hands clenched before her, clearly excited about what was inside.

Lis pulled the lid off to reveal sweet cakes like those her mother used to make, perfectly shaped into flowers. The smell was overwhelming, and her mouth watered instantly.

'My mother made them for you,' Mu-Phi said, sitting down again and grinning.

Lis lifted one to her nose and breathed it in before biting hungrily into it. She moaned with the pleasure of it, and Mu-Phi laughed. Lis pushed the box across and nodded, and Mu-Phi hesitated for only a moment before taking one.

'Thank you,' Lis said, her lips still cakey. Then she pulled out another. 'The best breakfast I have had in a long time.' And she bit into the second cake.

'Perhaps I should have made something more nourishing,' Mu-

Phi said, a worried look creasing her brow.

'I am not likely to survive the first year, let alone three, if I continue with the empress as I have. Let me enjoy what I can of life while I have it.'

Mu-Phi laughed and poured more tea. 'I think the prince will ensure that you are all you can be.'

'Really?' Lis asked with a mouthful of cake, and they both laughed.

Then Mu-Phi became very serious she bowed to Lis. 'Yes. On his life,' she said.

Lis woke from a dream where the whole world was burning around her to find that she was just as hot and dry in the waking world. The maid stood fidgeting by the bed and, despite being hidden in a dark corner, she could sense the prince reaching out for the magic in the room.

'What has happened?' she asked Mu-Phi in a hushed tone. Her throat burned, and she was desperate for water. As though sensing her needs, the girl knelt down beside the bed with a cup in her hand. Despite its heat, Lis gulped it down.

'What happened?' she repeated, looking past the girl to the corner.

'What did you dream of?' the maid asked.

Lis shook her head, sitting up and trying not to groan with the effort. She wasn't clear on what had happened in the dream, whether it was her or someone else that had caused the devastation, nor why it had happened.

'Magic,' the prince whispered, and she froze. Had she unleashed what her father had feared, and he had sensed her?

Lis squeezed her eyes closed, wondering what he would do. When she opened them, she squealed, for he was standing over her.

'Do not fear,' he whispered, too close. 'I have increased the number of hunters around you.'

Lis raised her eyes to the girl sitting beside the bed.

'I am not what you think,' Mu-Phi said.

'You are more than you appear to be,' Lis answered before she could stop herself. She looked up briefly at the prince, who tried not to sigh as he sat down on the edge of her bed. Was he too familiar?

'She is the only other person I truly trust,' he said. 'If I cannot watch over you directly, then Mu-Phi is the only one to be alone with you in this room.'

'The tutors?'

He shook his head.

'I don't trust your mother; she is too determined that...' Lis bit her lip. 'I am sorry.'

'I would rather you were honest with me.'

'Even though you think I ran away to Peng.'

'You did run away to Peng,' he said, standing.

She wanted to reach for him, but she didn't. 'Why are you here?'

'There is a sense of magic. It appears to be everywhere I go, and I can't find it or determine exactly where it is coming from.'

'You fear it,' Lis said.

'You don't know what they can do.'

'I saw a man form fire in his hand,' she said, leaning forward.

He nodded.

'What have you seen?' Lis asked.

'All the elements in some form or other, and then those who have tried to shape the minds of others.'

'Could they shape your mind?' she asked, fearful of something dark.

'I think my hunter abilities will help prevent it, but I don't know. Perhaps I am bewitched already,' he said with a smirk.

'Your mother would not appreciate you here, and the healer said I am to rest.'

'You don't appear to be getting much rest.'

Lis nodded and lay back. She was exhausted, as much from the dream as after her time being invisible. 'I should sleep,' she said, pulling the covers up.

The prince and the maid moved closer to the door to talk in hushed tones. She wanted to tell him he could stay, but then he was only next door. If she caused any flames to leak from her dreams into the room in the night, she would rather he wasn't there to see it.

Over the coming days the prince appeared in her room just as often as the maid. Her tutors had not returned. The dreams had become clearer in some ways, and much darker. Lis wasn't sure what side she was on. But she woke the same way from each one, feeling drained and hot and sure that she had watched the whole world burn.

It was after one of these dreams that the prince rushed into her room as she woke coughing and she was sure she saw someone on the other side of the doorway before it closed.

She glanced at the maid, who was fussing by the pot making tea, but neither of them seemed to notice him, so she wondered if he was a remnant of her dream. But once she had settled down later that evening and the prince left, satisfied that she was well although muttering about getting the healer, she noticed the man standing in the hallway again. The prince walked past him as though he wasn't there. He held his finger to his lips, and Lis squeezed her eyes closed.

The next morning, she jolted up from the bed as the prince arrived with a healer and the man, wearing muted colours, a lopsided smile and loose long hair, followed them in.

'She isn't sleeping,' the crown prince announced, his voice showing his frustration.

'I sleep,' she said. 'I have been having strange dreams that wake me,' she added, and the man no one else could see raised his eyebrows.

'You need your rest. It is the stress of your situation,' the older man said. 'I shall talk with the empress.'

'I need to return to my lessons,' Lis blurted. 'There is not enough time.'

'I do not think there is as much to learn as my mother thinks.' Lis turned to the prince as he spoke, and he looked lost for a moment. 'Perhaps there is more than I think.'

Lis laughed despite her head aching and her dry throat.

'Three days,' the healer announced to the room. 'If I am satisfied with your condition in three days, you may return to your studies.'

She nodded once and took the offered cup from the maid.

'I think the baths would assist in your healing,' he announced.

Lis looked straight to the prince, her heart suddenly pounding.

'Mu-Phi will be with you every moment, and I shall stand outside the door.'

She nodded and gulped.

'It is to help you relax,' the healer chastised, as though she was foolish to fear such a venture.

'I shall discuss it with the guards,' the prince said, leading the healer from the space.

'He told me what happened in the baths,' Mu-Phi said. 'Have you not been back?'

She shook her head.

'Ahh,' Mu-Phi said. 'My mother has made more cakes,' she added brightly, trying to change the subject completely.

'I feel like an invalid,' Lis murmured, watching the man walk the room. 'As though I'm not capable.'

'The prince thinks you are.'

The man stopped and looked at Mu-Phi, then back to Lis. There was something familiar about him, but she couldn't place it. Was he at the island she had visited? He wasn't the man throwing fire at the old tutor. A school, she realised. The answer had been before her all along and she hadn't seen it. Somewhere they could learn.

Lis looked down at her own hand, flexing her fingers and feeling her magic just below the surface.

What could she do if she had the opportunity to learn how to use her magic? What wonders could she create? She looked up slowly as the door opened and the prince returned. What horror could she wreak if she wanted to?

She sighed and looked at the man standing back from the prince. What did he want, and why hadn't she told anyone he was there? She looked back at her hands. How long until he dropped from the exhaustion of maintaining the invisibility and was discovered?

'They are ready for you,' the crown prince said, and she looked back to the maid.

They would have prepared the streets, cleared the people, just so she could travel to the baths. She stood, feeling a little wearier than she would like to admit, and the maid was beneath her arm, supporting her. The other man, she noticed, had also stepped forward.

As they moved out, the man unseen by the others bowed to her. When she followed the prince out and down the steps, it was harder than she imagined it could be. What did she do during those dreams that drained her so completely?

The litter sat just inside the main entrance, and a guard stood back with the curtain lifted. She smiled her thanks to him, noting how different it was to have him look at her. When the curtain dropped back into place, she was lifted smoothly from the ground and jostled along. She was unsure whether she was more nervous about what might occur at the baths or what the man left alone in her room might do. How long would he stay, and what did he want from her?

As they travelled, she could hear the prince and the maid talking. She couldn't hear what was said, but it was comforting that they were both with her. She felt a stab of guilt that she could like the prince. Yet he had been nothing but kind and had saved her several times already, while Peng had already forgotten her.

When the litter stopped and she was helped out, she stood for a moment too long inside the gate. The prince bowed once and disappeared inside. He returned after a little longer than she expected. 'I think he has checked it thoroughly,' Mu-Phi said, leaning in beside her.

She nodded and stepped forward as he emerged. With the maid at her side, she entered the royal baths. A lemongrass scent filled the steam, and she tried not to chew her lip.

Mu-Phi helped her out of her clothes and held her hand as she stepped down into the bath. Sure she could still see the blood in the water, she put a hand over her mouth at the coppery scent.

'It is safe,' the maid reassured her. 'There is nothing and no one here.'

Lis nodded and allowed herself to relax into the hot water. Mu-Phi moved to the side of the bath, and Lis could see her with a basket. 'I am getting some lotions for your hair,' she called back, her voice echoing strangely in the room. 'Do you want to wet your hair?'

Lis nodded, took a breath and submerged her head under the water. She ran her fingers through her hair and then opened her eyes. The water was dark, and she couldn't see anything. She broke the surface half expecting to see someone, but it was only Mu-Phi, smiling and indicating the step. She poured a lotion into Lis's hair and massaged it in vigorously.

After a little while, Lis allowed herself to close her eyes and relax. The maid poured water over her hair and repeated the experience. The hard fingers on her scalp helped relieve her tension.

Lis returned to her rooms in a relaxed daze, feeling calmer and ready for sleep. She had forgotten the man in the room until Mu-Phi had tucked her in and left, at which point he tapped her on the shoulder.

She stifled a scream and sat up slowly.

'You are never alone,' he whispered, his eye on the door.

'How can you stay as you are for so long?' she asked.

'That is not important. Are you unwell?'

'Tired, from my time as you are, and I have these dreams.'

'Can you tell me what you dream of?' he asked in a hurried whisper.

'It is not clear, but the prince is often there at the edges of my vision.'

He held up a hand, looking back to the door. 'He trusts you,' he whispered.

She nodded. 'He doesn't know.'

'When you can use all your skills, he may come to understand the good you can do.'

'He may trust me now, but he will kill me as soon as he knows.'

The man smiled then. A warm, genuine smile that made Lis want to smile with him. 'He cares for you.'

'Someone else told me the same thing, at the school,' she added, leaning closer to the man who was now kneeling at her bedside. 'But I'm not sure.' She looked towards the door.

His smile broadened. 'He has risked everything to bring you here, to have you close and ensure your safety.'

'I am the future empress,' she said.

'It is more than that.'

'What do you want from me?'

'I want what your prince does, to keep you safe. Although for possibly very different reasons.'

'And they are?'

The door opened quietly and the maid entered. It was only when she briefly glanced across at Lis that she realised Lis was sitting up. 'Are you unwell?' she asked, rushing over.

'No. Where were you?'

'The crown prince wanted…'

Lis held up her hand. 'You don't have to tell me,' she murmured, her face heating at the idea of them together.

'I will let you rest,' Mu-Phi said, backing out of the room.

Lis sighed.

'It is not what you think,' the man said, now standing beside the bed.

'You don't know what I think,' she whispered hoarsely. 'Or anything of who I am. There was another like me, a woman who took me to the school.'

He nodded once. 'The princess.'

'Princess?'

'That is a story only she can tell. We want you safe and strong. Neither of us are a risk to you.'

'I guessed as much,' she said. 'But there are others who do wish me harm.'

'They know what you can be.'

'I can't even learn to be a hidden princess properly. What else could I be?'

'You will see. I will leave you in the care of the crown prince. Rest. It will become easier.' He bowed low.

'Will the dreams stop?' she asked as he headed for the door.

He shrugged. Lis climbed out of the bed and opened the door for him. As he stepped into the hallway, she followed and noticed the prince and the maid talking in hushed tones by his door. The man turned and bowed low before her. With a grin, he strode past the crown prince without him even noticing he was there. She watched him walk along the hallway and down the stairs.

Was the overall feeling of magic blocking the prince's ability to pick up what was around him—or was this man, as she was, truly hidden from him and the other hunters?

25

Wei-Song sat behind the desk at the front of the classroom, evidence of the recent fight still scorched across the wall behind her. The young man she had sent to find the hidden princess rushed into the room.

'Your Highness.' He bowed before her, and she worried the girl had been lost.

She waved him up from his knees. 'Did you find her? Is she safe?'

Kei-Bi nodded. 'But it is hard to get close to her.'

'Guards?'

'The crown prince himself watches over her.'

'I am surprised the empress lets him that close,' she mused.

'The empress is not what she was. I am sure she feels the betrayal of U'shi, and the prince has coerced her into letting the hidden princess remain at the royal residence.'

'Do not presume to know the mind of the empress,' Wei-Song said sharply, and he touched his head to the floor before her. She tried not to sigh. 'The royal residence didn't offer enough protection to save the eldest prince,' she said. 'U'shi is with child then?'

He nodded.

'Has he placed a hunter close by?'

'He is a hunter,' the man reminded her. 'He has placed Mu-Phi as a maid, and he is just next door. He visits with her far too often, and I'm sure he looks in on her while she sleeps.'

'I heard stories of how he cared for her when she was found.'

'In a cell,' the man murmured with a shake of his head. 'Not the way to look after such a woman.'

'A woman who is intended to be your future empress.'

'She reminded me of that herself,' he said.

'You like her,' she said with a grin.

'She is struggling. I remember such a time myself. She has strange dreams, and she looks exhausted.'

'Did you learn anything else?' Wei-Song asked. She wondered at the dreams herself, but she wasn't going to raise that with this man. 'What of the others?'

'There was no sign.'

'Was the former hidden princess working with them?'

He shook his head. 'She only thought of herself, and spending time with the tutor. When she left the hidden princess to see her lover, it was by chance that they reached her in the baths.'

'Has he changed the guard?'

'He has added to it, but I think they remain essentially the same men.'

'Go and rest,' she said with a wave of her hand.

'What will you do?'

'What I must.'

'Could you not be what you thought this hidden princess to be? You have the skill.'

Wei-Song smiled bitterly. 'I am an unknown. She already holds the love of the people in this time. Even if the people don't know what happened to their prince, they hold the traditions close.'

'They could come to know you, if only…'

She held up her hand, and he stopped. 'I have heard of the visions, just as you have. I am not the hidden princess to save the people.'

He bowed low and left her. She looked over the papers before her, but she couldn't focus on the content. Long Lisabet was a girl who didn't know what power she had and didn't want to be in the position she was. But she was there, and it would be up to Wei-Song to ensure she answered her calling.

The dreams had stopped for Lis, because she was no longer able to sleep. Was the woman she had met another hidden princess? Did the prince know of her existence or identity? The man had not reappeared, and Lis knew that the healer would soon return to determine whether she was well enough to continue her studies.

She wondered just what they would attempt to teach her, and she hoped the prince was able to talk to his mother about what she needed. He seemed certain enough that she didn't have too much to learn.

She sighed and rubbed at her heavy eyes. He would be here soon enough. Despite his mother's strong words, he was always close. He had even started to take his breakfast with her. He would grumble as he had the day before that she still looked tired, and she wondered again what the healer would do if she was deemed too unwell.

But she didn't want to dream. The last one had left her scared. The prince had been clearer amidst the flames.

'Are you awake already?' Mu-Phi asked from the other side of the room.

Lis nodded and rubbed again at her face.

'Have you slept?' the maid asked, coming over and kneeling before her.

'I'm not sure,' Lis lied. The girl was loyal to the prince first. Although she was not to leave the room, Lis often heard their whispered conversations in the hallway. She had been tempted to sneak out to hear the details of their discussions, but she wasn't sure how it would affect her, and she didn't want to risk the prince discovering her.

She almost laughed at the idea. She had been so worried—her

whole family had—and yet she had walked past him using her magic and he'd had no idea.

'I will start your breakfast.'

Lis nodded and watched the girl move back to the kettle. She stoked the small fire beneath the pot and then silently left the room. Lis lay back and tried to keep her eyes from closing. Mu-Phi would report to the prince that she hadn't slept before she returned from the kitchens with her breakfast.

Lis could no longer fight the gritty feeling in her eyes, so she allowed them to close. A whole world sparked behind her lids, and she watched again as the world burned around her. Only this time, she didn't feel the heat. She could sense the flames, but they didn't touch her. She stepped closer to them, wondering at the lack of heat. The flames burned white before her, losing all hint of the oranges and reds, and the world went dark.

Then the sun shone bright in the sky, and Lis was standing at the school in a strange silence, as though her hands covered her ears. She moved through the corridors, looking over the artwork and wondering what they could teach her. Did she have an ability with fire? Was that why she dreamed of it?

But there was no one there to ask, and she sighed in the silence. Then she heard footsteps. When she turned, she saw a small child running past her wearing the grey uniform Lis wore as the hidden princess, her hair flowing behind her.

'It will be as it must be,' she called as she ran past Lis and disappeared through a doorway. Lis followed, but she couldn't find the child.

'What will?' she called into the silence.

'Everything,' the child called back, and then Lis woke.

She blinked into the light. As the door opened and she sat up, Mu-Phi entered with the prince following close behind.

He nodded his head towards her and took his usual place by the table. Lis threw the covers back and stood slowly. She felt more refreshed than she had before. and she wondered if she had slept for a long time. She felt warm, but not hot or dry. Mu-Phi rushed forward and put a robe around her shoulders.

Lis glanced over her shoulder at the prince, with whom she didn't feel as shy as she should. He had seen her in her undergarments before. She smiled her thanks to the girl and then sat down opposite the prince. He poured tea for them both as Mu-Phi moved one of the bowls she had carried in closer to Lis.

'You look well,' the prince said, confusion crossing his face as he looked up at Mu-Phi.

'You sound disappointed,' Lis answered, her voice clear. The heavy feeling of sleeplessness she had felt earlier, had lifted completely.

'You have looked so tired of late.'

'The healer returns today. I expect to be back to my studies.'

'Your days will be filled with tutors,' he sighed.

'That is why I am here,' she said, feeling the smile stretch her face. 'I am to learn, and there is much to cover.'

He nodded once, pushing food into his mouth. She watched him as he ate, and she followed his example. The food tasted different, as though colour had come back into the world.

U'shi watched the soldier walk past her cell. It was not a place she thought would ever be used again. And now she was the only occupant. She had not been in the small palace very long before she had been returned to the cold cell. The soldiers had marched her through the streets towards her new home. She had tried not to look at the people who openly stared and whispered about her, not too quietly. Never in all the world had she imagined this would be her life.

She ran a hand over her stomach and looked back at the man who watched her too closely. The other soldiers had stood silently, but this one watched her and moved about far too much. A nervousness prickled the back of her neck. She stood slowly and stepped closer to the bars.

'Who sent you?' she asked, her voice stronger than she felt.

He grinned at her before holding out his hand. She thought he might have a note or similar from her lover. She had no idea where Nizen was, or even if he had survived this long. She could remember the anger on the prince's face. The empress would have protected her—she knew what she was—but the prince's hate was too much for the emperor to ignore.

They should never have selected another, she determined as she stepped forward to see what he held in his hand. He was close to the bars, but he had not put his hand through, although there was sufficient room between the bars to do so. If she had been thinner, U'shi wondered if she could have squeezed through herself. But there was nowhere to go now and no one to go to.

He started to laugh when she reached the bars, and then he suddenly reached through and grabbed her wrist.

His hold burned her skin, and she shrieked. 'Don't you know who I am?'

He only laughed louder. U'shi tried to pull from his hold, but her arm burned hotter and she dropped to her knees. The heat pulsed through her.

'Magic,' she whispered.

'You are nothing,' he said, 'but a step between me and the princess.'

'I was your princess,' she snapped, despite the pain. She knew what she had been and what she should have remained. The country girl would not be what U'shi could have been as Empress.

'You were never my princess. You would have done nothing for this Empire.'

'I could have,' she said through gritted teeth as another wave of heat covered her body. U'shi felt a sharp pain in her chest and then in her stomach. She clutched at it as she doubled over, her arm still held above her. 'Stop,' she breathed. Her voice had no weight to it, no strength left. But the pain continued, and the heat intensified until the world went dark around her. 'Please stop,' she whispered. He released her, and her hand dropped back through the bars to her chest. There was nothing but fire and darkness.

The guard raced through the door, then stopped and bowed low as Lis jumped up from the table. She could see his hesitation as to whether he should step back and knock or continue. No, she could feel it. She took a deep breath and sat back at the table.

The prince opened his mouth to chastise him, but the guard motioned to the door, looking more at Lis than his prince. 'I think this best outside,' he murmured.

Lis looked to the prince as he raised his eyebrows.

'It is the maid, U'shi,' the guard said, and Lis could sense his heart beating fast.

She took a careful sip of her tea. The whole room seemed to buzz with magic, which she tried not to notice. The prince had climbed to his feet, and Mu-Phi stood directly behind her.

'Go on,' the prince said, his voice calm and level, as though there were nothing Lis could not hear.

'She is dead,' he whispered.

Lis put the cup down carefully. 'The tutor?' she asked, unsure why she needed to know anything of him.

'He was put to death last week, Your Highness,' the guard said, turning and bowing again to her.

She nodded, wondering when it had happened and why she hadn't been told. But then, she wasn't told very much. Lis stopped and took a deep breath; this was not the time to worry about what was shared with her. She had always known it would be very little. It was only because the crown prince worried for her that she was privy to such matters now.

She felt the crackle around him, as though he stretched and

hunted with his skill while standing stock still. She could taste it on the air, something beyond the prince and his searching skills. It burned like the flames of her dreams, and she wondered if she too had an ability to hunt.

'Magic,' the prince murmured, and the guard nodded.

'There are marks on her arm where she was burnt. But it was more than that. It appears to have pushed right through her, burning her from the inside.'

'How did we not know there was a fire bearer in the palace?' the prince asked, his level voice carrying his anger.

The guard shook his head.

'He walked right into the prison?'

'I don't understand how it was done. One soldier is missing.'

The prince huffed then, letting his frustration show, and he stomped to the door. The guard bowed again to Lis before following him out. It was only as Mu-Phi poured more tea that she realised the prince had said nothing to her before leaving.

'There is still magic here,' Lis whispered before picking up her cup.

'The prince will hunt it out,' the maid said, picking up his plates and placing them in her corner.

Lis was actually quite hungry, and she continued to eat as Mu-Phi folded the covers on her bed and poured ink into the pot. She also unfurled fresh paper on her desk. Lis watched her silently. She wondered if she should be sad for U'shi, but she couldn't feel anything for the woman who had made things so difficult for her. She hadn't wished such an end on her or her child, but she was more curious about what Mu-Phi knew of her future.

'What are you doing?' Lis asked.

'Preparing for your day,' Mu-Phi said, looking up from the desk with a confused expression.

'The healer is yet to come.'

'He will come soon. Although I know you haven't slept for days, you appear to be what you were.'

Lis nodded. Could one dream have turned her around so completely?

26

Lis was excited to see the healer enter the room, although his face was dark before he even focused on her. She wondered if she looked as bad as she had felt when she first woke, if the feeling of strength and control was just an illusion left over from the dream.

The high priestess following him in caused her heart to race, and she clutched her hands in her lap as they entered.

'Your Highness,' the healer said, bowing low before her. 'It is nice to see you are rested.'

She smiled her thanks, but she couldn't maintain it. Her eyes flickered to the woman behind him.

'She wishes to examine you herself,' he said, his voice tight.

Lis nodded once, to show her understanding. 'But you will examine me first,' she said. She had meant it as a question, yet it sounded more like a directive, and he smiled as he bowed again. He knelt before her at the table and placed a small cushion down. She wondered for a moment where it had come from, somewhere secret in his robes perhaps. She wondered what else he may have hidden away.

She tried to focus on his face, old and lined and kind. His narrow, pointed beard was white and, although it looked soft, she doubted it was. As tempted as she was to run her fingers through it, she maintained her stillness.

'Perfect,' he whispered. 'Did you go to the baths?' he asked, looking up at her.

She nodded and smiled. It had actually been quite calming once she had allowed herself to relax, and Mu-Phi had not left her side.

'You may return to your studies,' he said kindly, and she nodded her thanks.

'You are sure?' the high priestess asked. He scowled as he stood back and gestured to the patient.

She nodded her thanks and stepped forward. Lis's arm still rested on the cushion, but the high priestess placed her hand on her forehead. She closed her eyes and took a deep breath. Lis wondered just what this woman could sense in her. She could almost feel the buzz of magic as she did around the prince. Almost, but she wasn't certain. How many in the Empire had some magic they could explain as something else?

The woman smiled, and then it slipped from her face. Her brow drew together and although her eyes remained closed, Lis could feel them searching her. She held tight to her own magic, pulling it deep inside and imagining a wall between herself and the priestess.

The woman pulled her hand back with a frustrated sigh.

'Do you think her unwell?' the healer asked.

She shook her head and stepped back. 'She is not what I thought,' she said softly, but the frustration and anger was deep in her voice. The healer seemed to relax more at her words, and he nodded.

'You may do as you need,' the healer said with a bow. 'I must report to the empress. She is keen to visit with you and check upon you herself.'

'I would not want to be of trouble to the empress.'

'You are no trouble. You are her charge to train,' he said with a friendly smile, which Lis returned easily.

'I must pray,' the high priestess said, walking slowly from the room.

The old healer shook his head. 'They do as they like,' he said. 'She should follow protocol, but she sees herself above the rest of us—even the royal family.'

Lis stared at him, surprised by his honesty.

'She must bow and show respect,' he said. 'You must demand it,' he added more gently.

Lis didn't think she could take the priestess to task. The healer bowed and then backed out of the room. 'Thank you,' she called after him, and he paused in the doorway.

'There is no need for thanks. I live to serve,' he said before the door closed behind him.

Two very different people, Lis thought. She had a memory of her father being somewhat surprised that the high priestess had been involved in the Choosing, and she wondered if he had experienced anything with them during the magic war. She wouldn't be able to ask him now, but she wondered if the prince would be able, or willing, to answer her questions. Although she wasn't sure how she could phrase something like that so clearly.

Lis was sitting at the desk reading a text about the magic war when there was a gentle knock. The door opened, and the empress entered. Lis stood quickly from her place behind the desk and knelt before her. Tutor Na was a nice surprise following her in.

'You appear much better,' the empress said, looking Lis over and offering her a hand to stand.

'Thank you, Your Highness. It appears all I needed was rest.' Lis bowed again and noticed Mu-Phi watching her from the corner of the room. 'May I offer you tea?' she asked.

'We are here to serve you,' the empress said, then waited.

'Sit, please,' the tutor said, indicating the desk. Lis sat back down and closed the book she had been reading.

'What is it you study?' the empress asked.

'More on the magic war,' Lis said, placing the book back on the pile before her. 'I was curious about the role the priestesses played.'

'I do not know that they played any role,' the empress said

softly, still standing before Lis, and Lis wondered if she would stand and teach beside the tutor. 'They train far from the main islands of the Empire,' she continued, moving over and sitting at the table. Mu-Phi sat a cup of hot tea before her, and she nodded thanks. 'It was thought that there was magic there, but it was at the end of the war. There was little evidence other than the hunters, but they could not find the magic makers. It was not long after that the hunters declared they could no longer detect magic.'

'And so, the war ended.'

'Yes,' the empress said.

'But does that mean magic is gone?' Lis asked.

Tutor Na opened her mouth as though to chastise her, but the empress held up her hand.

'Living in this place, you have heard things,' the empress said, 'about the former crown prince, perhaps.'

Lis nodded.

'Remi feels strongly that there is still magic in the Empire, but he cannot produce it.'

'He is a hunter,' Lis said.

'Of great skill. And his brother's death touched him.' The empress looked away, and Lis could see the pain on her face. She understood that to a degree, thinking of her own mother. But to lose a child appeared out of balance, Lis thought.

'He worries for me,' Lis said softly.

'He does.' The empress sighed. 'But it is without reason, and it goes against so many traditions.'

'If he is the hunter you feel him to be, could it be that he senses something? And after what happened to U'shi…'

The empress's face hardened. 'The girl was silly, clearly a poor choice for the position,' she said, more to herself than to Lis. 'Her actions were not due to any magic, only lust.' She almost spat out the last word.

'Her de…' Lis stopped herself. The empress may not know of what had happened, and Lis didn't want to be the one to tell her.

She understood the connection the empress had to U'shi; she had trained the girl for so long. Lis wondered, suddenly, if she would ever feel such a connection to the empress. 'What are we to learn today?' she asked Tutor Na, trying to turn the conversation back to where they would all like to be focused.

'There is much that you already know,' the empress said, her voice sad and low, and Lis regretted mentioning U'shi at all. 'We have not worked with you as we should. We have not taken your former training and learning into account. You are not a child of eight to be taught to read.'

Lis opened her mouth in surprise, and the empress nodded slowly as she looked at the untouched cup before her.

'I have been too hard on you, and not because of what you are or who you are, but due to my own failings.'

Lis stood quickly from her desk and dropped to her knees before the empress.

'I am right,' the empress said softly, touching Lis's shoulder. Lis looked up when she did. 'It was my own grief and fear that led me to do as I did. It is not an excuse I should search for, but an apology.'

'No,' Lis breathed. 'You are Empress of the Rei-Een Empire. I am only a girl.'

'You are the empress to be, chosen by the future emperor to work at his side. It is my place as his mother to ensure that you are all you need to be. You already know how to read and write, you know the great families of the Empire—you are from a great family of the Empire.'

'I don't know that my father would still think that.'

'He was a good man. He still is. I would entrust my husband to no other during the war, and I trust my son with no other for his rule.'

Lis felt heat rise to her cheeks under the praise from the empress. What had occurred for her to change her mind so?

'Do you know the history of the hidden princesses?'

'A little,' Lis said, shaking her head.

'Once, the hidden princess was one of many. Instead of a Choosing at the age of eight, the eligible girls were all hidden away and trained. They were covered, as the prince covered you with the veil, so that they would be indistinguishable.'

Lis sat back on the floor before the empress, although she had heard something similar from Wei-Song.

The empress gulped and took a breath before continuing. 'They were all trained, all ready and perfect in their own way. Until they weren't.'

Lis bit down on her lip so as not to interrupt with the questions flooding through her.

'They were tested. In their knowledge, in their manners, in their understanding of the world. The best were then presented to the crown prince. Usually only two or three made it to that point, and he would select his favourite, usually based on how beautiful she was. He may have asked some questions, tested her himself in some way, and then a single hidden princess became the crown princess.'

'One,' Lis said. 'What happened to the others?'

'Put to death,' the empress said, and Lis covered her mouth. 'There was nothing else that could be done. For they would know what an empress knows, secrets and the like, and they may be a threat to the empress in the future. Of course, the tradition had to change, for a generation of girls lost was too much for the Empire to bear. And the noble families would no longer send their daughters. They lied about birth years and hid girls away.'

Lis nodded.

'What if the eldest child of an emperor is a girl?' she asked, unsure why she needed to know.

'It hasn't happened.'

Lis opened her mouth to ask another question, but she paused.

'Ask it,' the empress said.

'Has there been magic in the royal family?'

'Maybe long before it was the danger it became.'

'Hunters?'

'Remi is the first,' she said, standing.

Lis bowed again before her.

'I think you need something nicer to wear,' the empress said, her voice soft. She beckoned to the maid, who paused before stepping forward.

'The crown prince has ordered her to never leave my side,' Lis said.

The empress smiled and shook her head. 'Tutor Na will watch over you as you study; the girl will accompany me to select what you need.'

Lis nodded again, more to Mu-Phi than the empress.

They left the room, and Lis sat back, her mind racing at what she had been told of the hidden princesses. Had the prince known of this history when he suggested she wear the veil?

'Come,' Tutor Na said, indicating the desk.

Lis climbed to her feet and sat back at her desk.

27

There had to be some indication as to how the man had broken into the prison. The soldiers by the front gate were oblivious, and Remi was tempted to make them pay for the man's crimes. One of the guards had been killed, and Remi had decided he must have had something to do with it.

'I want to examine their bodies,' he told the hunter as they met inside the prison doors.

'They are both in the cell.' Hui Te-Sze bowed and led the way. The closer they got, the more Remi could feel the magic. It was like it surrounded him, although the cell was clearly the point of attack. He wondered if the man had killed the guard here in front of U'shi and how she might have reacted.

The burn marks on her arm were clear before he even made it inside the cell. Her eyes showed signs of burns as they stared unseeing at the ceiling. Neither body had been covered up. Remi had seen death before, but it saddened him here.

He had hated the woman for what she had done, and he was sure the affair with the tutor had started long before his brother's death. It was part of the reason he wanted to keep Lis close. They were too isolated in the hidden princess's palace. Too distanced from the rest of the Empire and the ways of the world. She needed to be around people. Remi shook his head and refocused on the woman before him. She would have been Empress if his brother had not died.

He squatted down beside her and held a hand over her head. He could feel the heat radiating from her still. The material of her gown, although simple and white, had melted to the flesh where a clear hand print was visible. He held his own hand over it to find it was similar in size. The magic still buzzed around it, thick and heavy and hot.

'Could it be that we can't sense them when they aren't using their magic?' he mused aloud.

'It may be the case,' Hui Te-Sze said. 'I can feel it here, so much of it, and I felt it when he unleashed it. I came running, but he was gone by the time I reached the cell.'

'How far away were you?'

Te-Sze pointed back down the corridor. 'In the office at the end,' he said. 'It came in a thick wave, but there was no sign and no trail when I arrived.'

Remi sighed. 'How did he get in?'

The hunter motioned to him, and they tracked back a couple of cells. He opened the door and led the prince inside. 'There is something here,' he said.

Remi could feel the magic, faint but present, and he wondered if the man had used it to enter the building a different way. He stepped away from the other hunter and pressed his hand into the wall. It was solid as he worked his way around. He stopped beneath a narrow window with two bars running across it, and he felt it strange that no other cell within the prison had a window. Remi stretched but couldn't quite reach it.

'Has this always been here?' he asked.

'I don't know.' Te-Sze shrugged. 'It has been too long since I frequented this place.'

'Lend me a knee,' Remi said.

The man knelt before him, one leg out so the prince could use him as a step. When he reached up this time, his hand closed only just around one of the bars before it disappeared in his hand and his knuckles scraped against the wall.

He jumped back down, looking at the damage to his hand. 'An illusion.'

'But is it a way in?'

Remi shook his head. 'Or a diversion.'

The hunter moved ahead of the prince out of the cell and called to the nearest guard. 'Search every room, every inch of every cell wall, and find where this man entered.'

The man bowed and disappeared. Remi turned back to the doorway as the window disappeared. Why were they back and what did they want?

'What do you want to do?' Te-Sze asked.

Where had they come from and why? Was this all to do with Lis, or was there another reason they were here?

'Sire?'

'There must be something,' he whispered, heading back towards the bodies in the other cell. He stood over the former hidden princess and wondered how his mother would take this news. Although it appeared that she was finally starting to consider Lis seriously, he was curious whether they treated all hidden princesses so badly.

'I need another hunter,' he said without looking up.

'If they are back, we are going to need a lot more.'

Remi nodded and wondered how he was going to explain this to his father. Even with what had happened to Ta-Sho, the emperor would not accept that they were back in the Empire or that they were such a threat. The man had seen the war, in some way. Although when Remi thought about it, he had heard more stories of General Long than his father.

'You wonder what the emperor will do,' Te-Sze said, and Remi nodded without turning.

'I'm not sure he will give us what we need to fight this.'

'Where do we start?'

'I want a hunter by the princess at all times,' Remi said. He looked up at the man's raised eyebrow before he looked down again. 'I mean another.'

'Sire,' the man said with a bow. 'I would be honoured to watch your bride.'

'First, send for as many hunters as you can find. We need to search this island completely. I need to find out what they want and what the former hidden princess might have been to them.'

'She had already been sentenced to death,' the hunter said.

'And yet she was to live until the child was born. Could she have let them into the bath house? She was so adamant that she hadn't. She was focused on her lover and had not considered the safety of the princess. But could it have been more? Could she have really wanted her harmed?'

'I shall do as you ask, and we can discover them together,' Te-Sze said, bowing low.

'Thank you,' Remi said with a sigh, placing his hand on the hunter's shoulder. 'I want to check on the princess for myself.'

The man couldn't hide his grin as he bowed again and left the prince still looking over the dead before him.

Remi entered the room without knocking and then stopped. He looked at his princess at her desk, her head bent over her reading. Old Tutor Jichun sat at the table, another parchment in his hands, his mother opposite, and Mu-Phi working away in the corner. Then there was a knock at the door behind him.

They all looked up at him as the door opened, and a trail of maids entered with trays of food. 'I thought we were to limit the number of people entering this room,' he said, his voice gruffer than he intended. When he glanced towards Lis, she dropped what she was reading and stood to bow to him.

His mother gave him a frustrated look, but she gestured to the table as the girls set the food down and disappeared. The empress then motioned Lis forward, and she stood beside the table. She was not wearing the usual grey the hidden princess had been in before, but a flowing silk gown in vibrant blues. He raked his eyes over her before his mother coughed and he realised what he'd done.

'Will you join us for lunch, Your Highness?' Lis asked. He looked back to her face and she smiled, although she didn't look comfortable. He wondered if she appreciated having so many here.

Despite her uncertainty, he nodded. The tutor stood from the table and indicated his space. He sat opposite his mother as Lis sat beside her. They remained silent for a moment.

'What have you been learning today?' he asked across the table.

'Trade histories with other nations,' she said, looking at the food in her bowl rather than at him. He realised that she hadn't yet picked up her chopsticks.

He nodded once to show he had heard. 'Do not let me keep you from your food.'

She shook her head and slowly poked at the bowl. His mother surprised him with a sigh.

'Should I bring the healer back? You do not eat enough,' she said.

Lis turned a friendly smile on her and indicated the empress's bowl. 'You should eat more yourself.'

His mother laughed, and Remi stared openly. When had he last heard her laugh? She then picked up some meat and pushed it into her mouth. Lis smiled and did the same, and he wondered what might have happened in the last day for such change to occur. Despite his intent, he had not returned to Lis after checking U'shi's body, and he hadn't taken his breakfast with her as he usually did. He had missed her, and he wondered if she had missed him or if she had been given the chance. Perhaps she spent her time with his mother now.

'I may need to go away,' he said.

Both women looked at him with the same look of disappointment at the same time, but it was his mother who spoke.

'You are not what you were,' she said before looking back to her bowl. 'You have responsibilities here.'

'There is a need.'

'No,' she said more forcefully. 'You will send another to do what you think must be done.'

'Is that what father would do?'

She nodded. 'It is, and you could do well by spending some time with him.'

Remi tried not to sigh. His father wouldn't see him, for he knew what Remi wanted and he wouldn't admit the truth. Would Remi be able to do as he needed to once he was Emperor, or would the world be different?

'Eat,' Lis said kindly. 'Please.'

He smiled, and the small group continued in silence. When they finished and the table was cleared, the tutor handed Lis another book.

'You may find this interesting,' he said, holding it out with respect, with two hands and bowing.

She smiled as she took it, then nodded as she read the cover before turning to the first pages. 'How far away are the Kingdoms of Engla by boat?' she asked.

'It depends on the boat,' Remi answered as the tutor opened his mouth. 'Why? Would you like to visit?'

Lis held up the book. 'Although I look at maps and I know where things are placed, I can't always judge the distances. If I have an idea by boat, such as how long it took us to reach the Palace Isle from my former home, I have a better sense of the world.'

He nodded once, noting that she had stated her island was no longer her home. She did it all while keeping her voice steady, but he wondered if it was an act.

'Ten days,' the tutor answered her previous question, 'by larger ship.'

Lis's eyes widened. 'So far. How did we know they were there to trade with?'

'There are some great stories of early explorers,' Remi said, and her face lit up.

'Tales,' his mother said. 'I suggest we stick to fact for now.'

Lis smiled and nodded low to the empress before her eyes flicked back to Remi's. He gave her a subtle nod. What would it hurt if he shared his books with her?

Lis felt actual joy at the idea of learning something new and for pleasure. She was sure the prince would bring her the book he spoke of as soon as he was able, although he didn't look as comfortable in her room as he had previously. She wondered if it was the number of people.

The empress took her arm with ease and guided her back to her desk.

'I would like to remain with you today,' she said softly in her ear, and Lis nodded before she let go.

She was enjoying the woman's company. Now that she was trying harder, she was kinder and, Lis realised, a nice woman. They could have been friends in another life, and she found a similarity in the empress to her mother. She continued to smile despite the heavy feeling now pushing on her chest. When she glanced up, the prince paused as though he could see her pain.

'You do not approve of my going,' he said to his mother, drawing her attention from the book Lis wanted to pick up. 'There have been some events,' he said slowly, 'that need my attention.'

'There are other hunters,' the empress said, picking up one of the books before Lis. 'I thought you may be of use to the princess.'

The prince actually looked a little lost for a moment, and Lis wondered if he would prefer not to be involved, for she had thought he might be.

'You know your history; you can support what she learns from the tutors.'

'I thought you didn't want me involved,' he stammered, a heat rising to his face. Lis wondered if it was due to his not wanting to help or the fact that he could. She looked down at the book the empress had indicated before her. She wasn't sure she wanted to know the answer. It didn't matter what either of them thought of the other, after all; she would be his wife no matter. But there was something she hadn't wanted to admit to herself.

She had grown to like these people. The banter with Mu-Phi, and the crown prince of a morning—it was comfortable. She had enjoyed the empress's company during the day, and she had learnt a lot from her in such a short time. Wondering if it would continue, she reached towards her hand and then stopped. No matter the friendship forming, she was just a girl playing princess until her training was finished. This was the empress of the nation, not her mother.

But as her hand hovered near the empress's, she felt something, like the faintest feeling of magic she had gotten from the prince. She wondered if this woman was something more. When she looked up, the empress seemed a little annoyed, and Lis pulled her hands into her lap. 'I'm sorry,' she murmured.

'It is not you,' the empress said quickly. 'You work hard. I worry about him.' She staggered a little, and Lis was quick to jump to her feet and offer the empress the seat. 'I feel a little tired,' she said, her hand at her temple.

'I don't think you are well,' Lis said quickly, indicating for the maid to come forward with water.

The empress took it too eagerly and then nodded slowly.

'I won't go,' the prince said, 'if it makes you unwell.'

She smiled up at him then. 'I don't want you to go, but that is not what makes me unwell.'

'I think we should call the healer,' Lis said to the tutor, motioning towards the door. As she did, it opened without a knock and the high priestess entered.

'Does it take so many to teach?' she asked, something sharp in her voice.

Lis tried not to show her displeasure at the woman's presence.

'Why are you here?' the prince asked with far less protocol.

'I am part of the teaching program for the hidden princess,' she announced. 'Are you?'

He nodded and turned back to his mother. 'Now is not the time for a visit.'

'Your Highness,' she said, bowing before the empress. 'Is it your head again?'

'You do need a healer,' Lis said. And the empress surprised her by reaching out and taking her hand.

'She only needs rest,' the priestess said. 'She has these headaches from time to time.'

'I agree with the princess,' the prince said firmly.

'Let me escort you to your rooms, Your Highness. You can rest, and then if you require the healer, I can send for him.'

The empress nodded and allowed the priestess to guide her from the room. Lis watched her go, an uncertainty settling in her chest. She had come to like the woman, and she didn't like the idea of her unwell. But there was something else, something around her that wasn't quite magic, but it wasn't quite right.

'What is it?' the prince asked gently beside her.

She looked up at him with a questioning expression.

'You look concerned.'

'I am concerned for the empress,' she said, trying to smile, 'I worry that…' She trailed off, unsure what else to say.

'What do you worry about?' he asked.

Lis shook her head and turned back to the tutor, who looked between the two of them and then bowed. 'I shall leave you with your reading, Your Highness. I shall return tomorrow.'

She bowed towards him, and Mu-Phi saw him from the room. Lis sat with a sigh at the desk before she remembered herself and the prince, and then she made to stand again. He surprised her by resting a hand on her shoulder. She stayed as she was.

'Will you go away?' she asked, unsure what she wanted him to say.

'Maybe mother is correct; maybe others should go.'

'Did you find something?'

The prince actually looked uncomfortable. 'You didn't tell me what has you worried.'

'You have me worried now,' she said without thinking. 'I am sorry, Your Highness. I have felt the pressure of a full day of study.'

'I shall let you rest,' he said.

'Stay,' she said quickly. 'I would like to know what has happened that might send you away. Although,' she added, looking back to the book before her on the table, 'I should not ask.'

'You tell me why you worry, and I shall share my findings.'

She nodded once. 'I worry that the high priestess is too close to your mother, and that she would not allow me to call the healer.'

'The priestesses have always done things their own way, although I understand that they have not behaved as they should with you. I shall send for the healer to attend her.'

'Thank you,' Lis said, bowing to the prince.

He looked briefly at Mu-Phi and then turned back to Lis. He stood almost over her as she sat at the desk, but she didn't feel threatened. He squatted down beside her, and she blinked away her surprise. 'U'shi is dead,' he said very softly, and Lis noticed Mu-Phi lifted her head from her tasks trying to listen. Although Lis wondered if the girl already knew all that the prince did.

'I heard the guard tell you earlier. You thought there was magic involved.' Lis waited, but when he said nothing, she asked, 'Did you find the killer?'

He shook his head and stepped away, turning his back to her. 'I can't sense them like I once did.'

'Are you sure it was magic?'

He nodded. 'A fire bearer. She was burnt from the inside.'

Lis covered her mouth at the idea.

'I should not have told you,' he said, stepping forward.

'I have no one to tell.'

'That is not what I mean.'

Lis had started to relax into this life, and she shouldn't have. There were still those with magic. Whether they wanted to help her or not, she wasn't sure, and she didn't know if there was more than one group of them. She was also kept from so much. Just as she had always been. Her father had not told her the whole truth of his time as a general. The man she had started to think of as a friend told the maid more than he told her. She was only a hidden princess, and she had to remember her station. For she had none until the training was finished.

No one would mourn U'shi; she was just a maid. Although she was sure the empress felt her loss, maybe more for the lost years of training rather than the woman herself. Lis looked back to the table, thinking of the friendly lunch they had shared, but they weren't friends and they were yet to be family.

'Mu-Phi,' she called, trying to keep her voice level although she felt like she was unravelling. 'Tea please.'

The girl looked to the prince before she nodded. It only seemed like yesterday that Lis could have made her own, serving her father at the same time. Her stomach roiled. She was trapped and must be careful, she had to remind herself. She no longer had a home.

'What is it? Are you unwell?' the prince asked.

Lis shook her head.

'I should not have told you such things.'

'No,' she murmured. 'I am not the one to tell.'

She could hear the sadness in her own voice, and she focused on the cup that was placed before her without picking it up.

'That is not what I meant,' the prince said, his voice harsh. It carried the same tone as when she had told him others had said that he cared for her and he had asked her who would make such claims. The words cemented for her what she knew to be true. One good day could not change what she was, where she was or the life that was planned for her.

She looked up at his expectant face, surprised that he wasn't scowling.

'You wish to find those who have done this,' she said softly, taking a sip of the tea to help smooth out her voice. 'I have to study.'

He opened his mouth and closed it again, then marched over and sat at the table. He waved Mu-Phi over, and she placed tea before him. Lis looked at him with open surprise. Was he to settle here?

'What has changed?' he asked.

'Excuse me?'

'You have shut down.'

'Shut down?' She could feel the anger building in her chest. Did he have no idea what her life was?

'Yes. Do you fear the magic so much?'

She shook her head.

'Talk to me,' he demanded.

Lis looked to the maid and then back to him. 'No,' she said, her voice carrying the same edge as his own. 'It is not my place.'

'Why, because I tell you something and then tell you no more?'

She shook her head and turned back to the book. What did he want from her? 'It is as though you have no understanding of the world,' she said in frustration.

'Oh,' he said, an amused smiled playing at his lips.

'Do you think your brother visited with U'shi as you do me?'

The hurt at the memory of his brother was clear on his face, and she wondered if he would ever tell her the truth about what had happened to him. Mu-Phi made a strange noise from her corner, but Lis knew she would back the prince.

'I am no one,' Lis continued as he watched her. 'I am a country girl with no home and no place in the world, unless I manage to finish my training.'

'And then you shall be my wife, the crown princess and future Empress of the Rei-Een Empire.'

She bowed her head to him. 'If I survive.'

'Is this just surviving?' he asked, standing from the table.

'You have no idea,' she murmured. Why had she told him these things? She wanted so desperately to disappear, but there was nowhere to go. She wiped quickly at the tear that betrayed her strength.

He was kneeling before her then, his hands on her knees, and she gaped at him.

'Your Highness,' she cried.

'I have touched your feet,' he said with a smile. 'You are more to me than a country girl, and you have a home.'

She shook her head. She had nothing. And if he knew what she truly was, she would follow U'shi to the gods. She had a strange thought; if she were to die too, would they give up on the hidden princess tradition and consider an alternative? Perhaps he could choose his own wife from those he knew. Again, Lis's eyes lifted to the woman in the corner.

She took a steadying breath. She was acting like a girl, and he was right—she was to be the crown princess. She lifted his hands from her legs and smiled. 'Would you have me behave as U'shi did?' she asked.

He shook his head and as he stood, she turned back to the desk. 'I have so much to learn,' she said, picking up the book.

'I shall send the books I told you of.'

She nodded her thanks without turning back to him. She was exhausted, and yet there was much occurring within the palace she would like a better understanding of.

He bowed low to her and then left the room. She didn't look up, although she wasn't concentrating on the words before her. Would she ever be what they needed her to be? For the past day, she had felt as though she could, as though it was an even playing field, as though they listened to her and respected who she was. Now she doubted that again.

A guard appeared in the doorway, and Lis looked up as the

maid nodded. Mu-Phi didn't ask permission, only bowed and followed the man from the room. After so many had been present for so long, the room felt too large and empty. But it was a nice change.

Lis sighed and rolled her neck. She looked over the books on the desk before her and knew she had a good general understanding of the Empire. She needed to learn the details. Whether she wanted this or not, it was what her life was. She stood quickly and moved to Mu-Phi's corner of the room, then refilled her cup. She carried the kettle to the burner at the table and blew life into the coals. She glanced only briefly at the door, but no one rushed in at the use of her magic.

She settled the kettle and the cup, then returned to her desk to gather the yet unread books on trade. She moved back to the table, sipped at her tea and read. As she finished each book, she put it down and picked up another. Some were easier than others, but as she submerged herself in the pages, she soon found the subject interested her.

There were many things they no longer traded for, and Lis wondered if the magic had been somehow involved in that change. Or at least the Empire's fear of it. It was why they grew the crops they did on Fifth, she was sure.

The lights were starting to fade when the maid returned and, as she opened the door, Lis felt a surge of magic follow her in.

28

'You have made yourself comfortable,' Mu-Phi said with a smile as she entered and then stopped, staring directly as Lis. She opened her mouth to ask something, then dropped suddenly to her knees, her eyes rolling back in her head. As she fell to the floor, Lis touched her hands together and disappeared.

The man standing in the doorway wore dark dishevelled clothes, and his face was covered by a black cloth. Lis held her breath. Another man followed, and she could feel the magic radiating around them. She only hoped the prince could also feel it and was not far behind.

The two men looked around the room before moving in opposite directions. One almost touched Lis as he walked past the table and towards the little cooking area the maid used. The other went towards her bed and behind the screen. She looked towards the door, wondering if she could make it out before one of them realised she was there.

She allowed a little magic to build in her hand, and neither of them turned. While hidden she could remain safe, as she was before, and even those with magic did not appear to sense her. The two men met again in the middle of the room and looked at each other silently as the maid groaned on the floor. Lis wanted to check on her, but she remained frozen to the spot.

Where is the prince? What will they do if they find me?

Time seemed to stretch on forever with them looking around the room. When they finally left, Lis heard a shout and a scuffle and a thump in the hallway. She wanted to take the chance to run, but Mu-Phi groaned again, so she put her hands together and knelt down beside her. A guard appeared in the doorway and disappeared again.

'Stay still,' she whispered, pulling a cushion from beneath the table and putting it under her head.

'What happened?'

Lis shook her head. She felt a surge of magic from beyond the doorway, then heard the fizzle as the magic was extinguished. She only just stopped herself from disappearing as she focused on Mu-Phi watching her and trying to get up. Lis shook her head. She turned back to the table and poured a cup of tea, the water still hot. Then she knelt down over the maid and helped her sit up enough to sip it.

Where, in the name of all the gods, was the crown prince?

The guard reappeared at the doorway and rushed forward. He knelt down beside Mu-Phi and looked over Lis.

'I'm ok,' Mu-Phi murmured and tried to sit up, but put a hand to her head instead.

'Are you hurt, Your Highness?' the guard asked.

'No. I hid as they came in, and they couldn't find me.'

'Where?' Mu-Phi asked, her hand over her eyes.

'By the bed,' Lis said without thinking or taking her eyes from the girl.

'Show me,' the guard said, standing.

Lis chewed her lip and stood. She should have thought this through. She couldn't tell the man that she had hid right where she'd been sitting at the table. She walked back towards the bed and the screen. There was a dark corner on the other side where she kept her clothes and a chamber pot. 'There,' she lied, pointing to it.

He nodded once, but his brow was furrowed.

Does he know I lied? Could he know what I am? 'Did you get them?'

'One,' he said, moving back to the maid. 'The other was killed.'

'What will happen to him?'

'Why?' he asked, his voice too sharp, and Lis took a step back from him.

'What happened?' the prince asked, his voice high and strained as he raced through the door. Then he stopped, taking in Lis and Mu-Phi, and he gave the guard a questioning look.

'We are all well,' the maid said from her position on the floor.

'You don't appear to be,' the prince said, squatting down beside her. 'Are you hurt?'

'She was hit on the head. I think we need the healer,' Lis said quickly, trying not to look at the guard who was still watching her too closely. Was this man another hunter with different senses from the prince?

'You look tired,' he said carefully.

'It is late,' she said, looking back at him, 'and I have read so much today. And then two men appeared in my room and hit my maid on the head, and I don't know what they would have done if they had found me.' She tried to sound firm, but the nervousness in her own words was clear.

The prince stood slowly and walked towards her. 'Go for a healer,' he said to the other man, then fixed him with a long stare when he didn't move. 'Do you want to explain it to her father?'

The man shook his head and left. Lis sighed with the relief. She was ready to sit down, but she really wanted to ensure Mu-Phi was safe first.

'Help me get her into bed,' she said, moving back to the maid. He followed silently.

They carefully eased Mu-Phi to her feet and then guided her to her bed. They laid her down, and the prince removed her shoes before Lis covered her. He sat carefully on the edge of the narrow bed.

'I just need sleep,' Mu-Phi murmured.

'No,' Lis said too loudly. 'Not after such a hit to the head. you need to stay awake until the healer comes.'

The prince looked up at her. 'You have seen this before?'

Lis nodded once. 'My sister fell when we were children. My mother knew that after such an injury it was not safe to go to sleep, because she might not wake up. She had a cousin when they were children who had done just that.'

The prince nodded in return. 'I have seen the same,' he said, shaking the maid by the shoulder. 'Listen to your princess,' he said. 'Stay with us, talk with us.'

'Who were they?'

He clenched his fist. Lis could see the anger in the way he held himself, but he maintained his calm façade. For Mu-Phi, she guessed, to help keep her calm. Lis wasn't calm. Her heart pounded too fast, and she still held magic tight in her fingertips, ready to use. Although she didn't know how she could use it to defend herself from such a group. She tried to relax and allow it to dissipate back into her. *Is that why the guard was so interested in me? Could he sense the magic?*

'He is a hunter,' she said softly.

'Yes,' the prince said, looking up at her.

'Where were you?' She didn't want it to sound accusatory, but it did. It wasn't his job to protect her, after all. There was a whole dedicated group of soldiers. She opened her mouth to apologise, then bit her lip as he put his hand up.

'I should have been closer,' he said. 'I had some work to do that had taken me across the island.'

'I am sorry,' she admitted. 'It is not your place to be here at all times. I understand you have much to do.' She bowed before him.

'I would rather know that you are safe. Mu-Phi, tell me what you remember.'

The maid had started to drift again, and she blinked wearily at him. 'I was doing as you asked when I had a strange feeling, so I returned to the princess and she was working at the table.'

The prince looked across to the table.

'She wore a strange expression,' the maid said, 'and then the world went dark.'

'A strange expression?' they both asked at the same time. The prince smiled; Lis didn't.

'How did you make it from the table to your hiding spot so quickly?' the guard asked behind her, and she turned to see him standing beside a healer.

'She has been hit quite hard,' Lis said to the healer instead, indicating the patient. The healer stepped forward as the prince stood, looking again at the table.

'Where did you hide?' he asked.

She pointed past her own bed. 'They were distracted.'

'How long were they here?'

'Too long,' she said without thinking, the fear still real in her chest, the bitter taste apparent at the back of her throat.

The healer turned and looked at her. 'I think you should sit down and I shall examine you next, Your Highness.'

She shook her head. 'I was not hurt,' she said hurriedly.

'You have had a shock. Sit, drink tea and I shall attend you.'

The healer was young and not one she had met before, but she appreciated his direct nature.

'She wants to know where they were taken,' the hunter guard said.

'I want to know how they got in,' Lis said, trying to sound stronger than she felt. She wanted to lie down and sleep it all away. She reached for the pot and poured herself tea. It was a little bitter, steeped too long, and she pulled a face.

'Perhaps water would be better,' the healer said from his work over the maid. Then he returned to talking to her in a soft voice, working through a series of questions.

'Change the water,' the prince said to the guard, and he raised an eyebrow. 'Or go to my room and bring the already hot water.'

The guard bowed and left.

'He does not trust me,' Lis said, sipping automatically at the tea again before putting the cup down.

The prince sat opposite her at the table and looked over the books covering its surface. 'What have you been reading?'

'Why will no one tell me about these men? They came into my room,' she said too loudly, the shaking audible in her voice. 'They wanted something. Was it me?'

'I don't know,' the prince said honestly. He reached across the table for her hand, but she pulled it out of his reach.

'How did they get in? How did they make it here? What if they had found me?'

'But they didn't,' the hunter said again as he lifted one kettle and replaced it with another.

'Cups?' the prince asked.

Again, the man looked at him as though he had asked him to do something he shouldn't have. Then he sighed and moved to the small area where Mu-Phi prepared the food.

'What if they had killed Mu-Phi?'

'She will be fine. I will send herbs for her to have in the morning, and she will rest now. I see no danger, but I will return to check the damage. They did not break the skin. She will be very sore for some days and will need to remain in bed.'

'Thank you,' Lis said, making to stand.

'Now it is your turn,' he said, kneeling before her.

She held out her wrist to him. He closed his eyes as he placed his fingers on her skin, then nodded slowly. 'You need some rest yourself. Drink,' he coaxed as the prince sat a cup of water before her. 'I shall send some calming tea for you tomorrow, and we shall talk more when I check on the girl.'

Lis nodded slowly. He bowed low and then left.

'You didn't answer my question,' she said, turning back to the prince.

'I will increase the guard.' He looked at the man still watching

Lis too closely.

'I'm not safe here,' she said. There was nowhere for her. Wei-Song flashed through her mind, and Lis wondered whether she would be safe with her, and what she could learn there.

'Of course you are safe.'

She was exhausted, and yet getting into her bed and being left alone was the last thing she wanted. She looked back to the maid.

'I will stay,' the hunter said, and Lis felt a shiver cross her.

'He will stay outside the door.'

'I will leave it open so that we might hear you if you call,' he said, somewhat kindly, but there was something else there. 'You did not call for help,' he said.

'And give myself away? I might not have been here when you finally arrived,' she said.

He huffed, bowed stiffly and went to the door. 'I want five men in the corridor,' he said sharply to the guard outside.

'He doesn't like me,' she murmured. 'Will they be able to stop them?' Lis looked to the window. There were more ways to enter this room than the door.

'You have not told me why you want to know what happened to them,' the prince coaxed.

'I want to be sure they won't return. I want to know where they came from, why they were here, what they wanted.'

The prince opened his mouth and then closed it, his brow furrowing as he chewed on his lip.

Lis shook her head. 'I understand that I am not worthy of this position.' She held up her hand as he went to speak. 'I know what I am,' she said more clearly. 'I want a better understanding of the world around me. You said magic was gone, and yet it is everywhere, seeping into every part of my life. Everyone is becoming suspicious of everyone else, and the war will begin again.'

'My father won't allow it,' the prince said.

'He may not have the choice. I want a guard in the room,' Lis surprised herself by saying.

'There is one,' he said, nodding towards the sleeping maid.

'And she is very loyal to you, but not much use in protecting me,' she said. Her words were bitter and she regretted them in a way, for she liked the girl.

'I will replace her with another.'

'You will leave her where she is,' Lis said, 'and send another.'

'Tomorrow,' he said.

'Then the hunter watches from inside.'

Remi looked back at the door. 'That is what you want?'

'I will not sleep; he might as well watch over Mu-Phi with me.'

'You would rather him than me?'

'I would have thought you too busy,' she said. 'Do you not have someone to interrogate, to determine their plan? Or were they both killed on the spot?'

He looked at her closely. 'How do you know?'

'I heard one die,' she said more quietly.

'This is not what I want for you,' he said, kneeling before her. 'You have come for the greatest opportunity, to learn so much, and yet you have been so unhappy here.'

'How can I be unhappy when I have been given so much?' Lis said, her voice thick with sarcasm.

Remi watched over her as she slept. It was nearly dawn before she had finally relented and gotten into bed, and the hunter had opened the door to find him standing there. He wasn't leaving her alone again, yet she had been right. He had so much to do.

After nodding for the hunter to go, he entered the silent room where Mu-Phi still slept. He sat gently on the edge of Lis's bed. She murmured and turned, and he wondered if she hadn't had the chance to sleep yet. She didn't want him watching over her. Not as he had.

Her hair had fallen across her face. He brushed it back, knowing what his mother would say. But there was something about watching her sleep, and although he should not have such joys until they were wed, he wished it every day.

As his fingers brushed her skin, she murmured, 'Peng,' and he withdrew his hand quickly. Her face crumpled, and a fat tear rolled down her cheek. She had lost so much. But he shouldn't be jealous of a man who no longer wanted her. Her destiny was set.

'No,' she cried, sitting up and startling them both as she came eye to eye with him in the dark. She slapped a hand over her mouth and then sagged as she started to sob. He pulled her close without thinking, as he had done in the cell not so long ago.

'Don't let them take me,' she murmured, clinging to him as she had done then. It was almost as though he could feel the fear running through her.

'I won't,' he promised.

She relaxed into his arms, and he wondered if she still slept and her request was a dream. Perhaps she thought she had asked someone else the question, and it meant something very different.

Her breathing slowed, and he knew she had fallen into sleep, whether she had been fully before or not. He made to lay her back down, but as he moved her away from his body, she jolted awake, her hands tight around his tunic.

He tried to smile into her frightened eyes. 'You need to rest.'

'You promised,' she said.

He nodded and allowed her to rest against him. It was comfortable with her in his arms, yet he was twisted somewhat. He ran a hand over her back and tried not to sigh.

He woke the next morning lying across the bed, his legs still hanging from the edge and the princess sleeping on his chest as though he was her pillow. The healer stood over him smiling and, as he made to get up, the healer held out a hand.

'She needs the rest,' he whispered. He moved off with a grin, and Remi thought it would be to see over Mu-Phi.

'When she has finished resting,' Hui Te-Sze said, not looking quite as impressed as the healer, 'the emperor wishes to see you.'

29

There were too many people in the throne room when Remi arrived. Advisors, personal guard, even his mother's maids—although he couldn't see her amongst the people. He paused at the back of the room for a moment before making his way forward.

'Is your princess safe?' the emperor asked.

He nodded and bowed low to his father.

The emperor cleared his throat. The gentle murmuring in the room disappeared into silence, and it was as though everyone took a step back.

'Your mother worried,' he said carefully.

'Where is she?'

The emperor gave him a hard look, but did not answer the question. 'It appears that you were correct.' He said it honestly, but Remi could feel the tension in his voice. It was clear that it hurt him to admit such a thing. He wondered if the rest of the group felt the same.

General Zho-Hou entered the room, and the movement and murmuring began again.

'I understand that one lives,' the emperor said, and the general bowed low beside Remi before nodding.

'I thought we could use him to determine how many they are and what they want,' Remi said quickly. 'I know it goes against the laws.'

The emperor nodded, almost absently. 'What have you discovered?'

'Very little.'

'He has asked to see the princess,' General Zho-Hou said, and a murmur started up around the room again.

'No,' Remi said.

'It may be a way to learn what it is they want. These attacks have been focused on her.'

Remi bowed low to his father, wondering how he could explain such a thing to Lis and how she might react. She had been so frightened the previous night. Although, she had searched for an understanding, and perhaps such a visit would give it to her.

He turned as his mother was announced at the door, then stopped. His mother was leading Lis towards the emperor. The entire room bowed to them and then stepped back further. Remi wondered for a moment if they would turn their backs on her as was the custom not so long ago, but then his hidden princess seemed to have been creating new traditions every day.

She bowed low to the emperor, and Remi was disappointed that she didn't take the chance to look at him, or give him any sign that she saw him.

'Your Eminence,' the empress said, bowing with her. 'We have come as you requested.'

He motioned them forward with a small inward curl of his fingers, and Lis straightened as she stepped forward. Remi felt he should stand beside her rather than at the side of the room, but he stayed where he was.

'Has it been explained to you what I would like you to do?'

Lis glanced then at his mother before she bowed again. Remi hadn't even had the chance to tell her; his mother must have entered her room the moment he had left it.

'And you will do this for your emperor?'

'Yes, Your Highness,' Lis said, her voice clear and calm. Remi wondered what the healer had given her. She looked as fresh as if she had slept all night.

'You will have men with you at all times. Your maid, is she recovered?'

'Not as well as we would like. I have left her to rest.'

He looked at the empress when he nodded agreement.

'General Zho-Hou will go with you.'

Remi stepped forward.

The emperor sighed. 'We know exactly where he is,' he said. His voice sounded tired, as though they had already had this argument. 'You may go,' he said, waving them towards the door, but his eyes were on Remi.

Remi bowed his thanks and walked beside his princess.

Once they were out of the main chamber, the general took position before them. Remi noticed the number of soldiers watching around them and travelling with them.

'Are you sure?' he asked.

'Yes,' she said, her voice strong, but she didn't look at him.

They continued in silence towards the prison, and Remi wondered if the world had changed so much that this place would be used more and more.

The steadying breath Lis took before walking towards the cell was the only indication that she was nervous, and she held her hands before her. When they reached the bars, she faltered as though she recognised the man inside.

He sat against a wall, nothing but straw on the ground before him. He was dressed as he had been the night before, only now his face wasn't covered. Remi could see her trying not to turn from the bars. As the man looked up at her, he stood quickly and then bowed low.

'I am honoured, Your Highness, that you would visit with me.'

'Who are you?' she asked, a confidence in her voice that Remi wasn't sure was there. He remembered her holding him so close only hours ago.

The man looked up at Remi and then back to Lis. She gestured for Remi to step back.

'This is not a good idea,' he said.

'I need to know,' she said. 'Please.'

Remi bowed and stepped back. He was still close, but the man from the cell couldn't see him.

'Thank you, Your Highness,' he said.

'Who are you?' she asked again.

'One of many,' he said.

She didn't like the response, for she pursed her lips.

'Why do you want to see me?' This was asked more quietly, and Remi sensed the nervousness returning.

'You are the only one who can help us.'

'Were you with those who took me before?'

A silence followed, and Remi wished he could see the man's face.

'How do you think I can help you?' she asked when he didn't answer her.

'You can die,' he spat.

The magic burned hot, and Remi quickly stepped out of the shadow between Lis and the man, pulling her away. The fire ball grazed his shoulder as he pushed her back. He turned, but she had his arm.

'Wait!' she cried. Out of view of the cell, still in Remi's arms, she called out, 'How will my death help you?'

'You will bring magic to the lands, where it will be as it was. We should rule this land with our magic. It can never be as it was.'

'How can I do that?' Lis asked, pushing past Remi towards the cell bars. 'Why me?'

'Because it is what has been seen.'

General Zho-Hou pushed his sword through the man's chest as he pushed himself against the bars. He cackled as the magic fizzled, and he dropped to the ground.

'No!' she cried. 'Not yet. I don't have the answers. Who has seen this? Who thinks this? Why is it me?' she called out, but the man was already dead. His vacant stare focused on the ceiling above them. Lis fell, but Remi still held her tight. She shivered in his arms.

'Get her back to her rooms,' the general said, and Remi pulled her to her feet and dragged her from the cell.

'He didn't tell me,' she murmured.

He caught Te-Sze's eye as she stood back from him. She patted gently at her face and brushed out non-existent creases from her skirt. She took a deep breath and then nodded. 'I'm ready.' And then she reached for his shoulder but stopped.

'It is nothing,' he said, rolling his shoulder. The fireball had only grazed his armour. Although he had felt the heat of it, it hadn't burnt him. 'You don't have to do this.'

'I can't go out looking like a frightened child, clinging to you.'

He smiled then, but she looked away.

Remi chewed his lip and then stepped closer to the other hunter. 'Find a priestess,' he said before he followed his princess into the sunshine beyond the prison gate.

The high priestess sat in quiet contemplation. The warm air around her was heavy with the scent of ginger from the tea and the hushed, slow breathing of the other priestesses in focused meditation. The empress worried her. She had been too easily softened by the plight of the girl. The high priestess knew exactly who the girl was and what she would become. The visions she had been granted showed her just how powerful the girl would be. And yet there was no sense of it.

She had threatened the girl, who had almost admitted to having magic, and yet she could not feel it. The high priestess needed more certainty, a clear manifestation of what she had been shown. She blew out a long breath and centred herself.

None of them used what they had. The young prince was more powerful than he knew, but he used his skills poorly.

She took a deep breath. She could feel the frustration washing over her, and it was not helping her focus. Other than the death of the man in the cell, there was nothing. He had told the hidden princess of the visions, and she wondered what the crown prince might do next to help her.

It had surprised her that he had wanted to keep the man alive, a small window into the world of magic. Was it for his princess, to answer her question, or was it to answer his own curiosities?

She felt the spirit flow through the room. The flicker of a shared image grew in her mind and then dissipated like a cloud of smoke. A distant knocking drew her attention.

She pointed to one of the girls as she opened her eyes and left the gathering. She would have to focus on her own destinies today. And find ways in which she could help the empress to see her point of view.

The girl reappeared in the doorway.

Everyone in the room opened their eyes and looked towards her. 'The princess has been told of a vision, and the crown prince requests a priestess.'

'You may go, child,' the high priestess said.

The girl bowed low. 'Thank you for your trust,' she said before disappearing back into the temple.

'Is she ready for this?' another priestess asked.

The high priestess nodded once. 'Let us return to our prayers.'

Lis leapt from the seat Remi had only just managed to settle her in when the priestess entered the room. She was young, but she wore the gold bands of someone fully trained. They would only send someone appropriate to watch over the hidden princess.

She smiled, and Lis watched her as she entered the room.

'You need me, Your Highness?'

'We were told of a vision,' Remi said.

'Why would you send for them?' Lis asked, her voice cold and accusing.

'They understand such things.'

Lis turned back to the young priestess and studied her for a moment. 'You know of visions?' she asked.

The priestess bowed.

'Do you have visions?' Lis asked.

'There are some who think our prayer takes us to a higher level of understanding,' the priestess said, her voice sweet and soft. 'We do not have visions, but they are provided to those who do by the gods, so I may be able to understand the meaning.'

Lis looked back to Remi, and he tried to smile.

'Who spoke of the vision?' the young woman asked.

'A prisoner, someone trying to harm the princess.'

'Did he say why?'

'He saw my future,' Lis said.

The priestess laughed kindly. 'He guessed your future, as we all can. For you are the hidden princess and you will become Empress of our Empire.'

'He was trying to get at you,' Remi offered quietly, and Lis turned a cold look in his direction.

'He said it was to do with magic,' Lis said sternly. 'And that I needed to die so I wouldn't return the world to what it was.'

'What it was?' the priestess asked.

'When we lived with magic in harmony, perhaps,' she added, looking to Remi. 'We did once, before the visitors, before the war.'

'There is no one with magic left, Your Highness, for such a world. Those few who have remained appear determined to continue to inflict harm.'

Lis silently watched her, her face unreadable.

'Perhaps we should pray together,' the priestess offered quietly, her face calm and serene.

Lis tensed beside Remi.

'I think prayer would help,' he whispered. She shook her head in a silent plea when she glanced at him, her eyes wide with the fear he had seen the night before. 'We will sit together with the priestess and pray for an answer,' he added.

The priestess seemed to shift uncomfortably for the first time. She nodded, but she looked annoyed, and Remi wondered if Lis had reason to fear them. The last time a priestess had been present was in her cell, and she had physically threatened Lis. It made him wonder what they did know.

'Do you know of any people who do have visions?'

The priestess looked at him with confusion.

'When I was a child, there was a story of an old woman from Fifth who could see your inner secrets, and another on Third who could read your future in your hand,' he said.

'Tricks and stories, Your Highness,' she said with a laugh.

'I have seen stranger things,' he murmured.

'You are a hunter,' she said. Her voice was clear and offered no argument. 'You have seen much that we have not.'

'You work closely with the gods; there would be things you have seen,' Lis said.

'My work, as you call it, is in worship. If only the gods would talk with us as you imagine,'

There was a gentle knock at the door, and the young healer entered. He bowed low to all in the room and then moved through silently to his patient in the corner.

'I will take my leave. If you have concerns, Your Highness, please come to me at the temple or send for me again.'

Lis didn't move, but Remi nodded as she bowed low and left the room. Lis seemed to sag with the relief as she left. Lis had leaned heavily into the table when the healer appeared, kneeling before her, a concerned look on his face as he took her wrist.

'You do too much,' he whispered.

'I have done nothing but walk today.'

Remi opened his mouth and then closed it. She had done far more; she had stood before the emperor, faced a man who wished her dead, maintained her control when a woman she feared was brought before her. Although he wasn't sure why she feared the priestesses as she did.

'You were to ensure she rested,' the healer chastised the prince.

'My mother took her to the emperor without my knowledge.'

'I am not a child,' she snapped.

'But you are precious,' the healer said, and she flushed at his words.

Was there something between them? 'You do too much,' Remi said to the healer. 'You presume yourself higher than you are.'

'I know where I am and who I am. Do you?'

Remi scowled at the openness of the man, then noticed Lis watching him closely. 'What do you think I am?' Remi asked her.

She looked thoughtful for a moment and then smiled. 'More than you think you are.' Her smile lit up the room around her, and he relaxed again. He needed to ensure that he kept her safe.

'Have you heard of visions?' the princess asked the healer.

'Do you have visions?' he asked Lis. 'It may be a sign of...'

'Of what?' she asked, leaning forward.

'Damage,' he said softly. 'It may be that the exhaustion and attack have affected your mind.'

'I'm not having visions,' she said, leaning back. 'I was told of someone else who had. Could it be something?'

'Outside of a problem with the mind?' He shook his head.

Lis seemed to fold in on herself. And without a thought, Remi indicated the healer move back. Then he scooped her up and laid her down on her bed. 'You need to sleep,' he said.

'It is harder than it sounds,' she whispered.

'Try,' the healer said, standing over her.

She relented and closed her eyes, although Remi was sure she would not fall into sleep as easily as he hoped.

The healer beckoned him closer to the door. 'I worry, Your

Highness, that her lack of sleep and stress has impacted her.'

'She is not the one having visions.'

The man seemed to visibly relax. 'But she isn't resting as she should. The old master would have me beaten if he saw her now.'

'She has responded better to you than anyone else,' Remi said, more to himself. At the look he saw on the man's face, he added, 'She is very stubborn.'

'Either way, she must rest.' He said it firmly, pointing at the prince's chest before he remembered himself and bowed, then left the room.

Remi turned back to the bed to find Lis sitting up and watching him. 'Rest,' he said.

She shook her head and made to get up.

'What if I bring you a book?' he asked, and she paused.

'You will read to me as though I am a child?'

'I thought you could read yourself, but if it were to comfort you...'

'I can read.'

He called the guard, who appeared instantly.

'Don't move.'

He raced from the room and into his own, where he scanned his books for the one he wanted. It took him much longer to locate it than he thought it would. He had a moment of panic when he thought it lost, but then it was almost as though it called to him from the piles of books on his desk, and he saw it.

He returned to her room to find her sitting up on the edge of the bed, and he sighed. He nodded to the soldier, who left. Then he stepped forward and held out the book. 'You can only have this if you get back into bed.'

She sighed, swung her legs around and lay down. When he handed her the book, she sat up again, and he threatened to take it away.

'The stories of the explorers.'

'And not the fiction my mother would have you believe.'

Lis smiled, settling back and opening the book.

He watched her for a moment and then moved over to Mu-Phi. She had not woken properly since she had been hit, and it worried him. As he squatted by the bed, she opened her eyes, and he gasped. She held her finger to her lips.

He looked back towards Lis to find that the book had dropped to the covers. He smiled, and Mu-Phi sat up.

'Who had the visions?'

He shook his head.

'I am not lying here for my own health,' she whispered angrily.

'I thought you unwell,' he said.

'I am not what I would hope to be, but I am well enough to do as I must. Did you take her to see the man with magic?'

He nodded.

'Was that a good idea?'

'Probably not, but it was my father's. The man wanted to see her, but I think it was only to scare her further.' He blew out a long breath. 'We don't know if what he said was true.'

'But it was the reason he came to kill me,' Lis said behind him, and he jumped. 'I am not a child,' she said, the hurt clear in her voice.

'I know that.'

'Do you?' she asked. He reached for her, and she stepped back. 'I trusted you, worried about you,' she added, looking at Mu-Phi. 'Yet you pretend around me, as though I am the one not to be trusted. Maybe I am not; maybe I am the threat to the Empire these people seem to think me.'

Remi opened his mouth and then closed it. He wasn't sure what he could say to convince her otherwise.

'Perhaps my mind has gone,' she continued, turning from them. She walked straight for the door, and when it opened the guard stood uncertain before her. 'I wish to visit with the empress,' she said.

The guard looked to Remi, who nodded, and the man bowed

before leading Lis away towards his mother's rooms.

Remi's head dropped into his hands.

'She is very determined,' Mu-Phi murmured.

'I can't seem to win with her. I think we make progress, and then she ignores me or questions me.'

'I should think you would like being challenged, ignored not so much.'

He glared at her, and she grinned.

'I am glad you like your princess,' she said, leaning back. 'I like the young healer; perhaps you should send for him again.'

'I think you could be returning to the duty you were called for.'

'There are more guards around the empress than the rest of the Palace Isle. If you are worried, follow her yourself.'

30

Lis was surprised by the lack of guards on the empress's door. The guard with her paused, as though she might not be in, before pulling the door open. The empress was laid out across the table, and Lis rushed forward. She shook her gently by the shoulder, and the empress murmured something, but her eyes remained closed.

Lis looked back to the door, but the guard had not followed her in. She was about to call for him when she realised the room was full of the buzz of magic. If she called out, she might alert more than the guard that they were there alone. She couldn't see anyone else in the room, yet she was certain there was something or someone present.

She hoped the prince would sense the same thing. When the empress groaned behind her, Lis stepped back and knelt beside her.

'Your Highness,' she whispered.

'Something is wrong,' the empress said.

'Are you unwell? I'll send for the healer.' As she made to move away, the empress grabbed her wrist and held her tight.

'They want you,' she said, her voice faltering. Lis dropped back down by her side.

'Who does?'

'They want the power. They want the magic back.'

'Do they want me to help them?'

'Some do,' the empress said, trying to lift her head, and she groaned again. 'Some want you to die.'

Lis looked at her seriously. 'You know what I am,' she said.

'I didn't at first, but I do now.'

'And you are not afraid?'

'I don't need to be. You fear more—being discovered, being slaughtered by my son.'

Lis nodded slowly. 'What do you want of me?'

'I want you to be the empress I know you can be. I want you to do all you can for my son.'

'The High Priestess is involved in this,' Lis said. It wasn't a question.

'They all are. They want the power, but I know of another group.'

'The princess,' Lis breathed.

The empress smiled at her, and her strong grip slackened on her arm. Lis took her hand. 'They ordered her killed, as was the custom. She, like you, was born at the end of this war, but the war continues.'

'Who killed Crown Prince Rei Ta-Sho?' Lis asked.

'I don't know.' The empress winced as she said it.

'Not Wei-Song or her people?'

'Never,' she said loudly, standing quickly from the table and then dropping back down. Her hand moved to her head.

'What have they done to you?'

'It is just a headache.'

'Which you have never had before, and now you have them constantly.'

The empress looked over Lis, smiled and put her hand to her face. 'You are so like her,' she whispered.

'I can feel the magic around you,' Lis said. Putting her hand over the empress's. 'Always around you.'

'Remi does not sense it,' she said.

'I think there are some forms of magic that can't be sensed by all the hunters. Wei-Song possesses such.'

'She can hide,' the empress said with a smile.

'As can I,' Lis answered. 'I wonder if it stems from our need to remain hidden. I have tried so hard to keep it deep within me. I stood beside your son, and he didn't know I was there. I wonder,' she continued. 'There is so much magic at the moment, a background buzz—are his senses distorted.'

The empress pulled her close. 'I fear it is too late.'

'We will find a way to stop them.'

'It is too late for me.'

Lis pulled back and studied the empress's frightened face. 'Where are the guards and the maids?'

She shook her head.

'Let me help you to bed. You need rest.'

'It will do me no good.'

Lis helped direct her towards the bed, and she sighed as she lay down.

'I thought you would have lessons, Your Highness,' a quiet voice said behind Lis, and she continued to focus on the empress rather than the high priestess.

'I came to visit and found the empress unwell and all alone. I thought it best I stay.' She turned, smiling sweetly at the woman. She hoped the priestess didn't try to threaten her again. If only she had some way of defending herself. A shield of some kind.

'I will watch over her,' the priestess said, stepping forward, and the empress groaned quietly behind Lis.

'I don't mind,' Lis said. 'It is a daughter's duty.'

'You are no daughter of the crown.' The priestess's hatred was clear in her voice.

'Am I not to marry her son? She will become my mother soon enough, and she teaches me as a mother would.'

The priestess turned angry eyes towards the empress. 'Does she?'

The empress grabbed at Lis's hand.

'Oh dear,' the high priestess said without expression in her voice. 'It appears that another evil man with magic has entered the royal residence.'

Lis looked around and then back to the priestess, who raised a hand towards the wheezing empress.

'No,' Lis screamed, pushing out with everything she had. The empress sucked in a deep breath.

'You have no power over me, little one. You are a Hidden; all you can do is hide from the world.'

'That is not all I can do,' Lis said, thinking of the times she brought the flowers out to bloom. 'I think I might be able to find things too.'

'What could you find?'

Lis searched the room, reaching out, trying to sense what else was there. A man stood against the far wall. The magic around him buzzed, and he grinned as though she couldn't see him. She pointed in his direction, and the priestess followed her finger before turning back.

'There is nothing there.'

Lis pointed again, and the priestess grumbled. The empress sat up sharply in her bed, her hand going straight back to her head as the man appeared.

'That was not a very good way to hide him,' Lis said. 'Maybe you aren't as strong as you think you are.'

'Do you think you can find things now?' she snapped. 'Knowing he is here will not help you. The empress will not protect you. She knows what you are. All those with magic must die, and she can't have brought one with magic into her son's life. She killed her own daughter to protect the Empire; she would do the same to you.'

'She may have,' Lis said carefully. 'But can the Empire afford another death by magic at this point? The people will fear it has returned. They will believe that you cannot protect them, that the gods cannot protect them.'

The priestess narrowed her eyes and pointed towards the

empress. 'You will be blamed for this.'

The man leapt forward, fire buzzing in his hands, and Lis knew that with his magic in the open, it was only a matter of time until the prince or another hunter arrived. She moved between the empress and the fire bearer.

'I will not let this happen.'

'Then you shall both die,' the priestess said.

He threw the fire, and Lis squeezed her eyes closed, wishing she could stop this. At the intake of breath from the high priestess, she opened her eyes. The fire burned around them, but both Lis and the empress were protected behind an invisible barrier.

'Who are you?' the high priestess growled.

'Just a hidden princess,' she said, trying to push the flames back as the heat that licked over the barrier burned her.

'No,' the priestess said.

The prince and the guards burst into the room. Hui Te-Sze pushed his sword straight through the fire bearer, who fizzled. The empress clutched at Lis as the high priestess turned on the crown prince. She threw her hand out and he ducked down, pushing his sword through her stomach as he slid forward.

Lis dropped onto the bed. She felt dry and drained and hot and sticky. The empress threw her arms around her and pulled her close.

'What were you doing?' the crown prince asked, coming over to the bed.

'Visiting,' she tried weakly, and the empress held her tight.

'You had your hand out,' Te-Sze said.

'She sensed them,' the empress said. 'She saved me. She told the priestess that she felt her magic, and then the man appeared and tried to kill us both.'

'But he didn't,' the hunter said.

The prince turned from Te-Sze back to his mother and Lis. 'You are a hunter?'

Lis shook her head and then nodded. 'I don't know,' she said. 'I could feel the magic buzzing around her.'

'A hunter,' he said slowly.

The empress's grip loosened, and Lis helped her lie down. 'Send for a healer,' she commanded, and the other guard disappeared. 'There was no one here, no guard, no maids.'

'How could your father not tell us this?' the crown prince mumbled behind her.

'We didn't know,' she said. 'I have lived on an island far from the world for so long. It was only when I was here that I could sense something. I didn't know that it meant I was a hunter.'

'Hush now, child,' the empress said, calling her back to the bed. 'It is well.'

'I'm not sure how,' Te-Sze said. He looked at Lis with wary eyes, and she realised he had looked at her like this before. He didn't trust her, and he sensed something in her as well.

'Maybe they were trying to threaten us,' Lis said

'The other man wanted you dead,' Te-Sze said, his sword still hanging in his hand. The blood dripped onto the body, making a larger pool of it across the floor.

'Is there only fire?' Lis asked.

'Sorry?'

'I have only seen fire,' she said, turning from the man to the priestess. 'What skill did she have?'

'We will sort it out.'

'Can I only sense the fire?'

'You recognised something in the priestess,' the prince said slowly, but he was looking over her much in the same way as the other hunter. She gulped under the pressure of his gaze. 'She threatened you before,' he said. It wasn't a question. 'Perhaps it was her you feared, and the man used her.'

'You heard the sound,' Lis said, watching him.

He nodded once.

'Your mother needs a healer,' she said, taking her hand.

'As do you,' the empress whispered.

Lis shook her head.

'Your hands,' she whispered.

Lis looked down at her hands. They weren't just red from the heat of the flames; they had blistered. The empress put her hand to Lis's cheek as she had before. 'You are my daughter,' she whispered.

A tear slipped from Lis as she put her own hand over the empress again, and the pain burned through her. 'What else is out there?' she asked.

The empress looked to her son. 'You need to tell her,' she said and then winced, putting her hand to her chest.

The healer entered the room, and Lis moved back so the old man could sit with his patient. He fussed for a while before Lis looked up at the young healer standing by the door. He motioned her out, but she shook her head.

'Let her rest,' the old man said, looking at Lis rather than anyone else in the room.

Lis bowed low, and the empress gave her a weak smile. Without looking at anyone else, she followed the young healer out and back to her own rooms. He indicated the bed and she sat on the edge, holding out her hands to him. He sighed before taking her pulse.

'Will she be ok?' she asked him.

'Thanks to you, it seems.'

'I worry that there is more to it than this attack,' Lis said without thinking. 'She has not been herself.'

'The healer will do all he can.'

Lis nodded silently.

'You will need ointment for your hands. I would prefer that you rest them—no writing—but I wonder if you would listen to me.' He sounded frustrated, and Lis nodded again.

'Is there something else I should know?'

She shook her head, still focused on her blistered hands.

He carefully wiped ointment over her palm and then wrapped a silk bandage around it. 'Rest,' he said, frustration clear in his voice, as though she were a naughty child who would not do as she was told. Had she been so difficult for this man? It wasn't her fault that she had been attacked. Although, she wondered, they were determined that she would not be Empress herself one day, so they would continue to fight her, to try to kill her. She didn't want others to be hurt in the process. Especially the empress.

Another tear ran down Lis's face as she imagined what the empress must have gone through to save her child. How she had told the world she had killed her own daughter, yet she lived. Lis imagined all that her parents had gone through to save her. Giving up their lives of comfort to live isolated on their island home. And for what? She was back in the middle of the capital, in the middle of a world they had tried to protect her from, and she was causing more trouble for the Empire.

'Your Highness, I...' the healer said as he stepped closer.

'What have you done?' the prince cried as he threw the doors open, interrupting the healer, who froze mid-step.

'I am sorry,' Lis said, climbing to her feet, unable to look the prince in the eye. She loved the empress like a mother, and she would not wish her harm.

In the silence that followed, Lis looked up to find both men staring at her. Fear caught the breath in her throat, and she stepped back, stumbling on the step and tripping. The prince reached forward, catching her by the hand, and she cried out.

He sat her down carefully on the edge of the bed and waved the healer forward. But she pulled her hands into her lap and shook her head.

'What is it?' the prince asked, looking at the healer. Then he stood quickly. 'Do you sense something on him?'

She shook her head as the healer stepped back before dropping to his knees.

The prince turned to her, and she looked down.

'You appear to sense some that I cannot,' he said, pacing around and then suddenly siting at her desk. 'What has happened here?' he asked, his voice too loud.

'I worry that the princess puts herself in danger,' the healer said.

'No,' Lis said. 'I was visiting. She has been unwell; I was worried.'

'For the empress?' the prince prompted, and she nodded.

'What did you see when you looked at me?' she asked.

He looked up, confused, and she turned to the healer. 'You both looked like you saw something,' she said, the fear straining her voice. 'What did you see?'

'You,' the healer whispered.

The prince growled as he jumped to his feet.

'What do you mean?' she asked.

'You are not what I expected,' the prince said.

'Another disappointment. Perhaps these fire bearers are correct and I should not be here.'

'You are more than you think you are,' the healer said.

Now it was her turn to stare at him. 'You don't know me,' she said. 'You don't know what I am. No one does.'

'Someone does,' Hui Te-Sze said, entering the room. 'It is why they want you dead.'

'As you do,' she said, turning angry eyes on him.

The crown prince stepped forward.

'I sensed something about you,' the man admitted, 'but I couldn't at the same time.'

'There is too much magic around.' She sighed. 'It blurs the senses.'

'How long have you sensed this?' the prince asked.

'Since that first time you reached out near me. I could sense something around you, a hum. Then it seemed to be everywhere,' Lis said.

'I have had that feeling at times, as though it is all around me and yet I can't sense anything,' the prince agreed.

Lis nodded.

'You felt Prince Remi reaching out?' Hui Te-Sze asked.

Lis nodded again. 'As I can feel you do now.'

The feeling stopped. 'How can you feel a hunter?'

'I don't know,' she said. 'I don't understand any of it.'

'There is something else,' the healer said, his voice soft and coaxing.

'I wonder if hunters have a kind of magic,' Lis blurted, and the man charged forward. The prince put himself between them.

'I am not one of *them*!' he shouted from around the prince.

'They used to be the same as us. People of this Empire.'

'You are taking the words of a mad man to heart now. You think this prophecy he talks of, where you will bring the world back to what it was, is true?' Te-Sze asked.

She shook her head, wanting desperately to disappear and run away.

'You would think your father would have explained things more clearly to you,' Te-Sze continued.

'My father didn't talk of the war or what he did.'

'I would be only too happy to enlighten you.'

'No one talks of magic,' Lis said. 'No one will voice what it is or was in case speaking of it will bring it back, and the fighting with it.'

The crown prince sighed.

'Tell me what is out there. Tell me what they have that they are so determined to use against me.'

Hui Te-Sze huffed.

'You don't think they want to harm me? Why do you stand outside my door so often?'

'Because the prince demands it.'

The prince looked to him. 'You don't think the future empress worth protecting.'

'I think she is one of them,' he said. 'I get a sense of something.'

'So you said. Perhaps it is because I am a hunter too,' she said, a confidence in her voice she didn't feel. 'Like the sense I get from the prince?' Lis stepped forward and looked between the two men. 'Unless you think the prince has magic?'

The anger was clear on the prince's face, but she was serious.

The hunter glanced sideways at the prince.

'When did you learn that you were a hunter?' she asked.

'As a child I could sense something in others, but it wasn't until later, when I was a soldier, that I realised the value of what I had.'

'Have you ever been wrong?' Lis asked.

'I can sense something or I can't. There is no wrong or right.'

'You aren't answering my question.'

'Once,' he murmured.

Lis waited.

'He was one of our own, but there was a hum about him always, and in battle it was stronger and...'

'You killed him,' she finished for him.

He nodded once.

'And there was no fizzle when he died.'

'He may have been one of those that are harder to detect. I've heard whispers of the Hidden,' Te-Sze said.

'The Hidden?'

He nodded. 'Nothing clear. It is thought this is the reason the war ended, not because the magic disappeared, but because we couldn't sense it like we could before. Like they knew how to hide it away. The Order of Huans, they came be known.'

Lis sat slowly at the table. She glanced then towards Mu-Phi and shot up again when she saw the empty bed.

'She has gone to her family.' The crown prince stood, and Lis clenched her fist before wincing.

'You need to rest,' the healer said quietly by the door.

'You may leave,' she said, turning her back on the room. 'You can all leave.'

'I think...' the prince started.

'And you can find another to stand at the door,' she said, looking at the guard. 'I would rather not be run through in my sleep because he thinks me something I am not.'

The crown prince sighed again. He bowed low and took the guard by the arm as they moved out.

31

Lis woke with a jolt, sitting bolt upright and throwing the covers off. Someone groaned, but she kept moving. She pressed her hands to her temples. Something wasn't right. There was an angry buzz filling her head and the world around her. What could they be doing, and why had no one done anything to stop it?

She was sure it was the background magic. There weren't just several—there were a lot of people with magic somewhere around the palace.

'The priestess,' she murmured.

She pushed open the door and found the healer sitting against the wall. When she pushed the door open completely, he fell against her legs.

'What are you doing?' she asked too loudly.

'The hunter won't watch you,' he murmured, rubbing his shoulder.

'And what good will you do?'

He opened his hand to reveal a small dagger, and she almost laughed at the size of it. 'You do realise that you would have to get very close to someone to use that? If they are throwing fire at you, it isn't going to do much good.'

'How is your hand?'

She brushed him off. 'How is the empress?'

'Resting. As you should be.'

'I can't,' she said, turning back into the room and stalling at the site of the prince. 'Were you watching me sleep again?'

'I keep thinking that you need protecting, but it may be that I need protection from you.'

'You also see me as a threat?' she asked. She was tempted to hide away then or show them what she was—do something spectacular that might force him to drive his sword into her. She wondered for a moment if she would hiss as the magic escaped, or if it was indeed different for the Hidden.

She opened her mouth to say something else, although she wasn't sure what she could say, but the prince held his hand up. Then the hunter ran into the room.

'What is that?' he asked.

'Why do you think I'm awake?' she snapped. 'It is burning through my mind.'

'Like a swarm of bees,' the healer said, and they all looked to him. 'I have work to do,' he mumbled.

Lis caught him by the sleeve, then groaned as the material pulled at her hand.

'Why has it built?' Lis asked as she relented and allowed the man to look over her hand.

'Who else is a hunter and has not said?' the guard murmured.

'People don't talk about such things in case we are thought to have magic. I like my innards on the inside.'

Lis smiled. In some ways, it was a comfort to know others were in the same situation. That they too feared for what they were. Although Lis wasn't a hunter; she could simply sense the magic. She wondered how many others claiming to be hunters were the same. Were they all Hidden? Or did it not matter?

Another soldier appeared at the doorway. 'I think with this level of noise, it is time to wake the emperor,' the crown prince said, 'and double the watch over the empress.'

'You think they will come for her again?' Lis asked.

'It is hard to know what they will do and who they may be after.

It was you they were trying to kill, and yet they didn't mind if the empress died with you.'

'You don't mind if they take me, as long as she is not harmed,' Lis said. Despite her understanding of just how little she mattered until the training was complete, it still hurt to be reminded.

She stepped behind the screen and then turned to find the prince standing behind her. 'Are you to help me dress now that you have taken my maid?'

He blushed and backed out of the space.

'I need to know what is out there and what threat it truly is. Whether the threat is to me alone or to the Empire.' She changed quickly and reappeared before the small group.

'I don't think this is a good idea,' the hunter said.

'Of course you don't. I might find something you have overlooked in all this time. I will go out with the rest of the hidden princess's guards. Or have you sent them all home to their families?'

The prince shook his head and then sent the hunter out of the room. She glanced at the healer, the small knife still clutched in his hands. 'You can come with me,' she said.

He nodded and then shook his head.

'You are to go without me?' the prince asked.

'I thought you needed to talk with the emperor,' Lis said, barely holding back the frustration she felt.

He nodded.

She shook her head and walked away from him. The soldiers in the hallway bowed and two moved along before her, the remaining two following behind. The healer looked between her and the armoured men behind them with some nervousness, but she carried on, thankful she didn't have to direct them and that they appeared willing to support her in this.

The cool night air when they emerged from the residence nearly shocked her back to reality. *What do I really think I can accomplish here? I have no idea how to fight magic. I can't even use my own to any real effect.*

The moon lay hidden behind clouds, a dim glow in the distance. Lamps and torches hung about the city, making little pools of light across buildings and walls and patches of street. Not a soul could be seen. A peacock called in the distance, and Lis wondered where it might be.

'Can you feel it?' she asked the healer.

He nodded, his face creased.

'You can't tell where it comes from?'

'No,' he admitted. 'It is as though it is all around us.' He stepped forward. 'Like it surrounds us. What is on the other side of the wall?'

'Water and rocks,' Lis said, thinking of the approach to the Palace Isle and that there was no way to get close to the wall other than the docks. 'There must be lookouts,' she said, pointing to the top of the wall.

'I can't see anyone,' the healer said.

'Let's get closer.'

'I don't think that is a good idea. But I see why you think it is.'

Lis stopped and looked at him closely. 'Who are you?'

'An idiot,' he murmured.

'Really?'

'Healer Yang,' he mumbled, giving her a cursory bow.

'Why are you here?'

'Because you dragged me out here and into the gods know what.'

She laughed. 'Why are you on the Palace Isle?'

'I came to learn. I had an affinity for healing, and the masters took me on as an apprentice.'

'Now you work as a healer for the royal family.'

'The lesser members,' he added.

She raised her eyebrows. 'When did you know you could sense?'

'When I got here. There has always been something around me, something around the Palace Isle, and it seems to be increasing. I wondered if it was you,' he said honestly. 'It started to increase when you arrived.'

Lis made to say something, but she thought she saw movement. The guards all stood behind her, waiting for orders.

She felt suddenly exposed, and she motioned a man forward.

'Your Highness,' the soldier said softly.

'I haven't a sword,' she said.

'Would you like me to stand before you, or do you want a sword?'

She looked up at him then, and he watched the world around them rather than her. He looked back at her briefly. 'Would you trust me with one?'

'I'm not sure you could carry it,' he said, turning his attention back to the world around them. 'You direct us and we'll protect you.'

'And me?' the healer, Yang asked.

'You have a sword,' the man said, but Lis could hear the laughter in his voice. 'You should stay close to the princess.'

She nodded and stepped forward.

As they got closer to the wall, the feeling of magic increased. She could feel it pressing on her, but she couldn't detect where it was coming from. Healer Yang wore a pained expression, and she knew he sensed the same. She paused, wondering if he was the same as her, and how she could find out if he was.

There was someone on the top of the wall, and she couldn't tell if it was a watchman or someone else. 'Can we get inside the wall?' she asked.

The nearest soldier stopped and looked at her seriously.

'It is very thick. Either it is solid, or there is space to move through inside.'

He sighed and indicated towards a watch tower that sat further along the wall. They moved as a group towards it. She wondered if they would be hampered by buildings jutting up against the wall, and if those inside the buildings had a way of getting into or through the wall. As they drew closer, she saw there was a walkway separating the dwellings from the wall. The walls around the houses and smaller palaces never touched up against the main wall of the island.

When they reached the base of the tower, Lis expected more light to spill from the wider structure above, but it was just as dim. A door was built into the wall that looked no different from any other part of it, and she knew she had been right. Perhaps she should have been learning about such aspects of the Palace Isle during her classes with her tutors.

The soldier stepped forward and banged on the door, and only then did Lis realise it had no handle. Silence surrounded them before the sound of footsteps drew closer. A heavy bolt moved somewhere on the other side of the door, and it squealed open.

Lis remained back in the group, but she didn't sense any shift in the magic as the door opened. The soldier stepped forward and explained the princess's fears in hushed tones. The man looked across at her and laughed.

'There is no way for any man to get inside the wall other than a watch door.'

'What if someone on the watch let them in?' she asked.

'It wouldn't happen,' he snapped, pulling himself up tall. He made to pull the door closed, but the soldier at the front put his foot in the way and glared at the man on her behalf.

'May I look from the top of the wall?' she asked.

The man sighed and pushed the door open wider. Lis stepped into the darkness beside him, and the soldier followed before the door was pulled closed behind her. She felt nervous at the idea. When the bolt slid back into place, she heard something else, a lock perhaps.

'Up,' the man said without ceremony.

Lis took a breath, lifted her skirts and moved up the wooden, creaking steps. There were far more steps than she was used to, and she paused to rest.

'Do you need assistance, Your Highness?' her guard asked. She smiled as she shook her head.

'I don't get as much exercise as I used to,' she said, starting upwards again.

It seemed to take a long time before she reached the starlit sky through a small trapdoor at the top of the stairs, where a soldier looked at her with surprise. She held her hand out to him, and he helped lift her up the final rungs to the top. With the guard not far behind, Lis stepped forward and leaned on the high stone wall. It came up to her waist as she breathed in the cool stone around her. There was no buzzing of magic.

She looked out across the water, reflecting the dull glow of the moon. This side of the island looked to the east and in the distance, she could see the mountains of Fourth. There were some boats out on the water, their small lanterns casting dots of light to show where they were.

'Fishing boats,' the man beside her said, and she nodded.

There were only five or so that she could see.

'What do you think?' the guard asked beside her.

'It is beautiful,' she said. 'But I can't feel anything here. Can I see inside the wall?' she asked the other soldier with them, and he shrugged.

She walked over the other side of the wall and, stretching across the thick parapet, she looked down at the healer and the other soldiers still waiting. They appeared nervous. She could sense the buzz surrounding the healer. She closed her eyes but couldn't feel anything else.

'So strange,' she murmured.

'This way, Your Highness,' the guard said, stepping down into the darkness beneath them again.

They had to help her down, and she dropped a short distance into the arms of the waiting soldier. 'I beg your pardon,' he said, a nervousness about him.

'It was required,' she said, hoping he could see her reassurance in the dim light as well as hear it in her voice.

They travelled down a flight of stairs. Then the soldier held out a torch, and she saw the narrow passageway that led off from it. She hadn't noticed it on the way up, but then it was dark and she hadn't been looking for it.

He moved ahead of her, the hallway lighting up with the torch he held. She heard something squeal in the distance, possibly a rat, and she shivered.

'Enough,' she called after a time. 'There is nothing here.' She also didn't want to go too far, for she didn't know what lay ahead of her. If only her father had told her more of what he had fought, how they had fought. She might know what she could do.

At least her head had stopped hurting, and she could feel nothing but the men around her. Why did there appear to be so much magic surrounding the palace when they couldn't find it?

They made their way back along the passageway and down to the base of the stairs. She heard the clicking sound of a lock before the bolt was slipped back, and she wondered what they would do if they were locked in here. It was a relief to be back in the cool night air after the stuffy hallways.

The healer looked just as nervous as he had before, as though they might run him through without Lis there to protect him. As soon as she made it out of the shadow of the wall, the overwhelming buzz of magic returned. She put her hand to her head.

'What are you saying?' the emperor asked, leaning forward on his throne as Remi knelt before him.

He tried to keep still, holding his arms out and his head dipped low. 'What I have been saying for some time. Magic is back.'

The emperor leapt from his seat. Although he had not been

dismissed, Remi let his hands drop. The emperor shook his head as he paced.

'I have felt it increasing. The princess felt it as well; it pulled her from her sleep.'

'The empress said she was a hunter,' the emperor murmured, still pacing. 'She is safe?'

'The empress?'

He stopped his pacing and looked at him seriously. 'The princess.'

Remi took a deep breath. 'She is somewhat determined,' he said. 'She has gone to investigate further.'

'Have you lost your mind completely? Do you not want to marry the girl?'

'Quite certainly. She is very different from any other girl I have met. She knows what she does, and I trust her.'

'Despite her not telling us she was a hunter.'

'She didn't know, didn't realise until she was here. Her father kept her protected on his island.'

'Hmmm,' the emperor hummed, looking into the distance beyond Remi. 'He is far shrewder than I ever gave him credit for.'

'He won the war; you rewarded him.'

'But I knew his heart wasn't in it. Perhaps he saw something in the daughter he wasn't sure of.'

'Maybe there are more hunters than we knew. Maybe they feared what we would do with them.'

'Maybe they hold magic of their own.'

'I would sense it,' Remi said too loudly, then bowed again to his father.

'And yet the girl has sensed more than you, and she is untrained, unpractised.' He sighed and sat down slowly on his throne. 'Who did she go out with?'

'Her personal guard.'

'Traditions already destroyed,' the emperor murmured. 'They would look at her.'

'Everyone looks at her. You brought her before the court. There is not one member of the court who has not seen her. Unless she should take the veil again?' he asked, more with his eyebrows than his voice.

'That has very different connotations,' the emperor huffed.

Remi felt confused for a moment.

'You should know your history,' his father scolded. 'It is from the days when we hid a whole generation and all but one survived.'

'I was aware of that,' Remi said.

'It was more about the not surviving that the history tries to forget. We don't want the world thinking we will kill her if she does not meet our expectations.' The emperor sighed. 'Your mother continued her training in tradition. Thankfully, we wed before the war started.' He rubbed his hand over his forehead, a small sign of his tiredness that he would not have shown if anyone else were in the room. 'I hope that I live long enough to see you wed.'

'Of course you will.'

'Unless those with magic are here to remove me from my throne. Although there was talk from the one you captured.' He turned seriously to Remi.

Remi nodded.

'You are sure that she is safe?'

'Do you mean safe from the magic, or not a danger to us?'

The emperor scoffed without answering.

'Mother trusts her. If it had not been for the hidden princess, then who knows what might have happened to her.'

'I do not want it cried in the streets,' the emperor said with a sigh.

Remi stood quickly and bowed low again to his father. 'Thank you, Your Highness.'

'You may have whatever resources you need, but you must remain discrete.'

Remi nodded and left. He wasn't sure how he could keep it

secret much longer. With the buzz that surrounded them, he was sure an attack of some kind was not far away. And if fighting started on the Palace Isle, the whole world would know that magic had returned.

32

Lis entered her room with the healer and half the guard following, then stopped. Wei-Song stood against the far wall, looking weary and worried, and Lis suddenly realised that others knew who she was and where she had come from. The boatman had called her 'Highness' and Lis had thought he was speaking to her. The healer made a strange sucking noise and when Wei-Song pointed to her hand, he turned to Lis.

'Are you well?' the guard asked.

He nodded mutely.

'I am tired,' Lis said. 'Could you check over my hand again? Then I would like to sleep.'

The guard bowed. 'I will not be far should you need me.'

She tipped her head and they left.

The healer looked at her with desperation, and she indicated that he sit at the table. 'It is well,' she said softly as the other woman stepped forward.

'Healer Yang,' Lis said, half looking at the door. 'This is Princess Wei-Song.'

She bowed to Healer Yang and then turned to Lis. 'Could you find anything?'

Lis shook her head. 'This isn't your doing, is it?'

The young princess looked taken aback. 'This is not the Hidden,' she murmured.

'Why can I see her when the guards could not?' the healer

asked.

'You have a skill you did not know,' Wei-Song told him.

'It is ok,' Lis said. 'You have a strong hunter skill.' She glanced back at the princess.

Wei-Song scoffed and indicated that Lis move along the cushion so she could sit down. 'You are a Hidden,' she said to the healer.

He looked at his hands and then back to her.

'You can tell what is ailing someone more quickly than others?' Wei-Song asked.

'I have trained a long time.'

The princess looked him over as though he were a boy.

'I can't have magic,' he whispered. 'The prince will run me through.'

'He can't sense you,' Lis answered.

'But you can.' The fear was evident in his voice.

'And I am also talking to a woman no one else can see.'

Yang opened his mouth and then closed it. He looked at her seriously. 'You have magic,' he breathed.

She nodded.

'Not everyone with magic is dangerous,' he mumbled. 'At least they weren't, and I'm sure you're not trying to...' He paused, unsure what to say.

'We don't know what they want,' Lis answered.

'They want complete power,' Wei-Song said. 'They want a world where only those with magic exist, and they would rule such a world.'

'That is why they want you dead,' Yang said, pointing at Lis. 'They don't want you to make it how it was, when magic was just part of the world and we all worked together.'

'You have heard these stories too?'

'My grandmother used to tell me how the world was before.' He gave her a small smile. 'She used to love the rain and when I was a boy, I thought that she made it just so she could stand in it.'

Lis smiled at the idea of an old woman standing in her own little rain storm.

'She died in her sleep, and I was sure she wasn't ill.'

Lis felt her heart rate increase.

'I was too young to be sure, but I think my father did it. I think she asked him to.'

'Better to go quietly, without bringing attention to her family, than to be slaughtered by sword,' Wei-Song said.

Yang nodded slowly. Lis looked him over. He must have been older than her, for this would have happened during the war, yet he looked no older than Ting.

'You don't believe me,' he said sharply, looking at Lis with hard eyes.

'I do,' she said softly. 'I wonder what we can do to prevent this war from starting again.'

'I don't think there is anything we can do to prevent it.'

Lis turned and took the girl's hand, and Wei-Song looked at her with surprise. 'I heard your mother is unwell,' she said quickly. 'Are you able to visit with her?'

She stood quickly. 'How do you know my mother?'

Lis waited, wondering if the princess truly knew who she was.

Wei-Song looked between the two of them, then bowed and stepped towards the door just as it flew open. She disappeared quickly through it before it could be pulled closed by a guard, and the prince walked past his sister without knowing she existed.

'I'm sorry,' he said, stopping and looking at them both. 'You should be resting.'

'I can't sleep,' Lis said. 'Will the emperor allow you to do as you need?'

He nodded, leaning against the desk. He watched the healer, who sat lower at the table. It would take time, Lis thought, for him to come to terms with what he was. Lis had known for her whole life that she had magic. She only hoped he did not do something silly.

'Should you still be here?' the prince asked Yang.

'The healer is yet to look at my hand,' Lis said. 'And he has just discovered hunter abilities. It has been a big day for us all.'

The healer nodded. Lis placed her hand across the table, and he unwrapped the bandage from it. He paused as he looked over it, and Lis looked down to see the skin nearly healed, the blistering gone and the skin pink.

'You appear to have some skill,' the prince said. 'I will let you rest, but I will be back with the sun to talk about what we need to do next.'

She nodded, her eyes still on her palm.

'Did you find anything when you were out?'

'An overwhelming buzz, nothing more. Has it subsided, or have I become used to it?'

'The latter,' the prince said. 'It is still heavy in the air and confusing all my senses.'

Lis nodded slowly. 'Rest.'

Once he had left the room, Lis lifted her hand and looked over the skin for herself. 'How did you do this?'

'The ointment,' Healer Yang said. When she looked up at him, he looked a little nervous.

'This has healed better than you would have thought?'

He nodded.

'Do you have a healing magic?'

'Don't say that,' he said too loudly, then leaned forward. 'I don't want to have magic.'

'It isn't so bad,' Lis said, remembering the fun she'd had.

'We are going to die,' he murmured.

'No, we won't.' She could only hope her words were true.

'How did they not see her?' he asked, waving his hand to indicate the room.

'It is a skill of the Hidden. We can literally hide.' She touched her hands together, and his eyes grew wide. She repeated the action. 'I can't show you, for no matter what I do, you can still see me.'

'But I could see something different. Like I know that you are there but aren't.' He shook his head. 'It is difficult to explain. Like the girl. I saw her, but there was something odd about how I saw her. I have thought that before,' he said, 'that I saw someone when others couldn't.'

'I can teach you, maybe, to do it too, but it is very draining.'

'You ran away,' he said, comprehension dawning.

She nodded and looked at the table.

'Is life so bad?'

'It was different at the hidden palace. With U'shi, and not seeing anyone other than my tutors.'

'It is what the hidden princess is—hidden.'

She laughed. 'So, I hid myself from the world and disappeared.'

'It is safer for you here, for the crown prince will not allow anything to happen to you.'

'I know he tries, but he may not be able to sense all threats. Like the high priestess.'

'I cannot believe that all of them are tainted.'

'I don't know, but we need to be more alert.'

'And I will stand guard,' he said, standing slowly and pulling his little dagger from his pocket.

'You need to rest,' Lis urged.

'As do you. Sleep. I'll rest here at the table then, for it won't be long until your prince needs you again.' Lis nodded and twirled slowly, her clothes changing, and he smiled at her. 'You could teach me that.'

'I don't know how I do it,' she said, climbing into her bed. 'But I could try.'

33

Lis woke to a noise that shook the whole world around her. The healer groaned as he jumped to his feet. He opened his mouth to say something, but he snapped his mouth shut as the guards poured through the door.

'Your Highness, we are under attack.'

'What do you want me to do?' she asked.

The prince appeared. 'Outside,' he cried at the guards.

'I'm not staying here alone,' she returned.

'My mother, stay with her.'

As the soldiers moved downstairs, she took the healer by the elbow and led him down as well. They pushed into the empress's room to come face to face with the princess and a sword.

She lowered it slowly.

'The crown prince sent us,' the healer said, looking around. 'Your Highness.' He moved to the bed.

She waved him off, but he took her wrist.

'Something is not right here,' he said, looking back to Lis.

She nodded.

'There is a taint. I can feel it, but I can't sense what has started it.'

'The high priestess,' Lis said.

'I could...' the healer said, looking at the princess, and the empress surprised him by grabbing his hand.

'You can see her,'

He tried to move back, but he couldn't release himself from her hold.

'It seems he is also Hidden,' Lis said softly. 'And he has great strength as a healer.'

The empress nodded, and the princess stepped forward. 'Let him look, Mother,' she whispered.

The healer chewed on his lip, but said nothing. As another explosion seemed to rock the building, he stumbled forward, his hands landing on the empress. She scowled at him, and Lis expected him to rush backwards, but he closed his eyes and left his hands where they were.

'I can feel it,' he whispered.

The building swayed again. They could hear shouts and the sound of fighting coming from just outside the residence as the building groaned above them. If Lis gave herself over to them, they might kill her and move on. But then, she might also be the first of many. She didn't know what else they wanted.

'Who has visions?' Lis asked the princess.

'Some do to varying degrees. Why?'

'Something I was told. Why don't you tire like I do?' she asked.

'Practice, channelling your magic, finding a way to use it without burning through it.'

'Would you be able to teach me?'

'I'm not sure we will get the chance.'

The empress groaned, and the healer sighed. He had moved one hand over her stomach and the other over her forehead. His eyes squeezed shut, as though he was looking at something far beyond what was in front of him. Lis rested her hand on his shoulder and felt the energy that flowed through him. She wondered if the prince would also feel it, were he to touch Yang.

'I can see it,' he whispered, 'but I can't heal it. I'm not strong enough.'

'You can feel him,' the princess said. 'He would be able to feel you. Give to him, and he can use us both to heal her.'

Lis placed a hand on his other shoulder and felt him straighten and strengthen under her hold. She closed her eyes and tried to tune into the feeling around the healer. Then she pushed forward.

She felt a final push or pulse from him, and then he went limp. They held him up, resting his head against the bed. The empress sat up and stretched before taking her daughter in her arms.

Lis leaned alongside the healer. She felt tired, but not as drained as she had been before, and not as weary as the healer himself looked.

'Three of you,' the empress said.

'The three of what?' the prince asked, throwing open the doors. 'It is not safe here.'

The princess stepped back, and the empress stepped forward. 'I'm not sure they can be moved,' she said.

The prince looked at the healer and shook his head.

'He has helped me greatly,' the empress said, taking her son's hands.

Another explosion shook the building and this time, Lis was sure it would collapse.

'Now,' the prince cried as another guard raced into the room.

The guard put his arm around Lis, shielding her from the building as dust started to fall around them like snow. The prince did the same to the empress. Lis barely caught sight of a woman, simply dressed, pulling the healer up and to his feet. Tucked under his arm, she guided him out.

There was a loud crack, and then it thundered. Lis was pulled forward by the guard into the bloody courtyard. She tried to stop, but he kept her moving forward. Bodies lay on the ground before her, soldiers and magic men alike. The empress drew in a sharp breath as they were pulled along. The building fell behind them in a rush of noise, and Lis pushed her hands over her ears. She didn't have many belongings in her room here, but what she did have was gone. She was thankful that Mu-Phi had been sent away, despite her anger at it.

The healer squealed, then looked at the face of the woman under his arm and squealed again.

'I may not be pretty, sir, but now is not the time.'

'You... you...' he stammered.

'My maid,' the empress said. 'She had only just started.'

Lis tried to stop and look around her, but the soldier kept her moving quickly. 'Where do we go?' she asked.

'Somewhere safe?' Yang asked behind them.

'Is there somewhere safe in all of this?'

He stopped dead and she almost slipped. Still moving with the momentum, the sudden stop was a surprise.

A man stood before them with a nasty grin on his face and a fireball in his hand. The guard raised his sword just as he let it go. Lis stretched out her hand, wanting to stop it as she had before, forgetting the danger to herself. But he was cut down from behind, a fizzle signalling his end, and the fireball faded as it hit her barrier. The strength behind it was gone.

'I want off this island,' Lis said, more to herself than anything, but as the guard turned to her, she realised she had said it aloud.

'That may be an idea,'

'No, get to my father,' the prince said quickly.

Wei-Song cried out as a blade caught her arm. The healer wrapped his hand around the wound, swung her to the side and stuck his little knife into the man standing before him. He fizzled as the blade penetrated his heart. As he slipped from it to the ground, the healer turned to Lis with a horrified look. She didn't know if it was because he had actually managed to save the princess, or if it was because of the sound the man had made when he died.

'Go,' the prince urged, pushing them forward.

As they made their way through the fighting, Lis recognised many of her own guards. Some more moved around them as they travelled, trying to protect them.

Lis wasn't sure how it happened, but they made it safely to the throne room. The world was much quieter, and she was surprised by the amount of blood that splattered their clothing. The guard still had his arm wrapped tight around her, as though he was too scared to let her go.

'What is this?' the emperor asked, turning away from his discussion with an advisor.

'Move more men to the doors—all the doors,' the prince directed, and the guards surrounding them disappeared. 'Where is Hui Te-Sze? Never mind, I have two more hunters here.' He waved at the soldier holding Lis, who then reluctantly let Lis go and raced away.

Without him holding her up, she found her knees couldn't support her, and she dropped to the floor. The empress rushed forward and took her in her arms.

'I heard you were unwell,' the emperor murmured.

'Nothing like a fight to get me out of bed, and the royal residence now lies in ruins.'

The emperor stood slowly and stepped forward. 'My love,' he said, helping her to her feet and pulling her into his arms. She appeared uncomfortable in such a place, or perhaps it was just that she was not used to such affection.

'Who is this?' he asked.

'Healer Yang,' Lis answered, 'and a hunter.'

The emperor grinned at him. His eyes barely travelled over the dishevelled girl standing at the back of the group, until she removed her hand from the wound on her arm and Yang and the empress rushed forward.

'Sit down,' the empress said softly.

'And this?' the emperor asked.

'Wei-Song, my maid.'

The emperor stammered, his mouth working before he could clamp it shut. Then he nodded slowly.

'Father,' the prince said. 'I think we should consider getting the women somewhere safer.'

'There is nowhere safer than here,' the emperor murmured, his eyes still on the maid.

'What is it?' the prince asked, looking to the girl.

Lis wondered if they could see the resemblance to her mother, although she had changed her appearance enough. She was wearing servant clothing now, and her hair was more simply pulled back.

'We were to name our daughter Wei-Song.'

'We didn't have a daughter,' the empress said, her voice tight, and the girl looked at her with a pained expression. She had done all she could with the lack of choices she had, Lis realised. Lis wondered what she might have done in such a situation.

Wei-Song tried to stand and gave a shaky bow to the empress, barely looking at the emperor. 'I shall take my leave.'

'You can't go out in that,' Lis said just as the prince stepped forward.

'You have been a great help to my mother; you must stay,' he said, his voice kind, and she looked to Lis.

The sound of fighting grew louder, and Lis knew the soldiers had not prevented them from reaching the throne room. She held her breath. Then the fighting crashed into the room, and the empress screamed. The maid stepped between her and the men flowing through the door, and the emperor pulled a sword.

Lis found herself shoulder to shoulder with the prince, although she wasn't sure what she could achieve. She had managed to protect herself a little with her barrier, but she didn't know what other skills she had—nor what skills these men had.

A storm grew quickly and swirled above her head. Thick, dark clouds moved through the rafters, blowing the lanterns and hangings. Thunder rumbled, and Lis bit back a scream. What would her father have done? What would he want her to do?

The prince had his arm out, pushing her behind him.

'I can help,' she offered, but she wasn't sure how.

'We don't need your sensing skills.'

Lis bit her lip. Rain was heavy on the air. She wondered if it would cause problems for the fire bearers if it were to fall from the clouds above. She didn't know enough about magic. She glanced back at the princess, standing as her prince was, only before her mother. Lis hoped they survived this so she could have a chance to learn from her. Although she doubted the prince would allow her to leave and travel to the school.

Men poured into the room, and Lis wondered if anyone had survived the attack outside. Lightning flashed through the room as the thunder nearly deafened her. As it faded, the empress screamed.

Lis looked around their small group, quickly being surrounded by the men in dark clothing, and she wondered if she could hide them all.

The emperor lay prone at the steps to his throne, his eyes closed. The healer raced forward, but a man nearby with fire made him pause.

'We just want the little princess,' he said, his voice clear despite the sounds of the room.

Lis stepped forward as the prince caught her arm. 'Will this end it?' she asked.

The man grinned. 'It will start it.'

The prince pulled her back beside him, his grip tight around her arm, and she tried not to wince.

'What have you done?' the empress cried.

'We have simply removed him from the fight. We want the hidden princess.'

The maid stepped forward and Lis shook her head.

'You have some skill,' one man said to the healer before glancing at the empress. The lightning cracked again, and the empress fell where she was.

Lis wanted to put herself between the madness and the prince. They could hide, although she wasn't sure how quickly Yang could pick it up. He appeared to have tapped into his healing abilities, although she doubted he knew how he did what he did.

The group of men around them took a step in. The air buzzed and crackled with the magic as it swarmed around them and the storm continued to grow above them. The crown prince stood with his sword outstretched, but there were too many.

As the group surrounding them moved closer, they backed into each other.

'Can't you do something?' Yang pleaded.

Lis didn't know of whom he asked the question.

'Can we protect them?' Lis asked.

'Who?' the prince asked, briefly looking sideways at her, his focus moving back to the men around them.

She tried to visualise her barrier around them, hiding them away and keeping them safe. Wei-Song suddenly took her hand, and Lis felt the surge of magical energy through her. If only she could hide them all—but she didn't know if that would save them. Just because they couldn't be seen didn't mean they couldn't be killed.

'Push,' Wei-Song whispered.

Fire crackled at the edges of the room as the storm swirled above them, and Lis closed her eyes. She tried to concentrate on what she may or may not have. She raised her hands out to her side as she opened her eyes, just as Wei-Song pulled the prince to the floor and the healer ducked down with them.

She pushed everything she had out from her, concentrating on protecting what was closest to her.

The effect was immediate. The magic men surrounding them were pushed violently backwards. Some hit the wall; others hit pillars or each other. In an instant, the storm dissipated and wispy clouds floated down from the ceiling before disappearing. Steam rose from some of the men lying around the room, but they remained still.

Lis hadn't heard the crackle or fizzle of their magic, and she didn't know if they were dead or not.

The space was suddenly filled with soldiers. Lis remained as she was in the centre of the room. Wei-Song reached up to take her hand, and the healer let go of her legs. She realised that he too must have lent his energy to her, as she had when he had healed the empress.

People fussed over the emperor and empress, helping them to their feet. They were lifting the unconscious men and taking them away. Did they not want to spill blood on the rugs of the throne room, or would they drag them to the prison? she wondered.

Lis looked at the prince, who was standing still and staring at her. He took a step backwards, and she looked down at the ground.

'We could run,' Wei-Song whispered.

Lis shook her head. 'My place is here.'

'Wei-Song,' the empress called, and the girl turned and knelt by her mother. The empress put her hand against the girl's face, relief evident on her own. 'Stay with me?' she asked.

The princess nodded, and as the empress was helped to her feet, she ducked easily beneath her arm and assisted her. A contingent of guards and ladies appeared to help her, although Lis wondered where they would go.

The healer stood slowly and placed his hand on her shoulder. Lis chanced a look at the prince again, just before he turned his back on her and left the room. She allowed the exhaustion to wash over her, and she stumbled. Yang caught her and, after a quick look around the room, led her to a step before the throne where he helped her sit down.

'What happens now?' he asked.

'I don't know,' she said.

34

Lis woke from a strange dream where the prince had held her close as they lifted high above the Palace Isle, looking down on it as though it were the map.

She blinked back the strange mix of panic and elation to find him standing over her with a sword held out towards her. He stared at her silently as she sat up, threw the covers back and swung her legs around.

The tip of his sword wavered just a fraction.

Lis sighed, the comfort she had felt in the dream dissipating. Her heart beat fast. She stood, and he stepped back. She took a deep breath. 'Please make it quick. I'm tired, and I don't want to linger.'

She waited, but nothing happened.

He stood as he was. 'You are one of them, and yet they want you dead.'

'Everyone does,' she sighed.

He shook his head and lowered the sword.

'That is why your father took your family away.'

She nodded once.

'He should have killed you.'

She stepped towards him. 'I know.'

'You are dangerous,' he hissed.

The sound of hatred stopped her steps. 'I don't know what I am or what I can do, other than hiding and making flowers bloom early.'

'And stopping a room full of soldiers determined to kill us all.'

'I just pushed them,' she said, looking down.

'How?' he asked, the sword forgotten. He stepped forward. But as she looked up, he stopped, and his curiosity was replaced with anger. 'You killed my brother.'

'I was on my island,' she said, and suddenly she wanted so desperately to be there again. 'Your brother was killed with fire, and I don't have that skill.'

'How do you know?'

'I visited his room when I was hiding.'

'This is why Hui Te-Sze is wary of you.'

'He seems to sense something you do not.'

'It doesn't matter what I sense; I've seen it.'

She nodded slowly. 'I wish you luck with the next hidden princess,' she said, bowing before him.

'Who would put their daughter forward with two dead?' he asked, his voice strained, raising the sword again with a shaky hand. 'They already lament the time, despite your knowledge and understanding of the world…' He stopped as she straightened and looked at him.

'You need to be very careful, Your Highness, for it sounds as though you might actually like me.'

'I've had to kill others I have known,' he murmured.

She stepped forward suddenly, pushing herself onto the tip of the outstretched sword. It was sharp against her skin. He pulled away from her and she grabbed the blade, wincing as it pulled through her hand. 'I am not worthy even of a quick end,' she murmured. 'I have watched you run through a man without thought.'

She felt the tip of the sword move to her flesh as he pushed against her, just enough to break the skin. She still held the blade tight, the sting of the cut trying to find its way into her consciousness, telling her to run.

'If you are hidden, can I still kill you?'

'Do you want to find out?' she asked, cocking her head. She no longer knew what she was doing.

'What is happening?' the healer asked from his sleepy pose across the room.

The prince didn't take his eyes from her.

'He is doing what he has to,' she answered for him.

The healer was on his feet, and the sudden movement had the sword push further into her. She maintained her position despite the sharp pain as it pushed deeper. She held her hand out to the healer, stopping him in his tracks.

'Are you the same sort of hunter that she is?' the prince asked Yang.

Lis shook her head

'You are hurting her,' Yang said, his voice stronger than she had thought he had in him.

'He is killing me slowly,' she murmured, trying not to look at her hand wrapped tightly around the sword, knowing that the blood dripped through her fingers. She wondered absently if the tip was doing the same to her stomach. Would it ruin the dress when she died? Would anyone worry for such a thing?

'Go,' Yang said.

She shook her head again, pulling the blade closer as Remi turned to face him. 'You know what she is?'

'I was there when she saved us all,' he growled, his eyes on the sword rather than the prince.

'Maybe you could talk him into doing this a bit faster,' Lis murmured.

'Kill her,' Hui Te-Sze called from the doorway, and the sword pushed deeper. The cool metal created a strange sensation inside her, as though she could feel every part of it. It was her hand that stung more as the sword cut deeper across her flesh.

When a groan escaped her, the prince looked at her with sudden fear and withdrew the sword. She dropped where she was, swatting away the healer as he raced to her. Her hand rested on her knee, a wide cut sliced through her palm and another across her fingers.

'I...' the prince started.

'You are not a good hunter,' she wheezed.

He turned to Hui Te-Sze and directed him out.

Yang knelt beside her, running his hand over hers as he hastily wrapped silk around it. She could feel the relief already.

A tear slid down her cheek, and she wiped at it hastily.

'He doesn't know what to do with you?' Yang said, looking back towards the door.

'He can't let me live,' she whispered, trying to stand and pushing her hand against her stomach.

'Where are you going?'

'To finish this,' Lis said, but he caught her arm and held her back. 'I can't live like this,' she whispered, leaning into him.

'You will need to for a time longer, because I don't think this is finished.'

'It is for him.' She wasn't sure why she felt such a loss with the prince's hatred of her. She had always known what he would do when he learnt of her true nature, and she had known she was nothing until the training was finished.

'I don't care,' the prince's angry voice boomed in the hallway just beyond the room. 'This is not over, and I want her watched. Surely your men can guard against a girl.'

Yang raised an eyebrow as she tried to stand back from him, but her knees were weak. More of her blood had leaked through her dress than she had thought was possible.

As she focused on her hand, Yang pulled her back to the bed, half carrying, half dragging, and then his hand was pressing down hard over the wound in her stomach. The pain lessened, and she closed her eyes.

She could no longer hear the prince outside her door. She wondered if the guards would stay, or if the hunter would sneak in during the night and finish what the prince could not.

She sighed at the idea of it. There was nothing for her in the Empire now. No home, no family, no Peng and now, no prince. Perhaps he would be content to lock her away until the new empress was crowned, and she could decide what to do with her predecessor. The old ways came to mind, where they were all killed but one. But Lis wasn't in prison. She was in a small room somewhere on the Palace Isle, maybe even in an old palace that once housed a hidden princess.

No one knew what she was or where she was, and she had no idea of what was to come.

ACKNOWLEDGMENTS

Darja and Kim at Deranged Doctor Designs (DDD) for facilitating absolutely brilliant cover design work and all the marketing extras. Thank you for your support and clear emails around what was needed from me to make the magic happen.

TWG members: Melissa, Matthew J Morrison, John Hargreaves, Sue Larsen, Nicholas Jansen and Chantelle Griffith for listening and support in all things writing related. Special thanks to Yasmin and Belinda for taking the time to read what I thought was a finished draft and making the story stronger.

Allison E Wright for wonderful editing work. Despite my Aussieness sneaking in, she carefully smooths out my words.

My parents, Francine and Ken Smith. Amazing, supportive people who I don't thank often enough. Thanks for keeping me grounded and being the best grandparents ever.

As always, Temwa for being my biggest supporter.

ABOUT THE AUTHOR

Georgina Makalani survives life as a servant of the public by hiding in her office at lunch time with dragons, witches, a laptop and a little bit of magic.

For more about Georgina and her books visit her website: www.theflowofink.com